"So tell me, Captain MacLachlan, what do you do for fun?"

Fun? Duncan had to think for a minute about Jane's question. How often did he do anything that he could call fun?

"I play basketball." Suddenly he was smiling. "I gave Judge Smithson a bloody nose with my elbow in one of our last games of the season."

Jane chuckled. "And you had the nerve to appear in his courtroom."

"He repaid me with an elbow to the gut. I dropped to my knees retching."

Her full-bodied laugh rang out.

"Like that image, do you?"

"I'm embarrassed to admit how much I do."

He was still smiling, something he hadn't expected to do in her company. She was irritating, all right, but also...not as unlikable as he'd thought. Smart, edgy, amusing. Still not a woman he'd consider romantically. But sexually?

Maybe.

Dear Reader,

Stories grow from surprising moments. This trilogy came from an image that lurked in my mind. I live in a small town where people know how to celebrate the Fourth of July. Our parade is a big deal, and bagpipers play while marching in kilts. One particular piper has lingered in my memory. He was tall, striking, auburn-headed and solemn, a hero if I've ever seen one. One day that not-so-important memory sent up shoots. I imagined three brothers walking shoulder to shoulder, all playing the bagpipes that are their heritage.

Alas, heroes have minds of their own. Duncan MacLachlan, the oldest son, declined to play the bagpipe. He was taught by his father, whom he bitterly resents, and he chooses to reject everything that came from a man he despises. And, darn him, Conall, the youngest son, feels the same. Only Niall, the hero of the upcoming book *From Father to Son*, embraces his Scottish heritage.

Despite his defiance, I fell for Duncan. He's a man to whom duty is all. He sacrificed his dreams when his brothers needed him. Romantic love is a foreign concept to him, and not one he intends to embrace. But aren't responsibility and duty rooted in a deep sense of caring? And what is caring but a kind of love? Oh, yes, it turns out that Duncan is quite capable of loving...once he meets a woman strong and fierce enough to defy him, command his respect and gain his trust. He might have been able to ignore her, if only she didn't need his protection. Naturally, Duncan feels it's his duty to provide it. And love has everything to do with it.

These brothers, damaged by a painful childhood, are some of my favorite heroes.

Enjoy!

Janice Kay Johnson

Between Love and Duty

Janice Kay Johnson

TORONTO NEW YORK LONDON
AMSTERDAM PARIS SYDNEY HAMBURG
STOCKHOLM ATHENS TOKYO MILAN MADRID
PRAGUE WARSAW BUDAPEST AUCKLAND

Recycling programs
for this product may
not exist in your area.

ISBN-13: 978-0-373-60682-5

BETWEEN LOVE AND DUTY

ABOUT THE AUTHOR

The author of more than sixty books for children and adults, Janice Kay Johnson writes Harlequin Superromance novels about love and family—about the way generations connect and the power our earliest experiences have on us throughout life. Her 2007 novel *Snowbound* won a RITA® Award from Romance Writers of America for Best Contemporary Series Romance. A former librarian, Janice raised two daughters in a small rural town north of Seattle, Washington. She loves to read and is an active volunteer and board member for Purrfect Pals, a no-kill cat shelter.

Janice enjoys hearing from readers. Please contact her c/o Harlequin Books, 225 Duncan Mill Road, Don Mills, ON M3B 3K9, Canada.

Books by Janice Kay Johnson

Other titles by this author available in ebook format

PROLOGUE

EIGHTEEN-YEAR-OLD DUNCAN MacLachlan saw from half a block away that his mother's car was in the driveway. So she was home. He didn't know if that was good or not. Man, he should have stopped to grab a burger somewhere. Mom wasn't likely to cook dinner tonight.

He parked at the curb, killed the engine and winced at the jerk followed by a barely muted *bang*. Mr. Kowalski next door glared every time he saw him now. Duncan always waved hello, even while thinking, *Live with it, dude.* Every penny he was making this summer was going in the bank to pay for tuition. There was no way he could afford to replace the muffler. He'd sell the car before he left for college at the end of August, anyway. Kowalski would have peace and quiet then.

Duncan loped across the yard, but found himself hesitating on the porch. He wasn't even sure why the reluctance. Who cared how many years Dad had gotten this time? Not him. They could throw away the key as far as Duncan was concerned.

Except, he guessed Mom did care.

Maybe. He frowned, his hand on the knob. She'd been strange lately. Worried about Dad, maybe, but…somehow Duncan didn't think so.

He gave his head a quick, hard shake. What? He was cowering at the thought of another chapter in the MacLachlan family soap opera? The *last* chapter, as far as he was concerned.

Five more weeks, and he was gone.

The sweet thought of freedom loosened his shoulders and he opened the door. "Hey, Mom," he called.

There was no answer. Surprised, he walked through to the kitchen and was more surprised yet to see that she was there, sitting at the table not doing anything. The radio was off; she didn't even have a magazine open in front of her. And no, she wasn't cooking dinner.

Dirty dishes in the sink showed that Conall had been around. So did the bread left on the counter, open so it could dry out. Peanut butter that should have gone back in the fridge. An empty milk carton lay on its side. Beside it was a crushed beer can. Duncan felt a rush of anger at the sight of that. Con was twelve years old. *Twelve.*

Was that what had Mom staring straight ahead, this weirdly unfocused look in her eyes?

Duncan didn't move past the doorway. "Mom?"

Slowly, almost as if painfully, she lifted her gaze and blinked; once, twice.

"Um...are you all right?" he asked.

Her face contorted, then smoothed again. He saw her swallow. "Your father was sentenced to ten years."

Duncan nodded. Dad had gotten five last time, got out early—the judge definitely was going to come down on him. He dealt drugs for a living; he deserved whatever they threw at him.

"Do you know where your brothers are?" she asked, in a seeming non sequitur.

Unease crawled up his spine with the quick *flick, flick* of a snake in the grass. Why was she so out of it? They both knew where Niall was. Duncan's fifteen-year-old brother was in juvie for possession. Only for a joint—it could be worse. With Niall, it usually was worse. This time, when they called, Mom had said, "He can rot there," and hung up the phone.

Around a constriction in his throat, Duncan said, "Conall was still asleep when I left this morning."

Only twelve, Conall had been out late last night. Duncan had heard him come in sometime after one. Mom wasn't even trying to control him anymore, which Duncan didn't understand.

"I left a note asking, if he didn't do anything

else today, he could at least leave the kitchen clean." Mom didn't even look toward the mess.

Duncan said awkwardly, "I can clean up."

Her eyes were focused now on his face. So intensely focused, he couldn't look away.

"I'm afraid——" her voice cracked "——you're going to have to."

"Do you, uh, want to lie down or something?"

She shook her head. "I'm done, Duncan. I can't take any more. Your father promised…"

He couldn't imagine why she would ever believe anything Dad promised. And she must have known for at least a year that he was moving drugs again. Duncan hadn't even heard them arguing. It was like she'd given up.

"I can't do anything with your brothers. You're an adult now. You don't need me anymore."

What was she talking about?

"I'm already packed," she said. "I wanted to stay until you got home. To…explain."

Explain what? He only stared.

"I'm leaving," his mother said flatly. "Your aunt Patty is in Sacramento. She told me I could stay with her until I got on my feet. I don't want anyone but you to know where I've gone."

"You're…leaving?" His voice cracked this time, as if he was a little kid and it was beginning to change.

"Yes. You should, too. Maybe Jed's parents would put you up until you go in August."

This was like an out-of-body experience. He watched himself standing in the doorway, gaping. Heard himself say, "But…Conall."

She shrugged. "He's not your responsibility."

"He's my brother."

His mother had aged. Between the moment he walked in the house and now, she'd added ten more years. She only shook her head. "There's nothing either of us can do for him, or Niall, either. Face it." She rose to her feet; her voice hardened. "I have."

"You're just…taking off," he said in disbelief.

"That's right." She walked toward him. He had to fall back to let her by. She paused briefly; he thought she kissed his cheek, although he wasn't positive. "You're a good boy, Duncan," his mother murmured, so softly he might have imagined that, too. A moment later he heard the front door open and close.

Her car started. She backed out.

He hadn't yet returned to his body. He was afraid to. The house was utterly quiet.

His father had been sentenced today to ten years in the Monroe Correctional Complex. His mother had driven away. Apparently she intended to keep going, all the way to California. She thought he should go upstairs, pack his things and leave, too, so that his brother Conall would come home to find no one.

There's nothing either of us can do for him, or Niall, either.

But he's twelve years old! A kid. Really, so was Niall.

Not your responsibility.

Then whose were they?

Duncan's heart was thudding as though he'd sprinted the homestretch of a five-mile run. His breath came in great gasps, like an old-fashioned bellows. His hands had formed fists at his sides.

Not your responsibility.

Then whose? Whose? he raged silently.

Upstairs he had a packet from the university. He was still waiting for a dorm roommate assignment, but he'd already chosen his classes. He was this close to escaping. The freedom had shimmered in front of him since he started high school and understood what he had to do to attain it. Good grades, scholarships, and he was gone.

The promise was so beautiful, he stared at it with burning eyes, understanding now what his mother had seen as she sat there at the kitchen table. Not the here and now, but what could be.

If only he, too, agreed that his brothers weren't his responsibility.

Duncan made an animal sound of pain and fell

to his knees. He pressed his forehead against the door frame and hung on.

There was a reason college and escaping home and family had always shimmered before his vision. That's what mirages did.

CHAPTER ONE

IT HAD BEEN A PISSER of a day, and Duncan Mac-Lachlan's mood was bleak. He had had to personally arrest one of his officers, a five-year veteran, for blackmailing a fifteen-year-old girl into performing an act of oral sex on him.

It didn't get any worse than that. Rendahl had betrayed the public trust. He'd also been so stupid he had apparently forgotten that his squad car was equipped with a video camera and microphone that uploaded wirelessly. Duncan grunted. Stupidity was the least of Rendahl's sins. Ugly reality was that he was a twenty-seven-year-old married man who'd blackmailed and terrorized an already frightened girl into fulfilling his sexual fantasy.

Duncan realized his teeth were grinding together and he made himself relax. The dentist was already threatening him with having to wear some damn plastic mouth guard at night. "Find another way to express your tension," Dr. Foster had suggested.

Today, Duncan would really have liked to express it by planting his fist in that son of a bitch's face. Hearing his nose crunch and seeing the blood spurt would have worked fine, if only as a temporary fix.

Instead, he'd gone by the book, because that's what he did. He'd been his usual icy self. His only consolation was the way Rendahl and his attorney both had shrunk from him. They'd seen something in his eyes that he hadn't otherwise let show by the slightest twitch of a muscle on his face.

To cap his perfect day, he'd held a press conference announcing the arrest while maintaining the girl's privacy. He had had to ignore most of the shouted questions. How did you explain something like this when you couldn't understand it yourself?

He'd come home and planted himself, cold beer in hand, in front of a Mariners game on TV. He'd gotten up for a couple of replacements, thought about dinner and settled for a sandwich. Purple and secretive, dusk finally crept through the windows. Duncan hadn't turned on a light, inside or out. The game hadn't worked any magic; he didn't know the final score and didn't care. At last he flicked the TV off with the remote and settled in his recliner, brooding.

How could such a lowlife have passed under his radar for five *years?* Gotten satisfactory ratings in annual reviews? Rendahl had fooled a lot of people. Duncan liked to think he knew the men and women who worked for him, even if there were seventy-four at last count. Knew their strengths, their weaknesses; what motivated them, what tempted them. Police Captain Duncan MacLachlan hadn't gotten where he was by misjudging people.

Dusk became night, and still he sat there, disinclined to go to bed, uninterested in reading or finding out what might be on television. The darkness wasn't complete, not with streetlamps, the Baileys' front porch light across the street, occasional passing headlights. It suited his mood to feel as if he was part of the night, invisible. Anonymous.

The recliner was comfortable enough that Duncan began to nod off. Rousing himself enough to get to bed seemed like too much effort. If he woke up later, fine. He let himself relax into sleep.

The tinkle of shattering glass shot him into wakefulness, instantly alert and incredulous. Unbelievable. Somebody was breaking into his house. He immediately understood why. He hadn't turned lights on and off the way he usually did. To somebody who hadn't seen him pull into the garage at six o'clock, it would have looked as if nobody was home.

He might get a stress reliever after all, he thought with black humor.

Duncan didn't lower the recliner; it might have creaked. Instead he reached for his weapon, which he'd earlier dropped on the side table along with his badge, and eased himself out of the chair. The fact that he'd kicked off his dress shoes was good. He could move far more silently in stockinged feet.

He used the light filtering in the front window to cross the living room without having to feel his way. The further tinkle of glass told him the intruder was brushing shards from the frame before climbing in. Or *while* climbing in. He knew it was the window in the utility room. Any second he'd hear...

Thud.

He'd left the wicker hamper of dirty clothes right in the middle of the small room. So his intruder didn't have a flashlight, or hadn't turned it on yet.

Duncan slipped down the hall and stationed himself to one side of the open doorway to the utility room. What he wanted to know was whether he had one trespasser, or more.

A dark shadow passed him. After a moment, he risked a look into the utility room. His vision was well-adjusted to the lack of light. Empty.

One, then.

He tracked the figure creeping down the hall then moved with a couple of long strides. Duncan slammed into the intruder and took him to the floor, where he held him down effortlessly and pressed the barrel of his gun against his neck.

"Police," he barked. "You're under arrest."

"What the...?" A string of obscenities followed in a voice that was high enough that, for a moment, Duncan believed he'd just flattened one of the rare women who did breaking and entering. The next second, he thought in disgust, *Oh, hell. It's a kid.*

"Hands behind your back," he snapped, and grabbed both wrists when the boy obliged. Scrawny wrists. He realized the body he was holding down wasn't very big. "All right, push yourself to your knees. That's right. We're getting to our feet." He helped—roughly. He nudged the kid a short ways until they reached the light switch. "Face the wall," he ordered. "Put your hands flat on the wall."

He turned on the light and was momentarily blinded. He didn't like that, but his intruder cringed from the brightness, too. Duncan waited until he could adequately see what he'd caught, then growled a profanity of his own.

"How old are you?"

Cheek ground against the wall, the Hispanic boy glared at him and stayed mute.

Duncan gave him a little shake. "Tell me."

The boy muttered something. Duncan shook him again.

"Twelve."

Well, damn. He hadn't caught even a small fish tonight. This was a minnow.

Book the kid? Call the parents? What if there weren't any?

He barely stifled a groan. *Decision time.*

THE BUILDING, DIVIDED INTO perhaps eight or ten apartments, was predictably ramshackle. Clapboard siding needed paint. Parking for tenants was on the street or in a very small dirt lot to one side, which was also home to a rusting hulk on cinder blocks. Another car, apparently ailing, had its hood up. Three men were bent over the engine. One had pants hanging so low, Jane Brooks could see way more than she wanted to. When she parked at the curb, another of the men glanced over his shoulder, but with a conspicuous lack of real interest.

She checked the folder on the passenger seat to verify the address. Yep, this was it. Number 203 was presumably upstairs. There was only one entrance, although fire escapes clung precariously to each end of the apartment house which, to her eye, didn't stand quite square.

She'd been in worse places.

Jane locked her car and made her brisk way in, nodding and greeting a very young, very pregnant woman who was trying to maneuver into one of the downstairs apartments a playpen that didn't quite want to fold the way it was supposed to. Jane held the door, smiled and chatted briefly in Spanish. She was lucky she'd taken it in high school. Currently, one-third of the kids in the local school district were Hispanic, up to half in two of the elementary schools, where instruction was in Spanish in the mornings, in English in the afternoons. She didn't quite consider herself fluent, but she was getting there, what with her volunteer work at the alternative high school and then with the Guardian ad Litem gig.

She was acting today as a court-appointed Guardian ad Litem. Her task was to interview the adults involved, or potentially to be involved, in the life of a boy named Tito Ortez. Tito's father was soon to be released from the Monroe Correctional Complex, and the judge would have to determine whether Tito could be returned to his custody. At the moment, the boy lived with his older sister, one Lupe Salgado, whose address this was. Eventually Jane would talk to Tito's father, of course, Tito himself and perhaps even teachers. His report card suggested he wasn't doing well in school.

The stairwell and hall were shabby but surprisingly clean. Upstairs she rapped firmly on the door displaying an upright metal 2, a listing 0 and a 3 that hung upside down.

"Venga," a voice called, and after only a momentary hesitation Jane opened the door to find herself in a cramped living room.

Two young, black-haired children sat in front of the television, on which a small green dragon seemed to be trying to puff dandelion seeds but was, to his frustration, setting them on fire. Both children turned to stare at Jane. The girl stuck her thumb in her mouth. An ironing board was set up in the narrow space between a stained sofa and the wall. A Formica table with four chairs and a high chair was wedged into the remaining space. The spicy smell of cooking issued from the kitchen.

Jane raised her voice enough to be heard in the kitchen. *"Hola. Me llamo Jane Brooks."*

A woman appeared, wiping her hands on a dish towel and looking flustered. *"Sí, sí.* I forgot you were coming. *Perdone."* In a flurry of Spanish too fast for Jane, she spoke to the children, then gestured Jane into the kitchen. She was cooking, she explained, and couldn't leave dinner unattended.

She did speak English, but not well; Jane made a mental note that living in a non-English-speaking household probably wasn't helping Tito's school performance. Jane and the boy's sister continued to speak in Spanish.

Jane was urged to sit at a very small table with two chairs while her hostess continued to bustle around the kitchen.

"You're Lupe?" she asked, for confirmation, and the young woman nodded.

Like the pregnant teenager downstairs, she had warm brown skin, long black hair and eyes the color of chocolate. She was pretty, but beginning to look worn. Plump around the middle, and moving as though her feet hurt.

Jane knew from the paperwork that Lupe was twenty-three. There had been other children born between Lupe, the oldest, and Tito, the youngest, but they were either on their own and unable to help with Tito or were in Mexico with their mother. Tito, Lupe explained, had stayed with his father because Mama thought as a boy he needed a man.

She shrugged expressively. "Then, one year after Mama returns to Mexico, Papa is arrested. So stupid! I called Mama, but she is living with an uncle and it is very crowded. So she begged me to keep Tito. Which I've done."

As if this household wasn't crowded. "You have children of your own," Jane said, with what she thought was some restraint.

"*Sí,* three. The little one is napping." She stirred

the black bean concoction on the stove. "My husband, he left me." She sounded defeated. "I work at La Fiesta and a neighbor watches the children. I can't depend on Tito. Maybe if he was a girl." She shrugged again.

"Do you visit your father at the prison?" The Monroe correctional institute was nearly an hour's drive away.

"Sometimes." Lupe sent her a shamed glance. "The money for gas... You know how it is. And my children have to come, too. I take Tito when I can, but it upsets him, so maybe it is good that we don't go often."

Jane nodded. Having a parent in prison was difficult for a child of any age, but for a middle schooler it must be especially traumatic. He wouldn't be the only kid in the school with an incarcerated parent, but he probably felt like he was.

"Is Tito any trouble to you?" she asked, and got a guarded response.

No, no, he was such a good boy, Lupe assured her, but then admitted that she didn't see much of him. She worked most evenings; tonight was a rare night when she was home with her children, and she didn't know where Tito was. With a friend, she felt sure. Would he be home for dinner? She didn't know, but doubted it.

They talked for half an hour, until Lupe was

ready to put dinner on the table and Jane realized she was in the way. She declined a polite invitation to join them and told Lupe she'd be in touch.

She was almost out the door when Lupe said, "Oh! I forgot to tell you about the nice policeman who has been spending time with Tito. Do you think you'd like to talk to him?"

Oh, yeah. She was definitely interested in hearing from him. Unless he was the father of a boy Tito's age, Jane had to wonder how he'd gotten acquainted with Tito at all.

"His name is Don…Can Mack…Lack…Land." Lupe tried to sound it out carefully, but grimaced. "That isn't right. I have it written down. *Un momentito, por favor.*"

She returned with a scrap of paper on which a bold hand had written "Duncan MacLachlan" along with a phone number. With a small shock, Jane recognized the name. Captain MacLachlan was regularly in the news. He was the unlikeliest of all mentors for a twelve-year-old boy.

Jane copied the phone number and thanked Lupe, then, thoughtful, made her way to her car. Aside from the intriguing and possibly worrisome involvement of Captain MacLachlan, she wasn't surprised by the visit, but she was dismayed. Clearly Tito couldn't stay long-term with his sister. He might have been better placed in a foster home while his father was behind bars, but there were never enough good foster homes, and he'd been lucky to have a family member willing to take him. Lupe's husband had probably still been around, too. Jane could understand why the placement had been approved, probably with a sigh of relief and a firmly closed file.

She drove a couple of blocks, then pulled over to make notes while her impressions were fresh. She jotted questions and directions to herself, too. What about the other siblings—perhaps one of them was now in a better position to offer a home to Tito? Find out what friends he was spending so much time with. Imperative to talk to teachers. Did he go to the Boys & Girls Club? After-school programs? Probably not at his age. Any other community organizations? She had no record that he'd been in trouble with the law, but she'd find out. Reading between the lines of what Lupe had said, Tito was ripe for exactly that. *MacLachlan?* she wrote in the margin. Was Tito in a juvenile court-ordered program of which the family court remained unaware?

The father's release date was only two weeks away, and Jane wanted to have a good sense of other possibilities for the boy before then. And, of course, she would make the trip to Monroe to speak with Hector Ortez. She had to do all of this around running her own business, however.

Lucky, she thought wryly, she had no social life to speak of.

Driving home, she tried to recall what she knew about Duncan MacLachlan. She'd never read or heard anything to make her think he was "nice." Although that wasn't fair.

In the department, he was only one step below the police chief. He was exceptionally young to be in that position, still in his thirties, Jane had read. He looked older, she'd thought when she saw his picture in the paper or brief segments from press conferences on the local news. That might only be because he was invariably stern. If he ever smiled, the press had yet to capture the moment.

She was a little disconcerted by how easily she recalled his face. She did remember staring at a front page photo of him in the local daily. She'd left that section of the newspaper lying out on her table for several days for reasons she hadn't examined but had to admit, in retrospect, had involved a spark of sexual interest. Not that she would have pursued it even if she'd met the guy in person—he was so not the kind of man she would consider dating even though courthouse gossip said he was unmarried. But that face...

The photo wasn't from one of his staged appearances; she suspected it had been taken with a telephoto lens, as he strode away from a crime scene. He was listening to something another man beside him was saying. His head was cocked slightly and he'd been frowning, more as if he was concentrating than annoyed. His face was... harsh. It might be the seemingly permanent furrows between his dark eyebrows and on his forehead that aged him. She'd had the probably silly idea that he could have been a seventeenth-century Calvinist minister—unbending, judgmental, yet unswervingly conscious of right and wrong.

Those Calvinist ministers probably hadn't had shoulders like his, though, or the leashed physical power that his well-cut suits didn't disguise.

So, okay, she'd never heard anything to make her doubt his integrity, but that still begged the question: why in heck was he interested in Tito Ortez?

On the notepad, she circled his name. Twice.

She would most definitely be finding out what he had to do with a rather ordinary boy whose father was about to be released from prison.

"SEE IF YOU CAN MATCH that shot," Duncan taunted, bouncing the basketball to the boy. He used the ragged hem of his T-shirt to wipe sweat from his face as he watched Tito move into position inside the free throw line and concentrate fiercely on lining up his shot. It was probably too far out for him; he was small even for his age and his arms were scrawny, but he didn't like to fail, either. Duncan had come to feel a reluctant admiration for his determination.

He bent his knees, the way Duncan had taught him, and used his lift to help propel the ball when he released it from his fingertips. It floated in a perfect arc and dropped through the hoop, barely ruffling the net.

"Yes, yes, *yes!*" Tito did a dance, and Duncan laughed.

"Very nice." He held up his hand for a high five, and the boy slapped it. "I'm being too easy on you."

"I've been practicing," Tito admitted. "It stays light so late. Now that I have my own ball." Duncan had given him one. "There's hardly ever anyone here in the evening. I have the court to myself."

They played soccer, too, and Tito was better at that, but for reasons mysterious to Duncan the boy was determined to become an NBA-quality basketball player. His father, he had admitted, was only five foot nine, and his mother was little—he'd held up a hand to estimate, and Duncan guessed Mama wasn't much over five foot tall—but *he* was going to be bigger than his father. He was sure of it. And he could be a point guard—they didn't have to be as tall, did they?

No, but Duncan suspected that six feet tall or

so was probably a minimum even for the high school team. Still, Tito was only twelve, and who knew? He might have a miraculous growth spurt. No matter what, he might excel in PE, and being good at anything could make a difference to him right now.

Besides...they were enjoying their occasional evening hour or Sunday afternoon on the concrete basketball court behind the middle school, or on the soccer field. Duncan often suggested pizza afterward, or sometimes a milk shake. Tito was slowly opening up to him, although Duncan was still unclear why he lived with his sister and where his parents were. He occasionally wondered uneasily whether the family might be here illegally; perhaps the parents were around, but avoiding the cop who was inexplicably befriending their son. He couldn't be sure and had decided from the beginning that he wouldn't go out of his way to find out.

Looking cocky, Tito passed the ball to him. Duncan drove in for a layup, easily evading the boy's feint at him. Tito tried to copy the move and thumped the ball against the backboard nowhere near the iron hoop. Scowling, he retreated and tried again, and again.

Duncan's cell phone rang. Irritated, he jogged over to where he'd left it outside the painted line on top of his sweatshirt. It was displaying a number he didn't recognize. He almost didn't answer, but a glance told him Tito was occupied, yelling at himself as he dribbled away from the hoop, then turned to begin a new drive.

Duncan answered brusquely, "MacLachlan."

A very feminine voice said, "Captain, my name is Jane Brooks. I'm a Guardian ad Litem for the family court. I understand you know Tito Ortez."

His gaze went straight to the boy, leaping to rebound another missed shot. Tito looked at him in inquiry, and Duncan held up one finger. Tito nodded and dribbled the ball in for another attempted layup.

"Yes," Duncan said. "May I ask what your interest is?"

"As I said, I'm..."

"A Guardian ad Litem," he interrupted. "I get that." And didn't like what his gut was telling him. Tito hadn't said anything about being involved in a custody dispute. Unless this had to do with the sister's children? Guardian ad Litems were always appointed to be a child's advocate— in fact, they were deemed the one person involved in a court case whose sole concern was the best interests of the child. "Does the case involve Tito?"

"Yes." She didn't embroider the bald answer. "I'd like to meet so that we can talk."

Tito had stopped and stood dribbling the ball,

watching him, although he was too far away to be able to hear even Duncan's end of the conversation. From the apprehension on the boy's face, Duncan realized his expression must have given something away.

"I'm with him right now," he said curtly. "Tomorrow morning…"

"Evenings are better for me."

He raised his eyebrows. Guardians ad Litem were paid, if minimally; many worked out of counseling services or the like. It would be normal to conduct business during the day.

Silence was an unbeatable tool for interrogation. He employed it now, and finally, grudgingly, she said, "I own a business. Dance Dreams."

He knew every business within the Stimson city limits, his jurisdiction, at least by sight. He'd never had occasion to step foot inside Dance Dreams, which sold dancewear, presumably including tap shoes and toe shoes, tutus and a lot of pink sparkly stuff that appeared in the window. Not his kind of place—and the juxtaposition of pink tulle and sometimes ugly dependency court hearings seemed to be a strange one.

Meeting Ms. Jane Brooks might be interesting.

"Evening, then," he agreed. "Tomorrow?"

"That would be great." She hesitated. "Shall we make it a coffee shop?"

"Why don't you stop by my place? We won't want to be overheard."

She agreed and he gave her his address. Duncan ended the call and returned to Tito. He conducted a lightning-quick internal debate and decided to say nothing yet. He'd find out what was going on first.

"Business," he said, then grinned. "What say we hang it up and go get something to eat? I didn't manage dinner and I'm starved."

"Pizza?" the boy said hopefully.

"Burgers." Duncan laughed at his expression. "Pizza next time."

Tito sighed with exaggerated disappointment. Somehow or other, he'd manage to force himself to chow down a cheeseburger, a good-sized helping of fries and a root beer float at a minimum.

Hey, maybe he'd have that growth spurt yet.

CHAPTER TWO

AT SEVEN IN THE EVENING, it was still full daylight in the Puget Sound area. Darkness wouldn't fall until eight-thirty or nine. The day had been hot for early May, and the heat still lingered when Jane arrived at Duncan MacLachlan's.

She loved his home on sight. It was distinctive enough she suspected it had been custom designed and built. The lot wasn't huge, but the houses on his side of the street all backed up to Mesahchie Creek and the greenbelt that protected it. Right here in the city, he had his own slice of wilderness.

The house was one story, sided with split-cedar shingles. Trim was painted forest green. From the driveway she could see interesting angles, bay windows and skylights, and a wooden arbor over a flagstone paved path that led around the side of the house.

Unable to repress a sigh, she got out. She was already afraid she was going to have the hots for him, and now she'd succumbed to his house before she even stepped inside.

I am unbiased, she reminded herself firmly. *I'm being* paid *to think of Tito first, last and always.*

She rang the doorbell and, as she waited, listened to the delicate music played by an unusual wind chime, long, thin shards of obsidian suspended from a branch of driftwood. It distracted her enough that she was startled when the door opened. She gave a betraying jerk, then felt her cheeks warm when she most wanted to be completely poised.

The man filling the doorway studied her thoroughly. "No wonder you opened the store. You were a dancer," he said, in the deep, somehow velvety voice she recognized from television interviews.

But his words helped her get a grip. "No."

"You look like one."

"I never had the opportunity," she said flatly. She held out a hand. "Captain MacLachlan."

He didn't smile. "Ms. Brooks." His very large hand enveloped hers for the briefest possible time considered civil. "Please come in."

She stepped inside, trying very, very hard to shut down her physical awareness of him, but not succeeding. It wasn't that he was huge; at a guess, he was about six feet tall, maybe even a little less. At five foot seven herself, she shouldn't feel dwarfed by him. It was that he had...presence. She couldn't think of any other way to describe it. He was the kind of man people would always look at first, no matter how big the crowd. Even when, like now, he wore neither uniform nor the kind of suit he was usually photographed in. He must have changed when he got home, to well-worn jeans, athletic shoes and a long-sleeved dark blue T-shirt that hugged broad shoulders.

He did indeed have a great body—lean and athletic. Not overmuscled, not thin. Perfect. His face wasn't model handsome, not by a long shot. He had broad, blunt cheekbones, a heavy brow, too many furrows and a crooked nose. His eyes were a wintry gray, clear and penetrating.

And, damn it, her knees wanted to buckle because he was *right there,* so close she could have touched him. *I did touch him,* she thought, and rolled her eyes at herself when he turned to lead the way into the living room. Apparently her inner teenager was alive and well.

Even though mainly focused on him, she was aware enough of her surroundings to know instantly that she loved the interior of his house as much as she had the exterior. Wide-planked wood floors, wooden blinds, cushiony leather furniture in a warm, chestnut brown underlaid by the contrasting elegance and color of Persian rugs. Bookcases, packed full, flanked a river-rock fireplace. For the walls, he favored art-quality photographs over paintings. Above the rough-hewn mantel hung a large framed photo of a bald eagle sitting on a snag above a river. The doors of an antique armoire stood open to display a large-screen television and, below, a fancy-looking audio system.

"Coffee?" Captain MacLachlan asked.

"Thank you."

He excused himself and disappeared, leaving her to wander and examine his books—an exceptionally eclectic mix of science fiction, thrillers, historical fiction and nonfiction that covered a gamut of subjects.

He returned with a tray and gestured her toward the sofa then sat across from her in a recliner that rocked forward as he added cream to his mug of coffee. Jane doctored her own with both sugar and cream then straightened.

"All right." His tone was abrupt, his expression uncompromising. "What's this about?"

She cleared her throat, going into professional mode. "Has Tito told you about his living situation?"

"I know he lives with his sister. I've talked to Lupe a couple of times."

Jane nodded. "Apparently his parents split up and his mother moved back to Mexico four years ago. She took three of Tito's sisters with her. There are a couple of other older siblings somewhere in the area. Tito stayed with his father." She gave a small shrug. "They both thought that because he's a boy, he needed a father more than a mother."

MacLachlan grunted. She couldn't tell what he thought about that rather traditional view.

"What happened to the father?" he asked.

"Three years ago, he was involved in a brawl at a tavern. He knifed another man, who died."

The police captain's face changed then. Hardened.

Jane continued, "He was convicted of manslaughter and given a five-year term. However, he's done what he needed to be released early."

He leaned forward and set down the mug with a sharp click. "Don't tell me anyone's thinking of returning custody to him." His incredulity was plain.

"He has every right to regain custody of his minor children," Jane said, as sharply. "There are no allegations of abuse or neglect. He was convicted of a crime unrelated to his family. He has continued to write and call Tito and likely his other children. He sees Tito as often as Lupe can drive him to Monroe."

"He's a convicted felon. A man with a demonstrated history of violence. Have you even met him?"

"Not yet."

MacLachlan made a disgusted sound. "But already you're his advocate."

That annoyed Jane enough to have her setting down her mug, too, so decisively that coffee
splashed onto the glass tabletop. "I neither said
nor implied that. I have been asked to assess possible placements for Tito. It's possible that his
father will be his best bet. In case you're unaware,
his current placement with his sister is far from
ideal. There may be other possibilities, and I will
consider those, as well. At the moment, I'm keeping an open mind." *Unlike you,* she didn't have to
say.

They glared at each other. After a moment he
gave a choppy nod, and she felt a glow of satisfaction because he was the one who had to back
down. She was right; he was wrong.

"What I'm doing," she said crisply, "is making
time to talk to any adults active in Tito's life.
Lupe gave me your name, although she seemed
unclear on how you'd come to be involved with
him."

He was exceptionally good at hiding his
thoughts, which perhaps wasn't surprising for a
cop. Jane found it disquieting to have to wait,
however, while he watched her with those cool
gray eyes and apparently decided what and how
much he was going to tell her.

He reached for his coffee again and took a long
swallow. Jane dragged her gaze from his strong,
tanned throat, and she was dismayed to feel her

cheeks warming again. She silently blasted herself. What was wrong with her? She *never* reacted to a man like this. Think how hideously embarrassing it would be if he noticed!

"He broke into my house."

Her eyes flew to his face. "What?"

He gave the faintest of smiles, and she bristled at the realization that he had enjoyed shocking her. "You heard me."

Jane opened and closed her mouth a couple of times. At last, she said cautiously, "That's how you met."

"Yes." Another of those smiles, barely a twitch of the lips. "The house was dark. I'd had a crappy day. When the Mariners game ended, I turned it off and I guess I fell asleep right here in my recliner. I heard the window break. I got my hands on him, discovered he's only twelve. He claimed that he'd been dared to break into a house. He insisted he's never done anything like that before." His shoulders moved in a barely there shrug. "I gambled he's telling the truth and didn't arrest him."

"Soo…" She drew the word out. "You became buddies instead."

This smile approached the real thing and she could have sworn she saw a glint of amusement in his eyes. The combination was enough to make her glad she was already sitting down.

"Something like that. I told him I wasn't letting him off the hook that easily. I could still arrest him at any time. I gave him a choice—spend some time with me and let me assess how honest he is, or be booked into juvie. Tito's a smart boy."

It seemed that Captain MacLachlan wasn't quite as hard-assed as he was reputed to be. Tito had, somehow, some way, gotten to him.

"You could have arrested him and recommended him for diversion." The diversion panels were made up of ordinary citizens who'd volunteered to serve. In lieu of a judge, they saw kids referred for minor crimes and were able to assign punishments. The program took a lot of pressure off the juvenile court, ensured young offenders had immediate consequences for their actions and gave them a chance to avoid having a conviction on their records.

"I could have," MacLachlan agreed. More slowly he said, "I probably should have." He frowned. "He looks like he's about ten years old."

Jane hadn't yet met Tito. She didn't say anything.

After a minute, MacLachlan released a sound that might have been a sigh. "I have two younger brothers who got in trouble with the law as juveniles. Tito reminded me of them. I thought I could make a difference for him."

The gruff, unemotional voice was completely

at odds with what he'd said. With his actions. Given all the pressure of his job, he had still somehow found time to spend with a troubled twelve-year-old boy.

Unless, of course... He *was* unmarried.

Her eyes must have narrowed. Hisfacialmuscles tightened. "No, Ms. Brooks, I am not sexually attracted to boys. Or men, for that matter."

Oh, man. Now her face had to be flaming red. It didn't even occur to her to deny that the possibility had crossed her mind.

"I'm sorry..."

He shook his head. "I'd think you were naive if it hadn't occurred to you. If you've been at this long, you've seen enough horrors that you *should* wonder," he said, with surprising gentleness.

"It does alter the way you look at people."

"Try my job," he said dryly.

"I can imagine." She hesitated. "I suppose that's why I was so surprised that you were making time for Tito."

"I've made more than I intended." MacLachlan was quiet for a moment. "I've had a good time with him."

"What do the two of you *do?*"

He shrugged. "Sports. Shoot some hoops, kick around a soccer ball. I feed him. I've eaten more pizza and cheeseburgers since I met Tito than I'd had in months." He sounded rueful. "He's so damn scrawny, I keep feeling compelled to try to fatten him up."

"His sister is petite."

"Yeah, the dad is short and the mother even shorter from what he says. I think some of the kids give him a hard time. PE has been tough for him."

"His grades aren't very good." Jane shuffled through her folder and found the most recent report card, which she handed to the captain. Their fingers touched, and it took determination for her not to react. Dumb.

He glanced at it, grimaced, then tossed it on the coffee table. So their hands wouldn't brush again? Jane picked it up and inserted it in the folder.

"He's a good kid," he said finally.

"Despite his nocturnal activities."

"According to him, his one-and-only adventure." A quick grin did amazing things to his face. "I scared the crap out of him."

Heart drumming, she thought, *you scare me, too*.

Unclipping the pen from her folder, she held it poised above the notepad. "Please give me your impressions of Tito."

"I won't betray his confidences."

Their gazes clashed.

"I wouldn't ask you to."

Although reluctant, he did talk. There were no

great revelations here; if he was to be believed, Tito was a funny, smart boy who sometimes acted younger than his age as well as looked it.

"Hasn't reached puberty," she diagnosed.

MacLachlan nodded. "Definitely not. No sign of beard growth or a change in his voice. He sure isn't adding any muscle."

"I suppose puberty is as hard for boys as it is for girls."

"It can be." There was that faint, rueful tone again, the one that made him unexpectedly likable. "Not for the guy who is shaving by the time he's in eighth grade and has all the moves on the girls. He's not the one hoping no one notices him when he sneaks in and out of the shower after gym, or the one who's trailing the pack on cross-country runs. The one shorter than all the girls."

She chuckled. "That sounds personal."

"No. It was my youngest brother. I suspect his lagging maturity contributed to him getting in trouble."

"Trying to prove himself."

He inclined his head. "The same way Tito was."

"Did you tell him about your brother?"

MacLachlan shook his head. "We're men. Men don't talk about our bodies or how deep our voices are."

She had to laugh. "Unless you're taunting each other."

Another flash of a grin came and went so fast she almost missed it. "Yeah. Unless."

She bent her head and, in self-defense, concentrated quite hard on her notes. "Is there anything else you'd like to add, Captain MacLachlan?"

"Duncan."

She looked up in surprise. "What?"

"You can call me Duncan."

"Oh." The name did suit him, sounding as gruff as the man. "Duncan."

"What's the next step?" he asked.

"I interview teachers, any of his other siblings, any other adults. Scout leaders, Boys & Girls Club employees and the like."

He shook his head. "I don't think he's involved in anything like that. My impression is, he's been forced to be a loner. His sister is too busy to push him into activities that might change that."

"Perhaps their priest…"

"She does drag him to church."

"Of course I'll be sitting down with his father. And, naturally, Tito himself." She hesitated. Maybe she didn't have to say this, but she felt compelled, anyway. "I'd appreciate it if you didn't discuss my visit with him. Or attempt to prejudice him in any way."

"You mean, suggest he might be better living with someone besides his ex-con father."

"That's exactly what I mean."

His face had returned to its earlier granite facade. "I think I can manage to keep my mouth shut, Ms. Brooks. Is the hearing date set?"

"Yes." She told him when.

He nodded and rose to his feet. "If that's all…?"

It was completely ridiculous to feel hurt because he was eager to get rid of her. Especially since she was relieved at the prospect of escape, too.

"Thank you for the coffee," she said formally, although she'd scarcely taken a sip.

He didn't bother with an insincere "You're welcome." All he did was walk her to the front door, say, "Ms. Brooks" and close the door firmly in her face.

Cheeks flushed again, this time with both humiliation and aggravation, Jane hurried to her car. *Jerk,* she thought, and refused to let herself remember those two astonishing grins.

WHEN SOMEONE HE DIDN'T KNOW wanted to talk to him like this, Tito knew it meant something bad was happening. After Mama went away and then Papa was arrested, lots of social workers came to talk to Tito and Lupe. Mostly they ignored Tito, though, even when they were supposedly asking him questions. He could tell that, in their eyes, he was only a little kid, so they didn't care what he said.

This time it was because Papa would be getting out of that place soon. Tito knew his father thought Tito would be living with him. He didn't know how he felt about that. Three years was a long time. He'd been so young the last time he lived with his father. He hated going down there, to the prison. Tito hadn't admitted to Lupe how much he hated it. He always slumped in the chair and mumbled when Papa asked about school or friends or whether his sister was taking good care of him and feeding him enough. Tito could tell Papa thought she wasn't, and that made him feel bad.

And now Lupe had taken him to the public library to meet with this Miss Brooks, who Lupe said had already come by the apartment to talk to her. Tito burned with resentment because Miss Brooks didn't know anything but would be able to decide things about his life. It made him mad that she'd talked to his sister at least a week ago but not to him until now.

"Tito," she said, when they went straight to the table in a quiet corner of the library where she had already been sitting. She gave him a big smile. He'd seen smiles like that before. He didn't return it.

"Lupe, thank you," she said. "Do you mind if I talk to Tito alone?"

This woman did speak Spanish, at least, he thought grudgingly. Lupe seemed to like her, but then she liked everyone except for that *idioto,* Raul, who lied every month and said he couldn't find a job only so he didn't have to pay child support. What kind of man did that make him? Not much of one. Tito worried that Lupe needed the money the state paid her to take care of him.

He sat down unhappily, across the table from the social worker woman, and his sister left them.

Miss Brooks said, "Tito, you can call me Jane. Would you rather speak in Spanish, or English?"

He shrugged and focused on the tabletop. Someone had written some bad words in ink. He rubbed a finger over them, and they smeared.

"Then let's make it English," she said, switching. "Since that's what you have to speak at school."

He shrugged again.

"You know your father will be released in two weeks."

She waited and waited, until he finally mumbled, "Yes."

She explained that the judge had asked her to talk to him and his family members and any adult friends—even his teachers—and recommend where she thought he should live.

"I know you're used to living with your sister now," she said, in a nice voice. "But she doesn't have much room, and she works evenings. It would be better if you had someone who could spend more time with you."

He did wish Lupe worked days instead. Tito didn't like Señora Ruiz, the neighbor who came over evenings. She ignored him and mostly paid attention to the little kids.

"How do you feel about it?"

Tito looked up at last. "What do you care?"

Her eyes were soft. Kind. They were pretty, too, blue but not cold. More like a flower.

"I do care. I want what's best for you, Tito. You don't know me, and you have no reason to trust me, but you can. I promise. *Te prometo*."

There was a lump in his throat. He struggled against it and finally nodded.

He still didn't answer very many of her questions. He didn't know if he wanted to live with his father! How could he know? And who else was there? Yes, he had a brother, Diego, but he was only twenty and worked the fields. He had dropped out of school early—not that much older than Tito was now. He never stayed in one place, and he didn't have a wife. Tito saw him only every few months.

When Miss Brooks said, "I spoke to Duncan MacLachlan," Tito looked at her in alarm.

"He didn't tell me."

"I asked him not to."

That tasted bad, like broccoli. He had *trusted* Duncan, who had caught him, *el stupido,* breaking into his house. What had Duncan said to her?

"He told me he wouldn't betray any confidences." She fumbled for another way to say that, but Tito understood and relaxed. He wished secretly that he could live with Duncan, but, of course, he wouldn't want a boy like Tito. Why would he? Tito wondered all the time why he was being so nice.

"Do you like spending time with Duncan?"

Tito smeared the words on the table some more, but he also nodded.

"He did tell me how you met."

Tito's head shot up, but she was smiling.

"Don't worry. It has nothing to do with where you live. I won't tell anyone else."

That lump was again in his throat. "*Gracias.* Thank you."

Still smiling, she said, "Here's my phone number, Tito. It's a cell phone, so you can reach me day or evening. If there's anything you want to say."

"Okay."

"I'll be speaking to your father next." She

asked him if there were other adults she should talk to, but he shrugged. He had friends, *sí,* but he didn't even know their parents. Truthfully, he didn't have many friends, but he wasn't going to tell her that.

She signaled and Lupe came over to them. Tito hadn't known that his sister had stayed. She looked so tired. He wondered if Papa could help her, once he got out. Would he be able to find work? If he couldn't, how would he be able to take Tito?

What would Papa think of Duncan? Tito felt a heavy sensation in his chest at the idea of not being able to play basketball and soccer with Duncan anymore, but if he had to live with Papa and Papa said no...

"Was it all right?" Lupe asked him on the way home, and Tito only hunched down in the car seat and shrugged.

He didn't know. He couldn't remember what "all right" was.

TELEPHONE TO HIS EAR, Duncan rotated his big leather office chair so that he was gazing out the window at the sky. His office was on the second floor of the new redbrick jail and police station. Right next door, attached by a glassed-in walkway, was the matching courthouse.

On the fourth ring, a woman said, "Dance Dreams."

Jane Brooks, of course. She had an intriguing voice. A little husky. Smoky. *Sexy, damn it.*

"Ms. Brooks. You've been dodging my calls."

A couple of weeks had passed since she'd come to his house, and never another word from her. He'd left her four messages on her cell phone. They had been increasingly testy, he knew.

"Yes, I have, Captain MacLachlan. As I thought I'd made clear to you, I'm unable to discuss my recommendations until I make them to the court. I'd welcome new information. However, you didn't sound as if you had any to offer."

He restrained a growl. "Have you talked to the father?"

"Yes, I have."

"And?"

"I'm afraid I'm not at liberty to discuss…"

He didn't even try to restrain this growl. "Ms. Brooks, do you or do you not want what's best for Tito?"

"That," she retorted with a snap in her voice, "depends on whether we're talking about what's best for Tito as pronounced by *you,* Captain."

"I've read the original police report on Hector Ortez's crime."

"As have I."

That surprised him.

She continued, "The trial transcript, too. Have you read that, Captain MacLachlan?"

He hadn't.

She waited politely. "No?" she said after a moment. "Since you're so interested, you might want to do so."

"I intend to."

"Good. Now, if you'll excuse me, I have customers."

He didn't know whether it was more insulting to think that she was lying about the existence of those customers, or that she wasn't.

Either way—she was gone. "Bullheaded woman," he muttered, hanging up the phone.

Duncan didn't like being bested by a pretty, feminine little thing who made her living selling, of all damn things, tutus.

Maybe not little, he conceded. She had the look of a dancer. Slender, small-breasted, graceful and long-legged, with the swanlike neck and unusually erect carriage he'd expect of one. In appearance, she was just plain feminine, with that mass of glossy hair the color of hand-rubbed maple wood, a sweet face and eyes of the darkest blue he'd ever seen.

All that, and the personality of a police dog on the job. Outwardly well behaved, sharp-eyed and ready, at the slightest excuse, to go for the throat.

He'd have expected as much if she'd been a defense attorney. But the proprietor of a dance shop?

Duncan might have been amused if he hadn't been so pissed. She'd made up her mind, all right. He suspected she had from the beginning, whatever she said to the contrary. She had every intention of handing Tito back to his father, whose main virtue seemed to be a lack of any history of domestic violence calls. Never mind that he'd stabbed a man to death in the parking lot of a tavern at two in the morning.

From the ache in his jaw, Duncan could tell he was grinding his teeth again. Swearing aloud served to relax his jaw. Maybe he'd recommend the technique to his dentist for other patients.

The rest of him hadn't relaxed one iota. He continued to brood when he should have been working.

At first sight, he'd had the passing thought that he might like to take Ms. Jane Brooks to bed. No more. He didn't care what color her eyes were, or how much he'd liked her long-fingered, graceful hands. He didn't object to social workers on principle, but he did object to idiots who believed in blood ties at the cost of common sense. He didn't have to feel a whole hell of a lot to enjoy taking a woman to bed, but he drew the line at one he held in contempt.

He swiveled in his chair and pulled out his computer keyboard. If Jane Brooks had kept him in the loop, he might have shared his intentions with her. As it was, she might be surprised by some opposition.

In his present mood, he hoped she was.

CHAPTER THREE

"THANK YOU FOR YOUR recommendations, Ms. Brooks." The Honorable Judge Edward Lehman peered at Jane over the top of his reading glasses. The judge had already greeted Hector Ortez, Lupe and the Department of Social & Health Services caseworker present in the small courtroom along with the recorder and bailiff.

Hector had been released a few days before. The decision had been made to hold this hearing immediately, before he had a chance to reestablish his relationship with his daughter and son on his own. Jane had had to hustle to finish all her interviews so quickly and put together a report for Lehman, but she was satisfied with the result if less than thrilled with any of Tito's options. She'd tried very hard *not* to consider Captain MacLachlan's outrage when she interviewed Hector at the correctional institute, but his voice and scathing gray eyes had stuck with her whether she liked it or not.

Now the judge continued, "I've received an additional opinion that I hadn't anticipated... Ah." He looked past her. "Captain MacLachlan."

With a sense of inevitability and rising aggravation, Jane turned her head to see Duncan MacLachlan entering chambers. Speak of the devil. Or was it *think* of the devil. The smallish space immediately shrank. He wore a crisp blue uniform today, as if he'd wanted to emphasize his position in the law enforcement community.

"Your Honor," he said with a nod.

Jane supposed the two men knew each other. Well, so what. *She* knew Judge Lehman, too. He was her favorite of the several family court judges with whom she'd dealt. She shouldn't leap to assume the two men were comembers of some kind of old boys' network.

"Apparently no one is represented by an attorney today," the judge observed, continuing after everyone shook their heads in agreement. "Ms. Salgado, do you speak English?"

"*Sí.* Yes, but not..." Lupe hesitated.

"Fluently? Perhaps we need a translator."

"I'm happy to translate anything Señora Salgado doesn't understand," Jane offered.

He determined that Jane was acceptable to Lupe as an interpreter and they moved on. He questioned her first. Was she able to keep Tito in her home if necessary? How did she feel about her brother returning to the custody of their father?

She explained that Tito could stay with her if necessary, but that it was difficult, given that she had three young children of her own, that she worked nights, that he had to sleep on the sofa.

"Yes," Jane translated faithfully, "I am happy if my brother can live with Papa again. I have tried to make sure they saw each other often enough so that they still know each other."

She heard a sound from her right that she strongly suspected was a snort from Captain MacLachlan, pitched low enough to escape being heard by His Honor.

The judge transferred his gaze to Tito's father, a short, sturdy man who she suspected might have Mayan blood. There was something about his face—the breadth of his cheekbones—perhaps, that made her think of statues she'd seen at a traveling exhibit of Mayan antiquities at the Seattle Art Museum.

Interestingly, Hector spoke better English than his daughter did. He'd been in this country longer, he explained; initially he had left his family behind in Mexico and come up here for work, then brought them when he could. He was an automobile mechanic. Lupe was his oldest child, and she'd found the language difficult and had left school when she was fifteen.

"I have already talked to the man I worked for, and he wants to hire me again," Hector told the judge. "He liked my work."

"So you do have employment." Lehman made a note. "Where are you currently living?"

He was staying with a friend, sleeping on the floor. The apartment was small and cramped, he admitted; two men shared it, and another was currently living there, as well. He would get an apartment or small house once he'd received his first few paychecks, but no one would rent to him until then.

Jane all but quivered, waiting for another snort—which didn't come. Apparently Captain MacLachlan had more self-control than to indulge himself a second time.

The judge talked to Hector at some length, and finally seemed satisfied. He flipped through papers in the file open before him and peered at one for a moment, then looked up.

"Ms. Brooks, appointed by this court as Guardian ad Litem to represent the interests of Tito, believes those interests may be best served by living with you, Mr. Ortez, once you've found steady employment—which it sounds as if you've done—and established a stable living environment, which may be weeks to months away. She feels it would be best for Tito to remain close to his sister, as he's been living with her for so long now, and to stay if possible in the same school. Ms. Hesby, do you disagree?"

The caseworker shook her head. "I'm fully aware that Señora Salgado has done her best, but I, too, believe Tito would benefit from more attention from a parental figure than she has been able to provide."

The judge addressed Hector, "Will you be living here in Stimson?"

"Yes," Hector said firmly. "This was my home before. My job is at Stan's Auto Repair on Tenth Street. Tito could walk there from school."

"Very good." He looked toward Duncan, which gave Jane an excuse to swivel slightly in her seat and do the same. "Mr. Ortez, are you aware that Captain MacLachlan has been mentoring your son?"

Jane thought there was some tension in Hector's nod even though he was smart enough to keep his thoughts hidden.

"The captain has expressed concern about the possibility of Tito living with you. He feels your conviction for a violent crime makes you an unsuitable role model for a young boy."

Streaks of red now slashed across Hector's high cheekbones. "I was defending myself only. I didn't mean to kill anyone. I don't usually fight. I'm not that kind of man."

Duncan said, "And yet you didn't deny, even

in your trial, that you had stabbed Joseph Briggs. That he'd made you, I quote, very mad."

Hector's brown eyes were hot now. "I served my time. I shouldn't lose my family, too."

"Can you keep your temper with a teenage boy who doesn't think he has to listen to his father?"

Hands planted flat on the table, Hector half rose. "I have other children. Ask Lupe! I have never hit my children."

"But you had a wife then." Duncan's tone was barely shy of badgering. "You earned the money and she raised the children. Isn't that right, Señor Ortez? But now you find yourself a single…"

Judge Lehman cleared his throat loudly. "Captain, Mr. Ortez, you may recall that this is a courtroom, not a forum for open debate."

Flushed, Hector sank into his chair. Duncan MacLachlan's expression didn't change. Jane could swear, even so, that he was basking in satisfaction because they had all—the judge in particular—seen the flare of rage on Hector's face. The captain glanced at her, and there it was in his eyes, unmistakable. He thought he'd introduced enough doubt in the judge's mind to swing the decision away from Hector.

"Captain, you're aware, I'm sure, how difficult it can be to find appropriate foster care placement for a teenage boy. Particularly if we insist that he stay within this school district." Judge Lehman's voice was ever so slightly sardonic. "Have you considered becoming licensed so that you could offer a home to Tito?"

It was all Jane could do not to applaud—or to laugh out loud. Instead, she turned a pleasantly interested face to Duncan, whose eyes had narrowed.

"I'm afraid that's not possible," he said. "You're aware, I'm sure, of how long and erratic my working hours can be."

The judge nodded. "I assumed as much. Very well. At this point, I believe our goal should be to reunite Tito Ortez with his father."

A broad grin broke on Hector's face. Duncan stiffened.

"However, I'd like to see the transition take place slowly. For the present, Tito shall continue to live with his sister. Mr. Ortez, I'm granting you generous visitation rights. However..." He paused, leveling a look over the glasses that had slid down his nose. "For the present, all visitation will be supervised. Ms. Brooks, are you available to do that supervision?"

She'd done that once before, in a contentious custody case involving two preteen children. "Evenings and weekends," she said, ignoring MacLachlan's incredulous stare.

The judge did the same. "Good. Mr. Ortez, I'm going to rule that you can see Tito *only* when

Ms. Brooks is present, or in your daughter Lupe's home when she is present—if, for example, you were to join your family for dinner. However, I ask that you not spend the night in your daughter's home."

Jane murmured a translation to Lupe, who listened intently.

"Do you understand?"

Hector nodded somewhat unhappily. He was no longer smiling.

"Tito cannot live with you until you have a suitable home in any case. This will give you an opportunity to build a relationship with your son. Let's reconvene in one month and at that point I'll speak to Tito, as well. I'll consider then whether you might be allowed unsupervised visitation or even whether Tito feels ready to live with you." He lifted his gavel and brought it down on the table with a brisk whack. Without ceremony, he gave a friendly nod, stood and strode from the room.

The bailiff guarded the door through which the judge had disappeared. The recorder paid no attention to anyone remaining in the room. After a moment, Jane pushed back her chair and stood, followed shortly by the others. Lupe and Hector hurried out, speaking in low-voiced Spanish. The caseworker waited for Jane and they chatted as they followed. Jane was very conscious of Duncan MacLachlan behind them.

She excused herself, said goodbye to Jennifer Hesby and slipped into the ladies' restroom, hoping she'd find herself alone when she emerged.

No such luck. Duncan was leaning against the wall waiting for her, his expression baleful.

He pushed away from the wall. "How can you kid yourself this is the right thing for Tito?"

"Children need their parents. Any social worker or psychologist will tell you that, for a child, maintaining a relationship with a parent is critical...."

"We're not talking about a relationship." He'd advanced far enough to be standing entirely too close to her. Aggressive. In her face. "This is a kid who has already demonstrated reckless behavior. You're talking about leaving him to the sole guidance of a man just released from prison after serving a term for a violent crime. Take off the rose-tinted glasses, Ms. Brooks."

She was damned if she'd retreat even a step. She met his angry stare with one as bland as she could make it. "I don't believe that any man's character is determined by a single act. I understand that you see enough of those single acts to..." She sought the right word. "To sour you. The fact remains, Hector Ortez *has* served his debt to society. He deserves a fair chance, and for Tito's sake I'm going to help make sure he gets one."

His eyes glittered with fury, surely out of proportion to their discussion. "For Tito's sake? Fairness to Hector has nothing to do with his kid! Tito needs someone who sticks to the straight and narrow. Someone who doesn't lash out every time he gets pissed. Someone who can set a good example and hold him accountable if he screws up."

She thrust her chin out a little farther. "Hold him accountable? Like you did? You cut him a break instead. Isn't that what you said?"

Plainly, he didn't like that. His shoulders went rigid. "You think what I did was wrong."

"Actually, no, I don't. I think what you did shows heart. You *didn't* judge Tito by one act. So why can't you do the same for his father?"

"Tito did something stupid. Hector murdered a man in cold blood."

"A man who was trying to kill him."

"Who had threatened him," he corrected. "You can't tell me there weren't alternatives. Would you have grabbed a knife and stabbed the guy if you'd been in that spot?"

Of course she wouldn't have. "His judgment was affected by alcohol."

His face was inches from hers now, his lips

drawn back to show his teeth. "Hector hasn't had a drink in three years because he couldn't get one. You trying to tell me you have faith he won't drink at home? That he'll always be sober when he's dealing with Tito? Have *you* ever seen what a kid looks like after his drunken father beats on him?"

She swallowed, then knew immediately he saw it as a sign of weakness. Of course she'd seen the aftereffects of parental abuse, but no, she didn't see the children until later, when the outward bruises had healed. But did he really think she didn't weigh risks? Damn it, she couldn't let him bully her; she couldn't.

"I don't think anyone is perfect," she said, and felt weariness. If only she could feel shining faith in someone. Anyone. "I do believe Tito's father is his best hope."

MacLachlan swore and finally—finally!—swung away from her. She held herself straight, resisting the temptation to sag with relief. He swung around as quickly to face her, but this time he was five or six feet away.

"Expect company, Ms. Brooks, when you supervise those visits. You want your solution to work. I don't trust you to recognize that it isn't. I'll expect to be kept apprised of each and every appointment. Is that clear?"

Anger rolled over her, starting with a hot

glow beneath her breastbone and spreading with stunning speed. "Certainly," she said. "If Judge Lehman instructs me to include you, I'll do so. Otherwise... If Tito doesn't invite you, it isn't happening. Is that clear?"

They glared at each other. After a moment, she gave a sharp nod, turned and walked out of the courthouse, refusing to hurry.

She was a little surprised, as she unlocked her car, to hear herself growl. A passing man, carrying a briefcase, gave her a startled glance. She was probably blushing as she got into her car and bent to rest her forehead on the steering wheel.

She couldn't remember when anyone had made her as mad as he did.

The only gratification that she could find—and it was tiny, barely a seed of pleasure—was a suspicion that she made him as mad,and that the experience was no more common or welcome for him than it was for her.

THREE DAYS LATER, Duncan found himself stalking along in the wake of Hector and Tito Ortez and Jane Brooks. Jane was chattering to Hector as if they were best friends. Hector responded occasionally with a nod or comment. Tito, to his credit, was the only one who seemed aware of the weirdness of the situation. Slinking along, trailing his father by a step or two, he was halfheart-

edly kicking his soccer ball. His head was bent,
his thin shoulders hunched. He had, earlier, given
Duncan one desperate glance and nod.

He and his father were apparently going to play
soccer in the field at the middle school. Duncan
didn't like anything about this father/son happening. He especially didn't like the father. He was
annoyed that Hector had chosen an activity that
was one of the things Duncan usually did with
Tito.

Most of all, he did not want to be physically
aware of Jane Brooks. In the three days since the
court hearing, Duncan had made up his mind that
he wouldn't be. She was attractive. So what? She
irritated him. He didn't like her. Dislike trumped
a pair of great legs or breasts that would nestle
like small birds in his hands. A throat so long and
pure he could only imagine how it would taste to
his open mouth. An elegant back and subtle curve
of hip. A perfect ass...

He tore his gaze from just that and let loose a
string of silent profanities. He didn't make a habit
of letting his dick do his thinking and he wasn't
going to start now. The fact that he was semi-
aroused because he was following her from the
middle school parking lot and she walked like a
dream was no excuse.

When they reached the sideline, Jane stopped,
letting Tito and his dad go on toward the soccer

goal and well-worn ground in front of it. Gaze fixed grimly on the duo, Duncan stopped a few feet from her.

Hector stole the ball from his son, raced ten yards and kicked it resoundingly into the goal. His teeth flashed white as he grinned at Tito, who was staring in astonishment. Hector gesticulated; Tito said something, maybe asked a question. Within minutes they were talking, then playing in earnest.

Without even looking at him, Jane said, "Lighten up."

"What?"

"I can feel you. You're a thundercloud."

"I can think of things I'd rather be doing this morning."

"Then do them," she said tartly. "Please."

"I told you I'd be here."

She made a huffing sound. "Do you really think I'm going to let anything bad happen to Tito? I may not carry a gun—" she aimed a pointed look at the one he conspicuously wore at his waist "—but I am quite capable of chaperoning, I assure you."

Duncan crossed his arms. "Cheering them on, you mean."

Tito whisked the ball by his father and scored a goal. Evidently delighted by the timing, Jane clapped and whistled. Her sidelong glance met a glower. Duncan clenched his jaw.

"Haven't you been playing soccer with him?" she said cheerfully. "You should be proud of him. Why aren't you cheering, too?"

Because I should be playing with him, not his father. Duncan believed that, but was also discomposed by the realization that he was feeling a pang of jealousy. He sure as hell wasn't admitting that to Jane Brooks.

"How often are we going to be doing this?" he asked, sounding grumpy even to his own ears.

"We? *I* will be doing this as often as I can. We've agreed to aim for twice a week, and Hector will be having dinner with Tito, Lupe and her kids a couple of additional evenings. I understand Tito's big brother, Diego, is around for a few weeks, too."

Duncan grunted. Tito had told him as much. The boy had sounded…wistful. He loved Diego and perhaps felt slightly in awe of him, but had said enough for Duncan, reading between the lines, to guess that Tito was also disappointed that his brother wasn't making more money or doing something important. Duncan had let the conversation drift so that the connection wasn't obvious before talking about how important Tito's grades in school were.

"You'll never get a really good job without

going to college or getting training in a trade," he'd said with a shrug. "No employer wants to hire a screwup. Someone who can't finish what they start."

Tito had looked thoughtful, for what that was worth. He was only twelve, not an age when he was likely to deeply contemplate life choices. Duncan knew that he was unusual in having set his eyes on his goal by the time he was ten or eleven. He had known he wanted success, respect, authority. He'd been determined to make good money so life wasn't uncertain. He'd been willing to sacrifice to get where he wanted. So it was possible. Tito probably didn't like feeling insecure, not knowing what the future would bring, any more than Duncan had at that age.

"I should have brought a lawn chair," Jane remarked. "I'll have to think of myself as a soccer mom. Snacks wouldn't be a bad thing, would they?" She pursed her lips. "A book, maybe."

She couldn't seem to resist needling him. Duncan said sardonically, "I thought you were being paid to keep your eyes on the father/son bonding process."

"I try to keep some distance when I do this kind of court-ordered supervision. I'm here, but not intruding on their time together. Fortunately, I'm really good at doing two things at once." Her smile was like a glint of sunlight catching a gun sight, serving as the same kind of warning. "I've been known to do three or four things at a time. I've read that women tend to be better at that. Probably because we're biologically programmed to watch the kids even while we've got dinner simmering on the fire and we're hanging the laundry out on the bushes to dry. Men, apparently, have tunnel vision in comparison. The studies are interesting, don't you think?"

"I can chew gum and walk at the same time, Ms. Brooks."

"Do you?"

At his fulminating stare, she widened her eyes innocently. "Chew gum, I mean. I hardly ever see adults chewing on gum."

What an unbelievably aggravating woman. "No," he said. "I admit I don't. I was speaking metaphorically."

"Oh." This smile was even sunnier. "And I had the loveliest picture of you in your uniform blowing a great big pink bubble."

He actually wanted to laugh. Duncan managed to focus instead on the soccer players; at the very moment Hector swept his laughing son into a hug. Any desire to laugh died.

"I'm going to sit," Jane announced, and lowered herself gracefully to the ground. She crossed her legs and bent to pluck blades of grass.

Duncan found himself wondering if she could

do the splits. The way her knees relaxed open as she leaned forward made him suspect she could. Not many women in their late twenties or early thirties remained that flexible. Had she been a gymnast rather than a dancer?

He moved uncomfortably. He didn't think he'd ever made love to a woman as limber as this one. He imagined lifting her legs over his shoulders as he...

Oh, hell. In self-defense, he walked away from her along the sideline, pacing almost to the end of the field before he turned and came back. She was watching him, he saw, although he couldn't tell what she was thinking. By the time he reached her, she'd turned her head and appeared to have put him out of her mind as she stuck her two middle fingers in her mouth and whistled her approval of something Tito had done with the soccer ball. Damn it, even *that* was sexy. How many women could whistle like that?

Spending time with Jane was not a good idea, Duncan was forced to realize. Annoying as she was, he did want her. But he was a man who lived by the rules he'd set for himself, and one of them was to make sure to never get involved with a woman whom he'd have to keep seeing when they were done. Jane's involvement with the court definitely put her on the other side of the line. But the alternative to spending time with her in the coming weeks was giving up on Tito, and he wasn't prepared to do that.

He could move ten feet away and pretend she wasn't there.

And look like a socially maladroit idiot, he thought ruefully.

With a sigh, he dropped to the ground a few feet from Jane and sat with one leg outstretched, the other knee bent.

"The kid's not bad, is he?"

"No, and neither is his father. Hector was telling me that he kept playing at Monroe. He says he was on his village team when he was growing up. He was good, but not quite good enough to go professional, to his regret."

"Tito and I have played more basketball than soccer." Man, did that sound defensive. Like he didn't have the guts to compete head-to-head with Hector. Angry with himself, Duncan continued, "I think maybe they're spending more time on basketball in phys ed. Tito obviously felt lacking."

She wrinkled her nose. "He's awfully short."

Duncan made a sound of agreement. "He's taken to shooting baskets for hours every evening. He's got determination, I'll give him that."

"It's a good sign."

"Yes."

Without turning his head, he could feel her gaze. He was reluctant to meet it. Sitting this close, he didn't like to think how he'd react to the rich, deep blue of her eyes.

"Why a dance shop?" he asked abruptly. "If you weren't a dancer."

She turned her head, began plucking grass again so that her shiny brown hair swung down to shield her face. Duncan waited patiently. It had to be a full minute before she said, "Because I wanted to be one."

"Then why weren't you?"

Jane straightened and tucked her hair behind her ear. If she'd been feeling something she didn't want him to see, she'd hidden it now. "Not all kids have those kinds of opportunities. I doubt Tito's sisters did, for example."

Was she saying her parents hadn't had the money to pay for classes? Duncan supposed that made sense. Those kind of extras were undeniably a luxury for a lot of families.

"By the time I was...free to do it on my own, I was too old for dance to be anything but a hobby." There was a tinge of something that he couldn't quite read in her voice. Regret? Or was it more acid? Bitterness? "I actually take classes now," she admitted, and this time she sounded a little shy. "For fun. And for exercise, of course."

"What kind of classes?"

"I started with ballet. Now I continue that at home. I have mirrors, a bar and mats. So I take other stuff. Jazz. Tap. Modern dance. Even belly dance."

Duncan heard the air escape his throat. He really wished she hadn't told him that.

"Although I'm not exactly the sultry type." She gave a one-sided shrug. "I guess I'm too skinny. And, well, not what you'd call exotic. I'm more girl-next-door."

"You?" He gave her an incredulous look. "I never had any girls next door that looked like you."

She blinked. Her eyes really were beautiful, emphasized by long, thick lashes only slightly darker than her hair. Which meant she hadn't had to use mascara.

"I... Thank you?" she said hesitantly. "If that was a compliment?"

"It was." He had to clear his throat to relieve the gruffness.

"Oh. Well." There was a pause before she murmured, "Who'd have thunk?"

Once again, he almost laughed. She'd had to ruin the touching moment between them.

"I'm full of surprises," he agreed.

Her smile was merry and less...sharp than the earlier ones. "Yes, you are. So tell me, Captain MacLachlan, what do you do for fun?"

Fun. He had to think for a minute. How often did he do anything that he could call "fun"?

"I play basketball." Suddenly he was smiling. "I gave Judge Lehman a bloody nose with my elbow in one of our last games of the season."

Jane chuckled. "And you had the nerve to appear in his courtroom."

"He repaid me with an elbow to the gut. I dropped to my knees retching."

Her full-bodied laugh rang out.

"Like that image, do you?"

"I'm embarrassed to admit how much I do."

He was still smiling, something he hadn't expected to do in her company. She was irritating, all right, but also not as unlikable as he'd wanted to believe. Smart, edgy, amusing. He might enjoy spending time with her if he wasn't so attracted to her. The combination was too threatening to a man who knew his limitations.

"Oh, it looks like they're done." She scrambled to her feet.

For an instant, Duncan had no idea what she was talking about. He was too busy taking in the sight of her long legs looking coltish even as she rose with the same grace she did everything. Skinny? No, she was willowy, slender, but definitely not skinny, which implied bony. Her curves were perfect, feminine.

Tito and Hector. That's who she was talking about. Duncan's head turned sharply and he saw the man and boy walking toward them. Tito had regained some reserve with his father, but not as much as when they arrived at the field. There was visible warmth between them, Duncan saw with narrowed eyes.

And he'd done a piss-poor job of observing them. He'd been too busy lusting after Tito's Guardian ad Litem, the woman who'd decided a murderer was a fine and dandy father for a boy already flirting with trouble.

Damn, Duncan thought in shock. Maybe she was right. He was known for his intense focus. Maybe he *couldn't* do two things at once.

CHAPTER FOUR

DUNCAN CALLED IN THE LATE afternoon a couple of days later to let Jane know he couldn't make it to Hector and Tito's second outing. She was disappointed, she knew, only because the whole thing was so ridiculously awkward. With Duncan there, her position felt less awkward. He was a distraction. Without him, she was left lurking like some kind of Peeping Jane.

Hector had taken Tito to a game arcade, which had the boy really excited. Hanging around the arcade, as noisy as it was, pretending she was interested in other people playing games while really keeping an eye on her targets, pretty much sucked as an evening's entertainment. She so didn't fit in. Plus, she'd been on her feet all day, and now for close to two additional hours, and she was beat and hungry and getting grouchy.

Finally she saw the two heading toward her. "You're still here?" Hector said, when they reached her.

She knew darn well he'd been aware of her

presence. "Of course I am," she said with a smile that felt fake.

He rolled his eyes, letting her know what he thought. He appeared oblivious of the anxious look his son gave him. "We're going for pizza now."

"Where?"

He told her, then walked out with Tito. Technically the boy should ride in her car, not with his father, but she was willing to give them the three minutes or so it would take to get to the pizza parlor. She saw them get into a battered pickup truck, then jumped into her own car and followed them out of the parking lot. Her cell phone rang as she turned into the pizza place behind the pickup.

She groped for the phone.

"This is Duncan," he said brusquely. "Is Tito still with his father?"

"Yes, we're going out for pizza now."

"I'll join you. Where are you?"

She rolled her eyes and probably looked as adolescent as Hector had, but she was conscious of relief, too, as she told Duncan where to find them. She hadn't been looking forward to sitting in a booth by herself. Maybe, she thought optimistically, Hector would invite her to join them. He'd already had time alone with Tito. If he wanted to impress her, he'd be a little friendlier.

But no. Father and son walked into the pizza parlor without even giving her the courtesy of a glance. She trudged after them. They had a spirited consultation and ordered, neither apparently interested in the salad bar. Then they headed for a booth, leaving her to order her own food.

Would Duncan be hungry? Would he want to share with her if he was? Who knew? She decided to be gracious and order a pizza large enough for both of them. If he didn't want any, she'd take the leftovers home.

She'd gotten her salad and drink and plopped herself into the booth right next to Tito and Hector's when she saw Duncan come in. He swept the room with a glance and homed in first on Tito and then her like a heat-seeking missile.

Jane waved him over. "I ordered a pizza. It's got pretty much everything on it. If you want to share, you're welcome. Anything else, you're on your own."

"Fair enough." He went to the counter, and soon returned with a salad, as well, and a drink. He slid into the booth across from her.

Jane had decided to let him sit facing the other booth in hopes he wouldn't be close enough to eavesdrop. She'd been trying, but was frustrated by the rapid-fire Spanish father and son were speaking.

Duncan was as intimidating as ever. Today he

must have been wearing a suit, although he'd left the coat in the car and had pulled his tie loose and unbuttoned the top button on his white shirt, which was rumpled. She was a little surprised to see that he looked tired. His hair was disheveled and his eyes bloodshot. He let out a breath that was almost a sigh as he leaned back in the booth.

"Bad day?" she asked.

"Average to lousy."

"Which part was lousy?"

His eyes met hers. "Do you really want to hear about my day?"

"We have to talk about something," she pointed out.

He grunted, displaying his excellent male communication skills. "What are *they* talking about?"

"I don't know," she confessed, keeping her voice low. "Well, I'm getting the gist of it, but they're talking fast."

"In Spanish," he realized.

"Yes."

"You speak it."

"Yes, but not well enough to keep up when somebody is chattering away at full speed."

His eyes narrowed. "Which makes you a lousy chaperone."

"There's no requirement that I have to hear every word they exchange."

With clear disapproval, Duncan said, "He

shouldn't be talking to Tito in Spanish. He needs to improve his English."

Jane sympathized, but felt compelled to argue. "Spanish is their native language."

"Which Tito can't use in school."

Suddenly tired herself, Jane pushed her half-eaten salad away. "Should I turn around and demand they switch languages so we can understand them?"

"That's not what I'm saying."

She studied him in fascination. "You're grinding your teeth. That can't be good for you."

He quit grinding and clenched instead. Strong muscles flexed in his jaw. Finally he set down his fork. "Thank you for pointing out the obvious to me."

Jane smiled. "I take it I'm not the first."

"No."

"Oh, well. I guess we all need a bad habit."

His expression relaxed and she thought she saw a glint of humor in his eyes. "What's yours?"

"Oh, I'm sure I have dozens." But did she want to admit any of them to Police Captain MacLachlan? "Ice cream."

One of those fascinating half smiles curved his mouth. "In large quantity?"

"When I'm in a bad mood, a pint of mint chocolate chip makes me feel way better."

"Since it's obviously not going to your hips, that doesn't sound like a bad habit. Only a habit."

"I suck on my hair."

He stifled a laugh. She loved what that did to his face. "You *what?*"

Oh, why had she told him? Resigned, she lifted the hank, a little bit stiff and clumped together, that provided her with comfort. As a kid, it had been the tail end of her braid.

The laugh burst out of him, low and deep. "Now that I have to see."

"I only do it when I'm by myself," she said with fraying dignity.

"That's worse than grinding your teeth."

"No, it isn't. I'm, well, soothing myself. It's like cracking your knuckles or nibbling on your fingernails. It's a nervous habit. I'm not suppressing an overflow of anger or hostility like you are." *So there.*

"If you had my job, you too might have some hostility that needs suppressing." Apparently unperturbed, he ate hungrily.

A number was called and Tito hopped up.

Duncan laid down his fork and said, "Hey, kid."

Tito looked embarrassed. "*Hola,* I mean hi."

Jane was aware that, behind her, Hector had turned to watch his son.

"Your pizza ready?" Duncan asked.

"Yes."

"Good." All amusement had left the wintry gray eyes when they apparently met Hector's over Jane's shoulder. "I hope ours will be soon. I'm starved."

The boy shuffled his feet and finally took himself off to fetch the pizza. Duncan kept staring what was plainly a challenge at Tito's father. Jane let it go on longer than she should have. Finally losing patience, she kicked him, hard, under the table.

"What the…?" He switched the hard stare to her.

She glared at him. "Enough already."

Tito returned, triumphantly bearing pizza. Jane looked away from Duncan long enough to smile at the twelve-year-old, who smiled shyly in return.

She realized that her number was being called, and slid out of the booth. "Will you behave yourself while I'm gone?" she asked.

Duncan's look reminded her painfully of ones all too familiar from her childhood, the kind that had once hammered at her self-confidence. Wow. And she'd been glad he was joining her. What had she been thinking?

He'd finished his salad by the time she returned with the pizza and two plates.

She didn't say a word, only helped herself to

a piece and then reached for a napkin from the holder.

After a minute, Duncan said, "Thanks for ordering for both of us."

"You're welcome." But she didn't mean it.

"My day was lousy because the city council is pushing us for layoffs and because one of two teenagers who were in a car accident last night died this morning."

"Oh, no." The morning news had mentioned the accident. A boy who'd barely gotten his license had been taking his fifteen-year-old girlfriend for a drive, even though in Washington State he wasn't allowed to have minors in the car with him unless an adult was also along. He'd apparently been showing off by speeding. They'd left the road and rolled several times before coming to rest in a large drainage ditch. "The girl?" Jane asked.

Duncan shook his head. "The boy. The girl's still hanging in there."

"Oh, dear. I'm sorry." She made a face. "When I have a lousy day, it means my receipts are down or an employee called in sick. Not that someone died."

Duncan took a bite and didn't say anything else for a long time. Somehow she knew he intended to, however, so she waited.

"The boy's mother is a dispatcher. She was at work when…" He stopped.

"Oh, no," Jane whispered again.

"Oh, yeah." He sighed. "It really brings it home. You know?"

"I can imagine."

He told her about how hard the responding officers were taking it, about how the car had been nearly flattened, about calling the boy's parents himself. And then he talked about the proposed budget and about the maddening inability of city council members to grasp the needs of the police department they took for granted. His voice grew hoarse. Jane ached to reach across the table and take his hand in hers, but she kept hers on her own side of the table.

We are not friends, she told herself, and had to repeat it. *We are not friends.*

Uneasiness stirred in her. She hardly knew Duncan. They were strangers sharing a pizza. So how had this conversation morphed into something so…intimate?

They were both startled to discover Hector and Tito stood beside their table.

"I'm taking my son home now," Hector announced.

Jane smiled, but injected steel into her voice. "I'd better do that, Señor Ortez. Tito, why don't you say good-night now?"

Hector's nostrils flared. "I can't drive my own son home?"

"Your visitation is supervised. You understand that."

"I'm a good father. I don't deserve to be embarrassed in front of my son."

She sympathized. This whole process must be humiliating for a man of any pride, but at the same time the arrogance in his stance and voice made her wary. They were still in the first week. Did he understand what he risked if he chose to be uncooperative?

"If all goes well, it's not for long," she reminded him, very conscious of Duncan across the table. He sat utterly still, but she knew without touching him that every muscle in his body was rigid.

Hector said some uncomplimentary things in Spanish, but finally left Tito with Jane and Duncan and stomped out, his displeasure evident in his body language. Tito waited, head hanging low, while Jane got a box and put the leftover pizza in it.

She offered it to Tito. "Why don't you take it home. The last thing I need is leftovers."

His head came up and she saw that she'd offended him. "It's not my pizza."

"Oh, I shouldn't have bothered with the box,

then. I don't want to take it home. Duncan, do you?"

He shook his head. "I'm having both lunch and dinner out tomorrow. Tito, are you sure you don't want it?"

Tito hesitated, suspicious, but finally grabbed the box. "If nobody else wants it. Yolanda and Mateo might like some."

Jane knew they were his small niece and nephew. She couldn't remember the baby's name, if she'd ever heard it.

"Good," she said with a big smile, and laid a hand on Tito's shoulder as they walked out, Duncan silent beside them. Somehow she wasn't surprised when he accompanied them to her car, waiting until Tito had gotten in and she'd opened her door.

"Nicely done," he murmured in her ear, so close she felt the warmth of his breath and heard him more as a vibration than actual voice.

"Good night, Duncan," she said firmly.

He bent to look into her car. "When's our next visit?"

Tito shrugged. "Papa said he would call."

"Okay. Let me know if you want to shoot some baskets in the meantime."

Tito nodded but didn't say anything. Duncan didn't allow himself to show disappointment or hurt, but she was very sure that he felt both.

"All right, Tito," he said in a voice that astonished her with its gentleness. "Good night." He nodded at Jane, waited until she'd gotten in and closed her door, then walked away.

JANE'S WEEK GOT EVEN MORE stressful as the court date for another case she'd taken on neared. It was a far more contentious custody dispute with both parents and one set of grandparents all using the children as a battleground. If she'd known she would be handling the supervised visitation for Tito, she wouldn't have done both, but it was too late now. The fact that she was so busy was her only excuse for not wondering sooner why Hector and Tito hadn't scheduled another outing.

Duncan's call triggered her alarm.

"What's going on?" he demanded in his usual charming style.

She injected an excess of sugar into her voice. "Why, hello, Captain MacLachlan. How nice to hear from you."

"Jane…" It was a clear warning.

Did the man have friends? Date? Or could he be charming when he chose? Jane grimaced. She was never likely to find out since he obviously had no interest whatsoever in anything but butting heads with her. And she ought to be amending, *Thank God*.

"I haven't heard a peep from Hector," she said.

"It's been four days."

Her gaze flew to the calendar that hung beside her desk in the small office at Dance Dreams. "I'll check and let you know."

After she'd ended the call, she considered whether to try to reach Hector or whether she should stop by Lupe's and potentially talk to Tito instead—or first. Or better yet, both. She'd be closing the store in fifteen minutes. Today, if she remembered right, was one of Lupe's nights off. It was likely, therefore, that Hector would be joining his family for dinner.

Stop by, she decided. *Surprise them.*

Or waste half an hour on the one-and-only evening she'd had all week without an interview scheduled for the other case for which she stood as Guardian ad Litem.

Still.

She was nearing Lupe's apartment house when she spotted Hector and Tito walking toward it. Tito was dribbling a basketball and they were talking. Feeling a headache coming on, Jane drove a circuitous route so that they didn't see her and parked around the corner. Then she hustled into the vestibule of the front door and waited, arms crossed, toe tapping in irritation.

They all but bumped into her. Worry flared on Tito's face, anger on his father's.

"What are you doing here?" Hector asked.

"Tito," she said calmly, "please go up to your sister's apartment. Your father and I need to talk."

Tito looked anxiously at Hector, then nodded and hurried inside. Jane didn't say a word until she heard his footsteps on the stairs. Then she said, "You've violated the conditions of your visitation with your son. I could go to the judge right now and tell him I think you shouldn't be allowed to see Tito at all."

He leaned toward her, his face flushed. "I'm allowed to have dinner with my children."

"You heard and understood Judge Lehman. You cannot spend time with Tito unless either I or Lupe are with you." She looked around ostentatiously. "Where is Lupe?"

"We went out only for a few minutes while she cooked."

"This isn't the first time, is it?"

His furious stare gave her his answer.

"Señor Ortez, I will be calling Judge Lehman tomorrow. I'm going to give you one more chance to comply with the order. However, you can no longer visit Tito at your daughter's apartment."

He slammed a fist against the wall to one side. Jane couldn't help jumping.

"*Hijo de puta*. This isn't right! I would never hurt one of my children. I've done nothing to deserve to be treated like some kind of monster!"

"Please don't swear at me." Doing her best not

to let him see that she was beginning to be frightened, Jane said, "If you love your son, you'll co-operate for one month. That's little enough to ask. If you can't do that, tell me now."

They stared at each other, his eyes dilated and red suffusing his face. His lips were drawn away from his teeth and he was breathing hard.

Jane held herself still, refusing to let him see that she was quaking inside.

He said finally, "I have no choice, do I? But I see now that you want to take my son away from me. Perhaps you want to give him to that police-man who was spending so much time with Tito. These visits—" he spat to one side "—they're nothing but a front, are they? So if I say later, I wasn't treated fairly, you can say, see? He had his chance. But it's a lie. Now I know."

"No," she said. "I promise you, Hector. Your future with your son is in your hands. If Tito doesn't come to live with you it will be your fault, because you didn't follow through with the judge's requirements. You can make this hard or you can make it easy. You can be smart. Why not be smart, Hector?"

He rocked on his heels. "Am I permitted to go upstairs and tell my family why I can't eat dinner at their table?"

She didn't dare back down at all. "I'll tell them."

With a vicious curse—in Spanish, thank God—

he punched the wall again and swung away. A minute later, Jane heard the cough and uneven roar from Hector's pickup, and then it accelerated past on the street.

She leaned against the wall for a minute and let herself shake.

"Well, that was fun," she said out loud. "To answer your question, Captain MacLachlan, *this* is what I do for fun."

DUNCAN WAITED UNTIL SEVEN and, when he still hadn't heard from her, called Jane's cell phone. When she answered, he said, "Well?"

"Has anybody ever told you your conversational skills stink?"

"You've hinted as much." He frowned. There had been something in her voice. Only tiredness, or had something happened to upset her? "So?"

She sighed. "About what you probably expect. Lupe couldn't say no to her own father. I caught Hector taking Tito out to shoot baskets without supervision."

Duncan swore. "Are you going to do anything about it, or did you issue a gentle warning?"

"Do I really give the impression of being such a pushover?"

She sounded offended enough, he was taken aback. *No,* he thought, Jane Brooks was anything but a pushover.

He'd been silent long enough she didn't wait for an answer.

"I've told Hector he can no longer see Tito at Lupe's apartment. No family dinners. He will see his son *only* under my direct supervision. Does that satisfy you, Captain?"

He didn't know. The same indefinable something was in her voice.

"How did he take it?"

"Not well," she admitted.

Duncan tensed. "He didn't lay a hand on you?"

"No. Nothing like that. Only said some bad words, complained we have no intention of really letting him have custody of his son and stormed away."

Duncan's doorbell rang. Frowning, he went to answer it. To Jane, he said, "I should have gone with you."

He was flinging the front door open to find his brother on the porch when Jane said, "Get real. That would have made everything way worse. He suspects you want to steal his son from him." After a brief pause, she said, "With reason."

"What the hell are you talking about?" he snapped.

Waiting with his hands shoved in the pockets of his leather jacket, Niall raised his eyebrows and grinned. Duncan glared at him and briefly covered the mouthpiece of the phone. "What do *you* want?"

"What's that supposed to mean?" Jane asked, sounding incensed.

"I wasn't talking to you. My brother's decided to drop in on me." With a grimace, he stepped to the side and let Niall in. He closed the door and started for the kitchen. "Jane, you know I can't have Tito. So what's this 'with reason'?"

"You love Tito. That makes you a threat to Hector. An understandable one."

"It's *bad* that I'm spending time with the boy?" he asked incredulously.

"No. Of course not. I didn't mean that. Only that I can see why Hector is afraid."

Aware of his brother watching him, Duncan pinched the bridge of his nose and momentarily closed his eyes. "I don't love him," he muttered.

"Are you sure?" Her voice had softened. "Sometimes we can't help ourselves." After a momentary silence, she added more briskly, "It doesn't matter, anyway. Hector needs to concentrate on his own behavior. His relationship with his son. That's what he doesn't quite get."

"*Quite?* Understatement."

"I was blunt. I can be."

Suddenly he was smiling, something he hadn't felt like doing all day. "I won't argue with that."

"Gee, thanks." Some of her spirit had returned. "I'll call when I hear from Hector. Okay?"

"Okay." The smile hadn't lasted long. Duncan found he was frowning. "Jane? Be careful."

"I will. But Hector's not like that. All he was doing today was venting."

Duncan ended the call feeling uneasy. Whatever she said to the contrary, he was betting Hector Ortez had scared her today. She *should* be scared when she confronted a pissed-off guy who'd barely gotten out of prison for having killed someone. Hector wasn't a big man, not a lot taller than Jane, but he outweighed her by fifty pounds or more, and a whole lot of muscle.

Better yet, she shouldn't be confronting someone like that.

It had been daylight, he reminded himself. It sounded as if she'd met Hector at Lupe's apartment house, which meant there had been other people around. And sharp as Jane could be, he'd also seen her exude warmth. Hector had seemed initially to like her.

She was probably right. Sober, Hector wasn't stupid enough to act out his rage.

Perturbed, Duncan realized he wasn't as reassured as he'd like to be. It was a good thing that he'd be there most of the time to deflect Hector's anger. She wouldn't like knowing he felt protective—*he* wasn't sure he liked knowing that he did—but there it was.

"This about the kid you've been hanging out with?" Niall asked. He'd peeled off his leather bomber jacket and gone to the refrigerator. He emerged with two beers in his hand.

Duncan took one. "How do you know I've been hanging out with a kid?"

Niall shrugged. "People talk."

"Goddamn it. What are they saying?"

"Not much. That there's a kid. Somebody thought you might have signed up for Big Brothers." Niall didn't smile. "I found that...unlikely."

Duncan studied Niall, three years younger than him. They weren't what you'd call close. They spoke. Occasionally one of them stopped by the other's house for a beer or they sat side by side on stools at the bar one block from the police station. Niall was on the force, too, a detective in major crimes. People were aware they were related, but they didn't have much to do with each other on the job, even though Duncan was, several rungs up the ladder, Niall's boss. He was still frequently bemused by the knowledge that his little brother, with a juvenile record as long as his arm, had become a cop. A good one, too. Probably because of his experience on the other side of the fence.

They were of a similar height and build, but Niall had their father's red hair. Auburn, in his case. He'd had freckles as a boy that were no longer visible. His gray eyes were often as cool as Duncan's.

"The kid's name is Tito Ortez. He broke into the house one night." Duncan told his brother the story, including recent events.

To his surprise, Niall said, "I remember the killing." He took a long swallow of beer. "I was close to an arrest on the guy who died. A real scumbag. Meant all that time I'd spent building a case was wasted. Down the tubes. On the other hand—" his quick grin flashed "—I didn't have to testify in court."

Duncan could identify with that. "Ortez claimed self-defense."

Niall waggled the hand that wasn't holding a beer. Sign language for "Could have been, but maybe not." That had been Duncan's conclusion, too. After catching glimpses of the anger Hector barely kept in check, Duncan was leaning more toward "maybe not."

"This Jane," Niall said, watching his brother.

"This Jane nothing. She's a pain in the ass."

"You smiled."

"I've been known to."

"On historic occasions." When Duncan said nothing, Niall let it go. "Conall called."

Duncan swallowed some beer, careful not to show any reaction. "Did he."

"He's involved in bringing down a drug cartel in Baja. Says he's getting a great tan."

The youngest MacLachlan brother, Conall, had always been hot-blooded and reckless. After their mother walked out of their lives, Niall had surrendered to Duncan's authority after a good scare—administered by Duncan. Conall, in contrast, had fought long and hard. He hated Duncan to this day. But so what? Duncan hadn't been trying to win his brothers' unstinting love and devotion. He'd been determined to save them from their father's path, and he had. Ironically, Conall, too, had become a cop, although in his case with the Drug Enforcement Agency. He surfaced from undercover occasionally to stay in touch with Niall.

Duncan wondered sometimes if he'd even recognize Conall if they came face-to-face.

Niall finished his beer and crushed the can. He let it fly and pumped his fist when it dropped unerringly into the recycling container. Duncan had a flash of memory: the two of them out shooting baskets at the school, dusk making it hard to see, but both of them reluctant to stop. They'd never talked much, only played. Communicated with body checks, high fives, grunts and laughs. Time on the court had been the best they'd spent together.

He'd been trying to re-create it with Tito, Duncan realized with a minor shock. Okay, he'd known in one way that he was, in a deliberate sense, but not that there had been an emotional component for him.

You love Tito.

He still shook off Jane's accusation. Of course he didn't. But...hell. He'd maybe wanted to go back. Have a redo.

Impossible.

"I'm taking off," Niall said, heading for the door. "I've got a date."

"Did you actually want something?"

Niall grinned. "Nope. Checking out the rumors, that's all."

Duncan shook his head in disgust, but walked his brother to the door. Night was settling. He stood on the porch and watched as Niall kicked his Harley to life and rode it away down the street. Duncan was already thinking about Jane.

Probably because he couldn't remember the last time *he'd* had a date.

CHAPTER FIVE

YOU BITCH.

Keys clutched tightly in her hand, Jane stared at the two words spray-painted on the back door of her store. The garish red paint was fresh enough to still be dripping. She had no doubt whatsoever that the nasty accusation was aimed at her. She had one full-time employee and a couple part-time clerks, but she opened the store herself almost every day.

Her mind leaped to her newest Guardian ad Litem case. The father and the grandmother were being particularly hostile. Jane wasn't done with her interviews, but she was already leaning toward recommending the mother have custody. She at least occasionally seemed to remember that the welfare of the two kids should be paramount.

After a moment Jane's mouth firmed and she unlocked the door. Thank goodness nobody else was here yet. Unless she was willing to share present and past cases—which she couldn't—calling the police wouldn't do any good.

Sticks and stones, she told herself. She'd been called worse, most of the time face-to-face. A couple of times, she'd received really ugly, anonymous phone calls. She'd shrugged them off, and spray paint on the door wasn't any worse than hearing the words, was it?

She let herself into Dance Dreams, dropped her purse into a drawer in her office, then filled a bucket with hot, sudsy water and went outside to scrub away the ugly words. She tossed the water into a weedy strip behind a garbage Dumpster, inspected the now-clean door with satisfaction then went inside to open the cash register.

A moment later she popped back out. What if the vandal had been dumb enough to toss the paint can in the Dumpster, complete with fingerprints? But when she clanged the lid open she saw that it was empty. The garbage had been picked up yesterday, and nothing had been dropped in there in the meantime.

Hector called midday and asked to spend much of the day with his son tomorrow, Saturday. Jane, wondering when she'd next have time to do any serious housecleaning, agreed that she could be available. Since she had no customers in the store at that moment, she called Duncan's cell phone and left a message telling him the time and place.

He returned her call in the late afternoon,

asking without preamble, "Was he a jackass again?"

"Huh?"

"There was something in your voice."

That made her blink. It was possible that when she'd left him the message she'd still been feeling stressed because of the nasty message spray-painted on the door. But how was it possible that Duncan had read her tone that accurately?

Knowing that he had, and that there had been a kind of gruff concern in his original question, momentarily weakened her. And *that* unnerved her. She had to do quick battle with the temptation to tell him what had actually upset her. Fortunately, she was strong enough to win. Of course she wasn't going to make a looming mountain out of a molehill, and that's exactly what would happen if she involved the police in something so essentially meaningless. Duncan was *not* the man to listen sympathetically. Nope, he'd launch a full-scale investigation.

"You're imagining things," she told him. Lied. "Hector and I had a civil conversation."

He apparently accepted her answer, which made her feel a little bit guilty. "He wants to take Tito to Camano Island State Park? What's he doing, packing a picnic?"

"Apparently. And they plan to go to the beach.

He says there's supposed to be an especially low tide. He thought Tito would enjoy the tide pools."

There was silence.

She felt compelled to say, "I actually thought it was a really nice idea."

Duncan sighed. "Yeah. It's just…Camano Island?"

It would be at least an hour's drive each way. She didn't suppose his life was any less stressful than hers.

"You don't have to go," she said without any real hope. Hope of what? Jane asked herself in the next second. That he wouldn't come? Or that he would?

Without hesitation, he asked, "Do you want to bring the picnic, or shall I?"

"I will. You'd probably try to poison me."

"It's really my turn. You bought the pizza."

She almost laughed at his lack of enthusiasm for the idea of bringing their picnic lunch. "I don't mind. Do you have any major likes or dislikes?"

They discussed food tastes briefly, agreeing that they both hated coleslaw and would agree to disagree on pickles. Considering she hadn't had time to do a grocery shop all week, Jane decided to go to a favorite deli in the morning before she picked up Tito.

"Why don't I drive?" Duncan suggested. "Does Tito go with you or Hector?"

"Me, this time. I need to make a point."

"Good," he said. "Where do I pick you up?"

"Home," she said and gave him the address. They agreed on eleven o'clock.

She hung up feeling slightly giddy. As if she had a date with Duncan MacLachlan. A real date.

JANE LAID OUT THE LUNCH she'd brought on a rough-hewn table in the picnic area set among old-growth cedars and Douglas firs, preserved when the land was set aside to be a state park.

As Duncan sat across from her, he said, "I knew an old lady whose mother told her that the whole island was once forested like this. She said the trees were so big, you could drive a buggy from one end of the island to the other beneath the canopy. There wasn't any of the scrubby undergrowth in those days."

"Really?" She looked around, her face showing pleasure and less tension than usual. Despite the presence of Hector and Tito, a short distance away at their own picnic table, Jane had relaxed a little.

He was a little surprised to realize how relaxed he'd begun to feel, too. Maybe this outing hadn't been such a bad idea. Tito had chattered excitedly the whole way. He remembered going to the beach when he was a little kid, he said, but it had been a long time ago. Duncan felt bad that he hadn't thought of something like this. No kid should live in a county that, while landlocked, was only a short drive from Puget Sound, and never make it to the beach. The trouble was, they didn't have a good public one much closer than this.

Camano Island was long and narrow, linked to the mainland by a bridge. The state park occupied land on the west side, looking across Saratoga Passage to Whidbey Island and, beyond that, the Olympic Mountains. Duncan knew that gray whales and occasionally orcas were seen in Saratoga Passage. He imagined what a thrill seeing a whale would be for Tito.

"Great potato salad," he said, and Jane smiled.

"I'd take credit, but, uh…"

"Snow Goose Deli?"

"Yep."

"Thought I recognized it." Apparently he and Jane had something in common besides detesting coleslaw. "I'm surprised Hector thought of this," he said after a minute.

"Me, too." She sneaked a glance at the pair at the adjoining table. "He's made some effort to be pleasant today, too."

"You must have scared him."

"Gee, thanks. Maybe it was my gentle ways that persuaded him cooperation beat butting heads."

Duncan was in a good enough mood to say, "Could be."

She finished her sandwich and took a drink of her diet cola. "Hector says hello when he calls. Goodbye, too," she said in a thoughtful voice.

Duncan grinned. "Huh."

Imagining what Niall would say to see his brother smiling—again!—was almost enough to wipe the grin from his mouth, but not quite.

"He doesn't assume I know who's calling, either. He's been known to say, Ms. Brooks, this is Hector Ortez."

"A considerate man."

"Occasionally even a gentleman," she agreed, a dimple in one cheek betraying her effort not to smile.

The teasing light in her eyes did something to Duncan that he was quite sure she didn't intend. She might irritate him now and again, but he wanted her in a way he hadn't wanted any woman in a long time. Maybe, he thought, disconcerted, ever. All that fire and stubbornness wouldn't be easy to live with, but taking it to bed was another story.

He moved uncomfortably now that his jeans had a tighter fit. "Should I be reading something into this?" he asked blandly.

The smile was definitely appearing now, but she managed to add a hint of doubt to her voice.

"I feel sure you know how to be a gentleman, too."

Did he? He'd grown up determined to survive. To escape. Maybe his mother had tried to teach her sons manners. If so, he didn't remember.

"Why are you frowning?" Jane asked. "Did I hit too close to home?"

Was he frowning? Yeah, damn it.

"Sorry. You got me thinking about something."

"Something?" Her head was tilted to one side.

"My mother." Strange, because he so rarely let himself think about her. "I was trying to remember whether she tried very hard to teach us manners, or whether she gave up early on."

"Us? Oh. You said something about a brother."

"I have two."

"You sound like your mother is dead," Jane said tentatively.

Usually he shut people down who asked about his family. For some reason he didn't want to do that with her. Their relationship had so far been abrasive but also honest. Maybe opening up some was a way of testing her.

He didn't let himself think about what the test results would mean.

"No. She walked out on us when I was eighteen. I haven't seen her since."

Her mouth opened in shock. "That's awful!"

"Yeah, it pretty well sucked," he heard himself admitting.

Eyes big and drenched with color, she studied him. "At least you were, well, an adult."

"I was," he agreed.

Had she heard the subtle emphasis on *I*? He saw immediately that she had.

"Your brothers?"

"Were twelve and fifteen."

"Surely you had a father."

Nope, he was in the slammer.

Time to cut off this line of questioning. He'd said enough already.

"No," he said briefly, wadding the paper that had wrapped his sandwich. "I was an adult. We managed."

"Dear Lord," she murmured.

He couldn't help the sardonic twist to his mouth. The dear Lord hadn't been around to help, that he could see.

"You raised them."

"Yes."

This time his answer was curt enough to send a signal. She stiffened slightly. After a moment, she carefully rewrapped the half of her sandwich that she hadn't eaten.

She took a bag of scones out of the basket she'd used to carry their lunches. "Cranberry orange."

"Damn. I'm glad I let you bring the food."

Watching surreptitiously, he was glad to see her mouth soften.

"You're welcome." Her eyes were cool when they met his, however. "I'm surprised you didn't bring some kind of listening device so we could hear every word Hector and Tito exchange."

Ah. That sounded more like the Jane he knew and... Didn't love.

"Maybe I'm recording them," Duncan suggested blandly.

Her laugh was low and, like everything else about her, too damn sexy for his own good.

"That wouldn't surprise me," she said.

From the other table, Hector called, "Are you ready to go to the beach?"

Jane swiveled on the bench. "Yep. Give me a second to put our lunch stuff away."

She repacked the basket and Duncan stowed it in the cargo area of his SUV. After a side trip to the restroom, they all headed down the path to the beach.

Split rails kept visitors from tumbling down the bank. Undergrown with glossy green salal, madrona trees with their distinctive, peeling red bark leaned precariously over the bluff. The salt-water scent was strong, probably because of the low tide. Duncan couldn't help breathing it in with pleasure. The sun sparkled on the water, and beyond the low, green sprawl of Whidbey

Island the Olympic Mountains were sharp and still snow-covered. A late-spring haze made them appear to float unconnected to earth.

The sun was warm on Duncan's face. He wanted to tilt his head back and soak it in. When was the last time he'd gone to the beach? Probably not any more recently than Tito.

Could be it was talking about his mother that brought her to mind now, but he had an oddly vivid memory of her taking all three boys to the beach. Not this one—the one in his memory was sandy. The sun was warm, though, even warmer than today. Conall had been a toddler, which meant Duncan was...no more than eight, he supposed. His mother had been laughing and pretty, nothing like the tense, pinched, controlled woman he better remembered. She'd drawn more and more inward as time went on, he understood for the first time. Hiding. From Dad? From all her failures, including her children? In recent years he'd thought of her as cold, but that wasn't quite right.

Ahead, Tito let out a hoot and bounded the last little way, skidding onto the gravel beach. Duncan smiled at the boy's eagerness.

I was as eager, that long-ago day.

When had he lost the ability to have fun?

"Look at that driftwood! Can I climb on it, Papa?"

"Of course you can," his father said. "But be careful. It's easy to slip."

Hector stopped and watched Tito scramble over whole trees, silvered by the salt water and cast by winter waves like so many pickup sticks against the island bluff. Duncan and Jane paused, too, but it seemed to him that Hector was pretending they weren't here.

After a minute Jane turned away from the others. She chose her own pile of driftwood and, to Duncan's amusement, straddled a fat log and then swung herself to her feet atop it like a gymnast on a balance beam. She walked its length then stepped onto a narrower log that lay at a slant. Duncan paralleled her, keeping his feet on the gravelly beach. Once she slipped and stretched her arms out to help herself balance. When she reached the top of the slope, she grinned at him in triumph.

"I'm queen of the mountain."

"Is that a challenge?"

She made a laughing face at him. "No, I don't want an elbow to the nose, thank you, anyway."

An elbow...? Then he remembered telling her about giving Judge Lehman a bloody nose. He grinned up at her. "Would I do that? I'm a gentleman, remember?"

She started to answer, but looked past him and called out in alarm, "Tito! What are you doing?"

Duncan turned, too. Hector was laughing and calling something up at his son. The boy had clambered high atop the heap of driftwood and was now swinging from the branch of a madrona that had grown from the bank at an angle. Bright red bark was crumbling onto his head and shoulders. Even before his mind consciously noticed that pebbles and dirt from the bank were showering onto the beach below, Duncan was already moving.

He brushed past Hector, who had turned to glower at Jane. Within seconds Duncan had leaped up the driftwood and reached Tito. He grabbed him around the waist and ordered, "Let go. Now."

"Why?" Tito protested, kicking at him.

"The tree's not strong enough to hold you." Once Duncan had the boy's feet planted beside him on a solid stretch of log, he pointed at the fresh tears in the bank. "See?"

"Oh."

The anger knotted in Duncan's gut wasn't for Tito, who was only a kid. Kids did dumb things. It was their fathers who were supposed to stop them.

Jane had reached Hector before Duncan did, though.

"If he'd fallen, he would have been badly hurt," she was saying.

Duncan was too mad to tell whether Hector's belligerent expression hid guilt.

"That boys need to play. To be physical." He sneered. "Women always want to baby their sons. You can't help yourselves."

Duncan grabbed his shoulder and spun him around. "You couldn't see that the tree wasn't deeply enough rooted to hold him? He'd have hit a log if he'd fallen and been badly injured!"

Hector shoved him hard. Duncan barely fell back a step, his anger suffusing him, blinding him. He'd known this son of a bitch wasn't good enough for Tito. If he had been, he'd have thought of his family before he got in the vicious brawl that resulted in a prison term. He would have put them first. Tito wouldn't have been left with no parent at all.

"Don't you put a hand on me," he said in a low, hard voice.

"You put a hand on me first!" Hector's face was inches from his. Violence boiled in the air.

For once in his life, Duncan didn't care. He felt like hurting someone. This pathetic excuse for a father needed a wake-up call. Duncan could provide it. He was snarling and leaning in even farther when Jane shoved her way between the two men, planted a hand on each chest and pushed.

"What are you *thinking?*" It was him she was looking at, not Hector. "Get a grip! Behave yourself." Finally she spared a fulminating glance for Hector. "Both of you."

Duncan staggered a couple of steps. He felt stunned, as though he'd taken a blow to the head. Had he really been about to slug a man who hadn't done anything but egg his kid on to do something that was a little bit dangerous? Duncan was always in control. Always. He was the original iceberg. He couldn't remember the last time he'd let himself feel much of anything.

"There's a child here! What a fine example the two of you set. About ready to get in a fistfight over nothing! Men!" Jane said in disgust.

Duncan saw that Tito had clambered down behind him and now stood staring at them with shocked dark eyes. He looked as scared as he had the night Duncan had drawn a gun on him.

Jane stalked over to Tito and swept him into her arms for a big hug. "Pretend you didn't see that," she told him. "I'm quite sure your father and Captain MacLachlan will be apologizing to each other and to you." She stared at them over Tito's dark head. "Won't you?"

Still in that state of disbelief, Duncan realized he'd have placed any of his officers under suspension for behaving with so little self-restraint. Thank God no one was near enough to have seen.

He groaned and looked at Hector. "Ms. Brooks is right. I overreacted. I thought Tito was about to fall and..." He swallowed and finished. "I acted out of fear."

Hector didn't look any happier than Duncan felt, but after a moment he dipped his head. "I thought what Tito was doing was safe. From here I couldn't see well."

Duncan turned and saw that it was true. Hector's view had been partially blocked. He probably hadn't seen the crumbling bluff. Which didn't altogether excuse him; he should have moved so that he could monitor his son.

But you can't watch them every minute. Duncan had tried, once the sole responsibility for his brothers was his, but he'd learned it wasn't possible.

After a minute Duncan held out a hand. Hector's eyes narrowed and he stared at it for a moment that stretched. Duncan was aware in his peripheral vision of Jane and Tito watching, the boy still held close to her. Perhaps Hector felt them watching, too, because finally he held out his hand and they shook. Their gazes met and held, still challenging, but Duncan saw traces of the shame he felt in the other man's eyes.

"Why don't you two go look at tide pools?" Jane suggested, giving Tito one last hug and then a gentle push forward. "Let's not waste a glorious day."

Duncan stood where he was and watched

Hector and Tito walk away, more distance between them than had been there earlier. He felt
guilty for that, and bothered because, damn it, it
was his fault the whole thing had blown up like
that.

At the same time, the fact that *she* had had to
intervene, that in this situation she held the authority, tasted bitter in his mouth.

Jane stood a few feet away looking at him.
Eventually she said, "Do you want to walk? Or
find someplace to sit down?"

He was still full of adrenaline and a complicated stew of emotions. "We can't go very far."

"Hector's not going to take off with Tito. We
can walk a ways down the beach."

Duncan gave a curt nod. They set out side by
side, by common consent staying close to the lap
of water. The smooth beach pebbles slipped and
slid under their feet. From time to time dried sea-
weed crunched underfoot. The sun was still high,
still warm, but Duncan felt cold inside.

"What was that about?" Jane finally asked.
Quietly, as if she really wanted to know. "I know
you don't like Hector, but..." Her sidelong glance
was uneasy.

Crap. The frustration at being in the wrong,
at having been called on it, still ate at him. She
could block him from Tito's life if she felt in-

clined. He hated knowing he had to answer her question.

What was that *about?*

Things he didn't like to talk about. Resented having to tell her.

He stared ahead, vaguely aware of some kids running and trying to get a kite aloft, of people in small clusters peering into tide pools, of some teenage boys lounging in a V formed by driftwood and drinking beer from a cooler.

"When I was growing up, my father was in and out of prison. He was a drug dealer. A real professional." His tone was ironic, giving away nothing of how he'd felt as a child with a father like that. "He never used. I guess that was one good thing. Dad was sentenced to ten years the day Mom threw up her hands and walked out."

"He wasn't there when you needed him."

He wanted to tell her that was simplistic psychobabble, but...she was right. "No."

"You were angry at your father, not Hector."

Duncan could tell she was thinking it out, wanting to believe his idiocy had been triggered by some deep childhood trauma. Because she wanted to excuse him?

He didn't deserve to be excused, detested being psychoanalyzed.

"Tito broke into my house. Did I tell you I pulled a gun on him?"

Jane stared at him, aghast.

"Where was his father when he was getting into trouble?" Duncan asked, the remnants of rage roughening his voice. "The same place my father was when my brothers were in and out of juvie. I can't excuse how I behaved, but you know what? Hector wasn't there when his son needed him, either."

Their hands brushed. Duncan realized that, sometime in the past few minutes, he'd become conscious again of Jane as a woman. Her supple calves and ankles, bared by cropped chinos. Long, narrow feet, toenails painted the color of spring blooming lilacs. The shimmer of sunlight off her hair, the curve of her cheek, those eyes.

She was gazing ahead now, looking troubled. Not as if she was reacting in any way to him. Hell, he thought, a few minutes ago she'd regarded him with disgust, and he couldn't blame her even as it made his skin crawl to know that he'd revealed too much of himself to her through that display of anger.

Finally she said, "But...Hector's trying to be there for Tito now." She stopped and they both looked back.

Duncan spotted the two immediately, Tito standing and his father crouched, both with their heads bent as they peered intently down.

"For how long?" he asked. "You've seen how easily he loses it."

"He's only been arrested the once. His older kids speak highly of him. He's got a temper, sure." In her pause, it was obvious what she was thinking. *So do you.* "You have to admit, this whole setup has got to be hard on his ego. He gets out of prison, thinks at last he has his dignity again, only to be told he can't even see his son without someone making sure he behaves himself. These aren't exactly ideal circumstances."

"No." Duncan could understand why Hector's pride felt rubbed raw right now. Which didn't excuse the way he'd failed his young son.

She stopped. He took another stride and realized she wasn't with him. When he turned to face her, she was looking gravely at him.

"You know you should back off. Leave this to me."

"I played right into your hands," he realized, feeling foolish. Not angry now, but...unsettled. With that one flash of blinding fury, he'd handed her power over him, and there was nothing he hated more than knowing somebody had a bit in his mouth. "I suppose you'll be calling Lehman come Monday morning and telling him I'm not dispassionate enough to be involved."

She kept looking at him for a disconcertingly long time. But finally she shook her head. "No.

I won't. What happened here today is nobody's business but ours. If you'd actually hit Hector, I wouldn't have had any choice, but fortunately it didn't go that far."

"I wouldn't have let it." He sounded hoarse, and wished he could be sure.

"Okay," she agreed, after only the tiniest of pauses. "Maybe we should turn around."

He nodded. They walked in silence.

"Do you want to look at tide pools?" he finally asked.

Her sigh wasn't meant for him to hear, he was sure. "We might as well," she said, sounding resigned more than pleased.

They'd been having a good day. He'd ruined it. No, he thought with a spurt of anger, it wasn't all his fault. Tito could have been hurt. Duncan had had to intervene, whether Hector liked it or not.

Whether Jane liked it or not.

The idea that they could have fun today—that had been doomed from the get-go. He didn't have fun, and this was why. It was hardly an epiphany to admit to himself that he couldn't let go of his sense of responsibility long enough to have genuine fun. Even as a teenager, he'd been too fixed on his goals. There would be time once he made his escape, he had promised himself. Except that then he hadn't been able to escape after all. Duncan remembered that sensation of his back bowing beneath the weight of the burden he had knowingly, grimly accepted: his brothers. He'd done his duty; they'd grown up. But had he ever felt light, free of the weight?

No, because by then he was a police officer, rising in the hierarchy, accepting new responsibilities. By then he'd seen so much that was grim, learned to view people in such a cynical light, feeling light, *fun*, was next to impossible.

And he and Jane weren't here to have a good time, he reminded himself. They were here to keep Tito safe. He'd done that.

To hell with Hector. Jane needed to get real.

They'd covered a distance while he brooded. He surfaced when she stopped and, like a child, squatted to peer into a shallow, rocky tide pool. A vividly colored starfish clung to one side and small pale crabs scuttled along the edge. Purplish barnacles grew from the rocks.

It wasn't the tide pool Duncan looked at, though. It was Jane, her face transformed by the simple pleasure of the moment. He felt something strange, and far more complicated than desire for a graceful, pretty woman. It reminded him unpleasantly of the stomach-clenching instant when he saw a speeding car swerving in and out of traffic and knew with absolutely certainty that an accident was going to happen and he had no way to stop it.

CHAPTER SIX

TITO HAD CARRIED A POCKET of happiness with him since yesterday, when Mr. Munro had handed out the graded quizzes in math class. It had stayed in his belly, a warm spot. He didn't usually have anything to brag about, but today he did.

He kept remembering the wait. Since Mr. Munro had started on the other side of the room, it took him a long time to get to Tito.

Usually Tito wouldn't care about the quiz. Half the time, he didn't bother doing the assignments. They weren't that hard, but he'd always thought they were boring. This week, though, Duncan had taken Tito home with him one evening and they had sat working on his math homework. Most of the time Tito didn't see what use any of the math they taught would ever be to him, but Duncan had showed him how he used the stuff Tito was learning right now all the time, and that had made him look at it differently.

Mr. Munro had finally reached him and laid the quiz in front of him on the desk. A big red A appeared at the top, along with the words "Good going, Tito!"

"Perfect score," the teacher said, with a friendly nod that made Tito flush with happiness. He shrugged and ducked his head to hide how he felt. But he carefully tucked the quiz in his book bag. He would pay attention next week, too.

Today he and Papa were to play soccer. Tito finally had his moment when they were walking toward the field and his father asked, "How was school this week?"

"I got an A on the test in math," Tito told him.

Papa gave him a big smile and laid a hand on his shoulder. "That's good!"

Tito could hear Jane and Duncan talking behind him and Papa. He wished he could tell Duncan about the A, too, maybe even show him the quiz, but he wasn't that stupid. His father wouldn't like it. To Papa, Duncan was like the police officers who had arrested him and the guards who had tried to humiliate him in the prison. They were all the enemy. Papa wouldn't be smiling if he knew Tito had gotten that A because Duncan helped him.

He'd had a chance to spend time with Duncan again only because Papa had gotten caught taking Tito over to the school unsupervised. Now they saw each other only twice a week. Once on the weekend, and once in the evening during the week. He didn't want anybody to know he was a little relieved. He liked knowing he could also shoot baskets with Duncan or even be by himself.

Who would care how he felt, anyway? he asked himself.

His father believed all should be the same as before he went away, but it wasn't. Tito wasn't a little kid anymore. He knew Lupe hoped he would go live with Papa, because her life was hard enough already. He understood, but it meant he couldn't talk to her. And even though Jane said she would listen to him, Tito didn't fool himself that he had any real choice. Everything happened *to* him, whether he liked it or not.

Mostly he was okay with it. Family was family. He knew that. So what if sometimes he thought he liked Duncan better than he did his own father? He didn't even know why Duncan bothered with him, or how long he would.

Right then his father, laughing, stole the ball from Tito. He'd rather play basketball. But, of course, they couldn't. Papa wasn't willing to play a sport that he wasn't so good at in front of Duncan. Tito knew that's why he made excuses and it was always soccer, soccer, soccer.

Lagging behind his father, wondering what Jane and Duncan were talking about, Tito suddenly realized he'd lost the happiness he had been hugging to himself. He didn't totally understand why, but knew it had to do with all these adults who each wanted something different from him.

Which Tito am I tonight? he asked himself, and now the glow in his belly was a smolder of resentment instead.

"MAYBE WE SHOULD START bringing our own soccer ball," Jane suggested, half-seriously. "We could take over the other half of the field."

"What?"

Good to know Duncan had forgotten she was even there. She'd been so conscious of him, she'd had the uncomfortable feeling that every cell in her body had swiveled his way, as if he called to her. True north. Meantime, his mind had been somewhere else entirely.

She repeated what she'd said.

He cast her an unreadable glance. "You play?"

"Anyone can kick a ball."

"You don't play."

Feeling inexplicably sulky, she said, "Forget it, okay?"

Great. Now he was noticing her. She kept her gaze stubbornly forward, but felt the familiar intensity of his assessment.

"Did you play any sports when you were a kid?" he asked.

"No."

"Why not?"

"Does it matter?" They'd reached the sideline. "I'm going to walk tonight instead of sitting. If I circle the field, I can keep an eye on Tito and get some exercise, too." Fingers crossed that he'd stay behind, she turned and walked away.

But no. He fell into step with her.

"Aren't you afraid you'll miss something?" she asked grumpily.

"Aren't you afraid Hector and I'll go at it if you don't stick around to supervise?" he asked, sounding curious and possibly amused.

"If you do, I can get you banned from these expeditions. That doesn't sound all bad right now."

"You're in a mood."

They reached the corner of the field and turned left. Jane could now see Tito and his father again. Tito was apparently playing goalie. She saw him make a halfhearted attempt at a save.

Odd, because she'd thought he was in good spirits when she picked him up at Lupe's. Had Hector said something that upset him? Tito's last glance over his shoulder before he joined his father on the field had been sullen, now that she thought about it.

She and Duncan reached the next corner and she turned sharply left again, walking fast. It annoyed her to realize that, with his longer legs, he was barely strolling while she'd probably end up puffing and panting in no time.

"No comment?" he prodded.

"About?"

"Why are you in such a pissy mood?"

She determined to make an effort. "I'm sorry if I seem that way. I have things on my mind, that's all."

Which was true. She'd been busy at work today; local dance schools were having recitals in the next month, and providing the costumes was lucrative for her. She loved watching giggling girls try on extravagant pink-and-purple leotards with stiff tutus, staring at themselves in wonder in the wall of mirrors. When she was that age, she'd dreamed of wearing something like that, of dancing on stage. She had known with all her being that she would be the epitomy of grace if only she could have ballet shoes. She would float like a downy seed head being lifted by a gentle breeze. Oh, how vividly she'd been able to see herself, knowing all the time that her dreams would never be real.

But her disposition had more to do with the nasty message that had arrived in the mail today. It had been a folded piece of eight-and-a-half-by-eleven colored paper, stapled to keep it closed. She'd torn it open assuming it was a flyer advertising a special at a local business, or perhaps a fundraiser for some nonprofit. Grateful to have a quiet moment to eat her sandwich and open the mail, she wasn't paying that much attention. And then she'd laid the paper flat and seen the message.

Bitch you think you can do anything you want but youll be sorry

It wasn't so much the words that had momentarily raised goose bumps; it was the fact that, in the best tradition of threatening notes, the letters had been individually cut out of magazines and newspapers and glued down. No punctuation. As she shivered, she had imagined someone—she had to believe a man—bent over a kitchen table, cutting each letter out with angry slashes. He'd have worn latex gloves, wouldn't he? Anyone who watched TV knew about fingerprints.

Nonetheless, Jane had lifted the message by the edges and dropped it into a manila envelope, which she tucked into a drawer. In case more messages came, and the tone became uglier.

"What kind of things?" Duncan asked, and she blinked, having to rewind her thoughts to remember what she'd last said.

I have things on my mind.

Oh, how tempting it was to tell him. She wished she hadn't had to see him so soon. For all the antagonism Duncan aroused in her, he also exuded strength. It had been a long time since she'd even dreamed of someone sheltering her, but she had a feeling Duncan would if she asked.

But...she still believed the message sender was only venting. "You'll be sorry" could mean anything, including "God will get you for this someday, when you're eighty-five years old and your time comes naturally." Whoever this was hadn't said "*I'll* make you sorry," which might have really scared her.

That wasn't really what was stopping her, however. It was the bad feeling she knew what Duncan's immediate assumption would be.

Hector.

And even though Hector Ortez was obviously volatile, she couldn't see him anonymously threatening a woman.

Frowning, she admitted even that wasn't what kept her quiet. What she didn't like was the implication that she couldn't take care of herself, that she needed a man—a dominant, dictatorial man, no less—to keep her safe. To meekly accept his authority in return for his protection.

No. She couldn't. She wouldn't. Her heart pounded hard at the very thought. She would never place herself in that kind of subservient role again. It alarmed her that she'd ever felt the temptation. Was there actually a part of her that *wanted* to reclaim any part of her hideous childhood?

"Oh... I'm finishing up my recommendation on

another case. It's not like Tito's. Everybody hates everybody. They all have attorneys," she said in a deliberately distracted tone. She shrugged.

"Don't tell me you're suffering doubts." The mockery in his voice was subtle, but it was there, confirming her decision not to confide in him— and ticking her off royally, too, even as she was shatteringly aware that it hurt to be reminded how little he thought of her.

Would he *sympathize* with the message writer?

Concentrating fiercely on the anger, Jane stopped dead, planted her knuckles on her hips and waited until he noticed and turned to face her.

"What's that supposed to mean?" she demanded.

He raised his eyebrows. "It was a question."

"Sure it was." She was really steaming now. "You don't think much of me, do you?"

Those cool gray eyes studied her. He wasn't sneering, she'd give him that. In fact, his expression was odd, as though he was disconcerted in some way. After a discernible pause, he said, "I wouldn't say that."

Jane snorted and started walking again. A good case of mad covered the hurt she refused to acknowledge and sped her steps until she was almost jogging.

She and Duncan were now circling behind the

goal Tito was still guarding. At that moment, Tito threw his body in front of the ball, and Jane called, "Great stop!"

He flashed her a grin, and she saw that he was starting to get into it. Despite her own mood, she was glad. Hector was trying, and this wasn't easy for either of them.

"You don't have to keep walking with me," she said frigidly.

"That's okay." He didn't sound bothered by their sharp exchange. "I don't mind stretching my legs."

They circled the field an entire time without speaking at all. Jane's tension gradually seeped away. Exercise was doing her good. She hadn't made it to a dance class in two weeks, which she hated. The half hour or less of stretching she was managing about every other day at home wasn't enough.

On the third circuit, Duncan asked out of the blue, "Did you grow up around here?"

"Are we going to make conversation?"

"Something like that," he said.

Suspicious of his motives, Jane couldn't think of any reason not to answer. "I'm from the Midwest. Iowa."

"Rural?"

"Small town."

"No Little League? Girl's soccer? Camp Fire girls?"

"Did I say I wasn't a Camp Fire girl?"

"Only guessing," he said mildly.

"You're right. I wasn't."

The silence wasn't at all relaxing now. She marched the length of the soccer field, Duncan effortlessly pacing her, before he nudged, "What did you do as a little girl?"

"Why do you care?"

His shoulders moved in a lazy shrug. "Curious."

She didn't answer right away. Her childhood was no great secret. She couldn't remember the last time she'd talked about it, though. It would make her feel naked, in a way.

With Duncan MacLachlan, of all people.

But he had told her about his father going to prison and his mother deserting the family, hadn't he? He wasn't asking for anything he hadn't given. The sting she'd felt earlier told her the truth; she wanted him to know her better. Maybe even to like her.

"I went to church. Bible study. I helped my mother clean and cook. I sewed my own clothing and eventually my sisters'." She couldn't help sounding flat. Which was fitting for the monochrome of her childhood. "My parents belonged to a weird little religious sect. No drinking, no dancing. Girls had to keep their bodies modestly attired. Their place was in the home."

"Surely you went to school."

She felt the softness of his voice like a touch. Apparently he recognized how emotionally perilous this territory was for her.

"Eventually, but only because of legal pressure. For a while, we were supposedly homeschooled, but we all failed the required tests, so the church elders surrendered and we were allowed to attend the public school. Never extracurriular activities, of course." She gave herself a shake, as if she could shed memories. "It was very restrictive, oppressive and depressing. Not abusive, though, if that's what you were thinking." Which was not strictly true, from her current perspective. Her father was an angry, rigid man who enforced his will with blows when he saw it as necessary. To her shame, she still, sometimes, winced away from a man's upraised hand. "I managed to hold out until I graduated from high school. One of my teachers helped me apply to colleges and even paid the application fees. I packed one suitcase, got on a Greyhound bus and was gone. End of story."

"Have you stayed in touch with your family?" Duncan asked, still in that relentlessly gentle voice.

She shook her head. "I tried. Father was angry

at the way I'd left. He decided I would be a wicked influence on my two younger sisters. He was probably right."

"So you don't know if they escaped in turn?"

Her fingernails bit into her palms and her hands ached from clenching them so tightly. "I do know. I've stayed friends with the teacher who helped me. She says both my sisters married within the church."

"I'm sorry," he said quietly.

"Me, too."

"Your mother?"

"Was a nonentity." From some distance, she heard herself laugh. It wasn't a pleasant sound. "Me, I guess I was born wild. As long as I can remember, I hated being told no. Girls don't run, or flop in the grass and feel the sun on their faces. They don't swim, or sigh over boys, or *think*." She said that with great ferocity. "They especially don't dance."

Mostly, her father had won, until the moment she got onto that bus, pressed her nose to the glass and strained to see her small hometown receding. She had secretly done forbidden things, but so rarely. And she'd known, bitterly, that she had lost her chance to play—she wasn't a child anymore—and most of all to dance professionally.

Her mother's face had faded in her memory, as

if it wasn't any stronger than her character. Her father, though, she could see as clearly as if he suddenly stood right up ahead, cold condemning stare as he waited for her to come to him. Tall—Jane had gotten her height from him. Thin, because he didn't believe in overindulgence of any kind. The burning eyes of a fanatic. Unfortunately, those were the color of hers. She hated knowing how much she'd taken from him.

For so much of her life, he had stood in for the God of the Old Testament, unforgiving and lacking any softness, even for his small daughters. Other parents might deviate from the harsh limitations laid down by the leader of the sect, but not Jane's father. Never Jane's father.

She was vaguely aware that she and Duncan had made another entire circuit of the field. That Hector and Tito had broken off playing and were waiting for her and Duncan to reach them. But the larger part of her was gripped by the past, by what telling Duncan about it made her feel.

"Was there a dance school in town?" he asked.

"A small one." She pictured the modest building, the mothers parking in front to drop off or pick up their daughters—had any boys in town dared to express a desire to dance? She couldn't imagine. "Probably not even very good." Although then she had believed it was the first step to the promised land. "But some of the girls I went to school with went. I saw them in their leotards. I started reading books in the library about dance. The pictures…" When she was allowed to research for school, she'd sidle between the stacks in the library until she was sure no one was looking. She knew where the books on dance were shelved. There had been one big, coffee-table type with glorious color photos of some of the great prima ballerinas performing. Such longing would grip her when she gazed at those pictures. It was a terrible, physical wrench to close the book and return it to the shelf.

She sighed. "Of course, I wouldn't have made it no matter what. Wanting isn't enough. I'm too tall. So it was always unrealistic."

"But you dreamed," he said, so softly. "Dance Dreams."

"Yep." They were nearing Hector and Tito, and she was hugely relieved that this conversation was over. Not sorry they'd had it, exactly; Duncan had been considerably more understanding and kinder than she'd expected. Maybe telling him had even been cathartic—but that didn't mean she hadn't hated every minute of remembering.

She raised her voice. "Have fun, guys?"

"Si," Tito said, betraying the fact that he'd been speaking Spanish with his father. "I mean, sure."

"Well, I'm sweating as much as if I'd played,

too," Jane said lightly. "So what now, Dad? Please tell me we're going somewhere I can get something cold to drink."

Hector laughed. He was a nice-looking man when his teeth flashed white and the crinkles beside his eyes deepened. The laughter fit him better than anger did.

"Yes, I promised Tito a root beer float. There's only one place for that, *si?*"

"Sí." Stimson had its very own ice-cream parlor, a longtime institution decorated with an appropriate, 1950s theme. Poodle skirts, hula hoops, three-toned cars with tail fins.

"Captain MacLachlan," Jane said, "I trust you plan to treat your date right and buy her a root beer float all her own."

She liked his smile entirely too much. It transformed his face even more than Hector's smile did his. Guarded to sexy.

"Yes, Ms. Brooks." He crooked an elbow for her. "I do believe I could buy you a root beer float."

She pretty much had to lay her hand on his arm, didn't she? Skin to skin, since he wore a short-sleeved tee. Saying something meaningless and cheerful to Tito, she pretended not to notice the jump of muscles beneath her fingertips. As quickly as possible, she withdrew her hand, hoping that Duncan believed in her blithe good humor, but knowing after only one swift glance from his watchful gray eyes that he wasn't fooled at all.

Well, so what? Jane told herself. He couldn't possibly guess how very vulnerable she had felt by the time she'd told him so fiercely that, most of all, girls didn't dance.

Although he had sounded awfully thoughtful when he murmured, "But you dreamed."

The fact that he might have seen more than she wanted him to did not mean that he was a sensitive guy. Heck, no. He was sharp, discerning. But she told herself with a sinking feeling that he wouldn't hesitate to use any advantage he gained over her in their battle over Tito's future.

The lure of ice cream or no, tonight she could hardly wait to get away from him.

INSTEAD OF SLEEPING, Duncan lay in bed trying to figure out a woman who puzzled him more the longer he knew her.

At first, he'd dismissed her as a classic busybody. One with a body that turned him on, sure, but basically a do-gooder confident *she* knew best.

Now he had a suspicion that she didn't only dream about dance, she dreamed about perfect families, too. Maybe she hadn't been able to do a damn thing to reshape her own to her satisfaction, but by God she'd fix other people's families.

She'd be insulted if he called her naive, but in a way she was. One of the things that made him edgy, though, that kept sleep at bay, was the delight he saw sometimes on her face when she looked at Hector and Tito. A sort of incandescent faith that Duncan couldn't remember ever feeling.

It was one of Jane Brooks's many contradictions. Cynicism and faith. A very adult sensuality alongside the ability to let herself feel childlike wonder.

What he couldn't figure out was how well Jane understood herself and her own motives.

He grunted a half laugh. How well did anyone, including him? Face it, he'd gone with instinct where Tito was concerned. Maybe, in his own way, he'd been trying to have a relationship with this kid that he hadn't been able to with his brothers. So who was he to judge?

What he couldn't feel was any of her faith. Even during the best times with Tito, Duncan hadn't kidded himself everything would turn up roses, that Tito would bond with him, take every word of advice he offered, end up valedictorian at the high school and starting point guard on the basketball team, and, hell, get into Harvard. Duncan had listened to his gut and been willing to try. What he couldn't do was *believe*. Not the way Jane clearly did.

She was the damndest woman, he thought in frustration, looking at the shifting shadows on the wall as a car passed outside. He'd lay money down that the attraction he felt wasn't one-sided, but she gave no signals whatsoever that she would welcome him making a move. Because they were in an adversarial position? Because she was determined to be professional? Or because she didn't like him?

Funny that should bother him, when he'd been convinced for so long that *he* didn't like *her*. And when he so rarely gave a damn what other people thought of him.

So why couldn't he get her out of his mind? Why was he aroused only because he was thinking about her?

Duncan swore out loud, something he didn't remember ever doing when he was supposed to be settling down to sleep.

He hadn't lost sleep over a woman since he was a teenager, not unless she was an embezzler, a drunk driver who'd killed a kid or maybe an aggressive defense attorney. He did have a type for sexual involvement, and it had nothing to do with hair color or bra size. Duncan liked women who were undemanding, who were happy with a nice evening out and a satisfying hour or so in bed.

Ludicrously enough, he realized he was smiling at the idea of a "nice" evening out with Jane. The only thing that kept their encounters close to civil was the fact that they were chaperoned by Tito and his father. Most of the time, he and Jane managed to have an argument, anyway.

What kept him restless was a bone-deep certainty that taking Jane to bed would be a whole lot more than "satisfying," pallid as that sounded, and with a little luck it would last longer than an hour or so, too. It would be the difference between eating to fill the stomach and having a gourmet dinner with extraordinary flavors—tart, sweet and everything in-between. It would be breathtaking, unforgettable...

And it wasn't happening.

He knew without asking that she wasn't a woman who had meaningless sex, and he didn't have the emotional makeup to have any other kind.

An insidious thought crept into his head. Did she have sex at all? Given her upbringing? Or had she gone the other way around, left home and gone crazy making up for everything she'd missed?

As passionate as she was in some ways, as self-aware, he couldn't imagine that she hadn't explored her sexual side. He was willing to bet, though, that her current life was as barren of romance and sex as his. Running a small business didn't allow a lot of spare time to start with, and he'd seen her consult her calendar to schedule these outings with Tito and Hector. There were daily appointments scribbled in. Unless she had someone waiting at home….

No. Duncan refused to believe that. She didn't wear a ring, and she'd have mentioned her husband or partner's name in passing. She wouldn't have flirted with him—and that's what they were doing some of the time, however much they might both pretend it wasn't. She wouldn't shiver when he laid a hand on her, flush when his gaze settled on her mouth. No. Whatever else Jane Brooks was, he believed her to be a woman of integrity.

And that was the most troubling thought of all, for a man who hadn't really trusted anyone since his mother abandoned her family when they needed her most.

"Oh, for God's sake!" He flung back the covers and reached for the lamp switch. If he couldn't sleep, he'd read. Watch some late-night television. Do anything but lie here getting worked up about a bullheaded woman who happened to push his sexual buttons.

He looked at the couple of books sitting on the bedside table and felt no interest in either. Going downstairs to find something more likely to grab his attention, he thought, *You could quit. Admit that the kid doesn't have many alternatives and his father may be the best one.* Jane would no doubt be relieved. He wouldn't have to see her anymore. This strange longing that she'd awakened in him would subside and soon be forgotten. The visits would go more smoothly without him around to make Hector bristle.

But Duncan knew he wouldn't do any such thing. He couldn't let go of his deep suspicion of Hector, a man who'd given in to his temper when he should have been thinking about how much his kids needed him. And while Duncan didn't love Tito—Jane's suggestion was ridiculous—he did feel a sense of responsibility for him. He'd made a commitment of a sort, and he lived up to his commitments.

He grabbed a book from his unread pile almost at random and headed again to bed, taken aback by the relief he felt.

Of course he had to keep spending time with Jane.

For Tito's sake.

But a moment later he grimaced. He didn't let other people get away with that kind of dishonesty, and he sure as hell wasn't letting himself get away with it. Not when he knew the truth.

He wanted to keep seeing Jane. He wanted Jane, period.

CHAPTER SEVEN

"I GOT ANOTHER A ON MY MATH test this week," Tito said.

Duncan laid a hand on the boy's shoulder and squeezed. "Good going! You don't need help, then?"

Tito held himself proudly. "No. The fractions, they're easy now."

Duncan had suggested a walk this evening rather than their usual sports. He'd intended to suggest they go to his house later and crack the books, but apparently that wouldn't be necessary. Tito's grades in English and Government needed to be addressed, too, but helping with those subjects was a little harder. Mostly, Duncan thought, what the boy needed was to develop his language skills. They could do that by talking.

So he'd driven them out of town to a stretch where they could walk along the flattop of the dike that confined the Skagit River. It was running high and turgid. Snow had lain low in the Cascade Mountain foothills until this couple of weeks of sunny, unexpectedly warm weather.

Snowmelt had pushed some of the region's rivers into flood stage. They'd been relatively lucky with the Skagit, which hadn't breached any dikes.

"Papa says he'll take me fishing," Tito said after they had walked in silence for a distance. "Do you fish?"

Duncan shook his head. "Never had the time or inclination. Maybe not the patience, either."

Tito grinned. "I think I can be patient."

"I think you can, too." Duncan thought of the dedication the twelve-year-old had given to improving his basketball skills. Practicing night after night, instead of running around with friends. That demonstrated both determination and patience.

"Your papa didn't take you fishing?" Tito asked diffidently.

"No." Duncan hadn't told him that his father had also served time in prison. Perhaps he should; it might help Tito understand that he didn't have to follow in his own father's footsteps. But this didn't seem like the moment. "He…was away a lot when I was growing up. My mother drove me to baseball practices, Boy Scouts." Things he'd taken for granted while still angrily certain his parents had both let him down, he thought, cringing at the contrast with Jane's sad childhood.

"Your papa… He taught you nothing?" Tito sounded disbelieving.

"He taught me to play the bagpipe." Dad had had all three boys playing at one point. Duncan couldn't help grinning. They'd made the most god-awful noise imaginable.

The boy's face crinkled in puzzlement. "Bagpipe?"

Duncan explained some of the history of this strangest of musical instruments. Tito listened with polite incredulity. Amused, Duncan admitted that some people cringed and covered their ears at the wail of a bagpipe. *Music* wasn't the word they'd use to describe the sound that emerged.

"MacLachlan is a Scottish name," he said. "My father's father—my grandfather—immigrated to the United States, like your father did. My dad was born here, but he spoke with an accent. Not as strong as his father's, but there." Funny, he hadn't remembered that lilt for a long time. It was a part of what had made his father so charming, so instantly likable. "The bagpipes weren't originally Scottish. A type of bagpipe is mentioned in the Old Testament. It's likely the ancient Greeks had them. I saw a picture from a medieval manuscript showing men playing the bagpipes in the twelth or thirteenth century. People forget now that they weren't always Scottish, though." Tito listened with enough interest that Duncan continued, telling him about the Battle of Culloden, in

1748, when the pipes stirred the Scottish troops to arms. They had been banned by the English, considered dangerously inciteful. "When we get to the house, I'll show you some pictures."

"Do you have your own bagpipe?"

"Yeah, someplace. I probably have my father's, too." Duncan didn't think he'd taken them, the one time he showed up after getting out of prison. That meeting had been short and disagreeable. Dad had deluded himself that he'd be greeted with open arms, despite not having heard from any of his sons in all those years. He'd aged extraordinarily; Duncan remembered mostly feeling so angry his vision had blurred. But there had been a sickness inside him, too, as he'd fought the need to beg, *How could you have done this to us?* "My brother Niall still plays. Have you heard of the Highland Games? There's a bagpipe competition," Duncan said.

So far as he knew, Conall had never played after Dad went to prison that last time. But Niall had stuck doggedly to it despite Duncan's dislike of what the bagpipes represented. He'd expected his brothers to reject their father and memories of him, good and bad. Duncan had seen Niall's determination to play as defiance. He still didn't know whether it really was, why Niall had needed to hold on to their roots in a way Duncan didn't. Duncan had seen his younger brother marching

in a parade wearing the Clan MacLachlan tartan
and playing music so haunting it raised prickles
on Duncan's nape. He'd felt something strange.
Regret, maybe.

"If you're interested," he continued, "maybe
he'd play for you sometime."

Tito nodded with enthusiasm. "I've never heard
of this bagpipe. I didn't know you could make
music from a bag."

Duncan only laughed. "Nothing that ever came
out of one when I played could be called music."

They must have walked two miles along the
dike, meeting a few other hikers or joggers, several with their dogs. Tito looked wistfully at the
dogs and said that he wished he could have one.
Papa said maybe, when they had a house.

"You getting to know him?" Duncan asked,
careful to sound casual.

Tito shot him a look that Duncan could only
call wary. He shrugged and mumbled, "Sure."

"Are you glad Jane and I are there, or do you
wish we weren't?"

Head bent, the boy seemed to be concentrating
on his feet. His "I don't know" was a mumble,
too.

Duncan had hoped he'd talk frankly about his
feelings, his worries about his father. Maybe that
was asking too much.

"Do you like Jane?"

The head came up, but Tito gave another jerky shrug of those narrow shoulders. "She's okay."

"She's fierce in defense of what she believes." Tito's forehead furrowed.

Duncan tried to explain what he meant.

"Una guerrera," Tito suggested. Looking to see if Duncan understood the Spanish, he said, "That is like…a soldier?"

"A warrior." Duncan smiled. "Yes, I see her that way."

"It's true that when she was mad at you and Papa, she fought." After a moment, sounding sad, he said, "I wish Lupe could be like that."

"With three children and no husband, she may be too tired to be a warrior. Or perhaps making enough money, cooking, taking care of her children and you, too, means that she is one in her own way. You know, nobody would have blamed her if she had said she couldn't take you in."

He watched Tito think that over and finally nod.

"Sí. I hate Raul," the boy said furiously. "He always has excuses. He doesn't even give Lupe the money he's supposed to."

"You're right to be angry," Duncan said after a minute. "For your sister's sake." He glanced at Tito's averted face. "This Raul, does he see his children?"

"Sometimes he comes by and gives her a little

money, then pretends to be glad to see them. I wish he never came."

"I don't blame you." Duncan made a mental note to do a little research on Raul. If he was earning money, by God he should be paying what he owed to the mother of his children. Duncan might be able to do something about that. Ease Lupe's burden a little.

"Look!" Tito said suddenly. "An eagle."

Sure enough, a bald eagle swooped low over the river, snatched at the water and rose in triumph with a wriggling fish in his talons. Tito watched in awe. "Did you see how fast he was?"

Duncan chuckled. "'He' might be a 'she' you know."

Face suddenly merry, Tito exclaimed, *"Una guerrera!"*

The laugh deepened in Duncan's chest. *"Sí.* Like our Jane." More quietly he added, "Or Lupe, bringing home food to her young."

He was glad to see Tito looking thoughtful.

THIS WAS THE NORTHWEST, so it was no great shock when sun gave way to rain. Not gentle spring showers, but unrelenting rain, timed to flatten the daffodils that bloomed not only in yards but in vast fields. The Skagit River delta was famed for growing bulbs, mostly daffodils and tulips. The Tulip Festival brought tourists and dollars to the region. Unfortunately, spring weather in the Puget Sound area was fickle. Everyone was hoping the current wet front moving through would pass on its way before the more fragile tulips began to open.

Hector had decided, since outdoor activities were impossible given the weather, that this evening they would go out for burgers and then to a movie. Jane was less than thrilled by the choice of an action movie, and even less happy about the idea of seeing it brushing shoulders with Duncan.

One small blessing was that no more unpleasant messages had been delivered that week. Could it be because she'd given her recommendation to the judge regarding the three-way battle for custody of the two elementary-age kids? In a way, she was out of it now. Too late for threats to influence her decision.

Except, neither message had exactly constituted a threat, she reminded herself. *Sticks and stones.*

Ruefully, she reflected on how many times she'd used the childish words to reassure herself recently.

What annoyed her was the level of tension she couldn't seem to squelch. She never arrived to open her store without bracing herself when she approached the back door. Every day, the moment the mail arrived, she quickly thumbed through it instead of tossing the pile casually aside the way she usually did. Relief would rush through her as she thought, *Not today.* She'd taken to hurriedly looking outside the front door, too, well before 10:00 a.m. when she opened, in case the next message was more publicly delivered.

She should be reassured by the week-long silence, but she wasn't.

Tonight, despite having worn a raincoat, Jane got wet getting from her car into Lupe's apartment building, and then out again. It hadn't seemed worth opening and closing an umbrella for such a quick dash, but she found she was shivering by the time she was in her car.

"Ugh. I'm ready for summer," she muttered.

Tito shook his head, spraying water like a wet dog.

"Gee, thanks."

He grinned. "Lupe says if we don't like rain, we should move somewhere else."

"Well, Lupe's right, but I have a successful business here, so moving isn't that easy."

Tito and she beat everyone else to McDonald's. Hector, dripping, was five minutes behind them. Hector and Tito had reached the front of the line and were ordering before Duncan showed up. He hadn't made it home to change, Jane saw. He wore one of his well-cut suits, this one a dark charcoal, with a white shirt and dress shoes.

She half expected to see that he'd made it in unscathed by mere weather, but no; rain glistened on his dark hair and spotted the elegant fabric of his suit coat.

He got into line behind her and eyed the overhead menu board without enthusiasm. "Couldn't we at least do fish and chips?" he said in a low, plaintive voice.

She laughed at him.

"Pizza or burgers," he muttered. "Pizza or burgers."

"*I* haven't had a hamburger for ages," she told him, feeling more cheerful than she had all day. "Or fries. I love French fries."

He grimaced at her order, but gave a similar one. He offered to pay for both, but she politely declined and took care of her own meal. This was so not a date.

As always, Tito looked embarrassed when Duncan greeted him. Hector offered a curt nod. They took their food on trays, stopped to get drinks, then chose a booth in the busy restaurant that was sandwiched between two already-full booths. Jane couldn't honestly blame them. It would be hard to relax with the duenna and her dark shadow hovering.

By the time Duncan's number was called, the two of them had to sit some distance away. He looked resigned rather than irked, however. With a groan, he set down his tray and slid into the booth. "God, what a day."

"And here I figured crooks would stay home, cozy and dry. Rather like my customers did," she said, wrinkling her nose.

"The crooks may have stayed home, but I'm sorry to tell you the average citizen didn't. When he got behind the wheel of the car, he didn't slow down, either."

"Oh, dear." Washingtonians should know how to drive in the rain, but somehow they didn't. Maybe too many of them were transplanted Californians.

When she said as much, Duncan grunted. "Too many people are idiots. That's a simpler explanation."

She laughed. "Will you be quoted as saying that in the *Dispatch?*"

"If it would make people slow down, I would. One of those idiots killed himself and his twenty-three-year-old son going over eighty miles an hour on the highway, weaving in and out of heavy traffic. That mess belonged to the State Patrol, not us, thank God, but it spilled over because the highway was shut down for almost two hours."

"Which meant everyone tried to detour through town."

He gave another unhappy grunt. "Speeding, of course, because they were frustrated."

"I heard there was an ugly accident. I didn't know that somebody died."

"The only good part is that no one else was severely injured."

He told her more about his day as they ate. She reciprocated, even though her tidbits felt so trivial next to the tragedies that occupied him.

But I deal in dreams, Jane reminded herself. Dreams counted, too.

She was embarrassed to realize how hungry she was for the sight of his face as they talked. Why it was so sexy with all the careworn lines, she couldn't have said, but then thought—no, his face was sexy *because* it was worn. Because those lines made visible the burden he carried and the fact that he cared.

And then there was his mouth, so often unrelenting but occasionally quirking into those startling grins. And the eyes, cold and dangerous as black ice one minute, soft and mysterious as a winter mist the next.

His hands…

Jane gritted her teeth. *Oh, boy. I'm in deep trouble here.*

When Hector and Tito appeared beside their table, she was startled enough to have to suppress a squeak. How embarrassing was it that she hadn't once glanced toward them. Would she have noticed if Hector and Tito had left without stopping? Would Duncan? She didn't think so. Although *he* had likely been brooding about the tragic consequences of people's carelessness, not the curve of her lips.

"Tito would like to drive with me to the theater," Hector said stiffly.

Yanked back to her responsibilities, Jane tried to remember if Hector's truck had decent tires but couldn't. Oh, for goodness sake! She wasn't the boy's mother to worry about things like that.

"Sure," she said, without looking at Duncan. Soon enough, they would have to let go. Tito would probably end up living with his father and neither she nor Duncan would have any say whatsoever in his life. "We'll be right behind."

Frowning, Duncan watched them go. Then he turned his gaze to her. "Why don't you come with me? I can bring you to get your car after the movie."

Jane didn't let herself be tempted. "The theater is halfway home for me. I'd as soon drive."

He nodded and rose, taking both their trays.

They were apparently parked on opposite sides of the lot and separated as soon as they got outside. The rain had, surprisingly, let up a little, but Jane hurried, anyway. Either she was still damp enough to feel the chill, or the rain wasn't that far from turning into snow, unusual but not unknown in May.

She reached her car and had already inserted the key in the lock when she saw that something had splattered on the windshield. Her heartbeat picked up and she took one step to see better.

Oh, God. A spiderweb of cracks radiated from a center in the windshield, as if…as if a head had smashed it. Right where *her* head would have struck in an accident. Diluted by the rain, blood ran in crooked rivers down the shattered glass.

Her mouth opened on a scream, but it might have backed up in her throat. Jane had only one thought: *Duncan.* She turned and ran.

SHOULDERS HUNCHED AGAINST the drizzle, Duncan was unlocking his SUV when he heard running footsteps. He spun to face the threat, his hand reached for his weapon. He was shocked to see Jane tearing across the parking lot toward him, water splashing beneath her feet.

He had only seconds before she reached him, long enough to see that she was distraught. Operating on instinct, he opened his arms and she flung herself at him.

It was more of a collision than an embrace. He closed his arms around her and swung her toward the body of the SUV while he searched the parking lot for whoever had scared her. Headlights moved over them as a car pulled out, but, clinging to him, she seemed oblivious.

"Jane," he said urgently. "What's wrong?"

She mumbled something against his chest.

He backed off enough that she had to lift her head.

She blinked a couple of times. Rain soaked her face like tears. "I'm being stupid," she whispered. "It was just…"

"*What* was 'just'?" Duncan said in exasperation.

"My windshield. Somebody broke my windshield."

"You mean, a vandal?"

She didn't say anything for long enough, his eyes narrowed.

"Yes, but…maybe not exactly."

His suspicion crystalized, and he hustled her around the SUV to the passenger side where he opened the door. "Get in."

"Where are we going?"

"To look at your car. Where else?"

A moment later, he got in as well and slammed his door, shutting out the wet night. The sodium lamps made the lighting diffuse and yellow. He realized how very still she sat, her elbows pressed to her sides, hugging herself. She was shivering.

Swearing, he turned on the engine and cranked up the heat, for what good that would do in the immediate future. He steered in the direction she'd come from. "Where are you parked?" he asked.

She gestured, and he spotted her car. After pulling up behind it, he shook his head when she reached for the door handle. "Let me take a look."

Duncan didn't like what he saw. It wasn't only the damage to the windshield that had scared her, he knew immediately; it was the red dye or paint or, hell, maybe real blood that had diluted to pink in the last trickles on the windshield and where it had washed onto the hood. This wasn't as simple as a teenager enjoying the act of randomly smashing car windows and windshields in a parking lot.

To be thorough, Duncan inspected all the nearest cars. None had been damaged. Then he went to his 4Runner and got in.

The heat was starting to kick in, but small trembles still shook Jane. He sat there for a moment.

"I doubt it's blood."

"No. It's, um, probably paint. Maybe spray paint."

"And you guess spray paint because…?" He waited.

Finally she looked at him. "I've had a couple of other, um, incidents recently."

He had to clamp down on anger that was out of proportion. "Incidents."

"Yes." Her eyes were colorless in this light,

dilated perhaps from shock. "Somebody spray-painted a message on the back door of my store. And then, well, I got a nasty note in the mail."

"You called the police, of course." He knew damn well she hadn't.

She shook her head. "They were...unpleasant but not exactly threatening."

Not *exactly*.

"What did they say?" He sounded one hell of a lot more patient than he felt.

Turning her head so she was no longer meeting his eyes, she told him.

"Unpleasant," he repeated, an edge in his voice.

"Neither was really threatening." Her eyes rolled his way. "Exactly."

He was really getting to hate that word.

"'Bitch, you'll be sorry' doesn't strike you in any way as a threat?"

She'd recovered enough to glare at him. "Well, of course it could be! But it isn't necessarily, either. The person might only mean that I'll regret whatever it was I did. I mean, there are always consequences..." She petered out under the force of his disbelieving stare, then straightened her shoulders and said, "No matter what decision I make as Guardian ad Litem, somebody is left unhappy. I'm not the most popular person around."

"Was Hector here before you?" Duncan asked slowly.

"I knew you'd ask that!" she stormed. "I knew it! That's why I didn't tell you about the other incidents."

"Was he?" Duncan asked, implacable.

"No! No, he wasn't. Which doesn't mean a thing. He had no way of knowing I'd let Tito go with him. If he were going to do something like that, he wouldn't want Tito to see."

Duncan unclenched his jaw. "You're sure about that? Maybe he was disappointed you said yes. Maybe he *wanted* to see your face when you walked out to your car. Did you ever think of that?"

"No." She met his stare defiantly. "Hector didn't do this."

"And you know that because…?"

"He's not like that."

Maybe he should have stifled the disparaging sound, but why?

At least she didn't look scared anymore. Now she was mad. "He's getting what he wants, all right? Why would he do something this stupid? If somebody had seen him whacking my windshield, he'd have lost his son for good. Tell me why he'd do that?"

Duncan could think of a lot of reasons, none rational, but he also, grudgingly, had to admit she was making sense. Hector *was* getting his way. Two more weeks and they'd be in front of the judge again. If Hector behaved himself he'd likely have full access to his kid, and custody as soon as he had a decent place to live. This *would* have been a stupid thing for him to do.

Which didn't mean he hadn't done it. Resentment and hurt, pride and rage at authority weren't easily corralled by common sense.

"All right," he said. "I'm going to call someone. We'll get your car towed to somewhere it can be worked over."

"My insurance will replace the windshield."

"Fine. But not until we make sure there are no other surprises."

She shivered. "I didn't look inside."

Duncan had, and had seen nothing, but he wasn't going to tell her that.

Instead of phoning dispatch, he called his brother, who sounded surprised to hear from him.

"You busy?" Duncan asked.

"Uh…is this important?"

"Yeah. I have something I'd like you to handle if you can."

"It's work."

"Yes."

"Aren't you home?"

"No." Duncan sighed. "This has to do with that boy I've been spending time with. Tito Ortez." He gave a very short synopsis of what he and Jane were doing at McDonald's, then told Niall about the two previous "incidents."

"A Guardian ad Litem," his brother said thoughtfully. "She probably pisses a lot of people off."

"So she tells me."

"Okay," Niall said, all cop. "Sit tight. I'll arrange a tow, too."

"Thanks."

It felt strange to be grateful he had his little brother to call. Not that there weren't plenty of competent detectives on the Stimson Police force, but this crime felt personal to Duncan. A frown gathered on his face at the thought. Not only personal to Jane, but to him, as well. Because she mattered.

Too much.

No, that was ridiculous. Of course he felt differently than he would if she were a stranger who'd happened to be eating here tonight and who'd come racing to him for help. Jane was… not a friend. But something like that. They might have started as adversaries but they'd become allies of a sort. She was easy to talk to when they both let down their guards. When they didn't, he enjoyed sparring with her.

Face it. He felt more for Jane Brooks than he did for most of his friends.

Besides which, he still suspected Hector had set up this little surprise for her.

"If it wasn't Hector," he said into the silence, "how'd somebody know this was your car? Why not do it outside your store?"

"I parked in front today." She was hugging herself again. She moved a little, maybe restlessly, but maybe not. She might be shivering again. "Usually I park in the alley. I have a spot there, next to the Dumpster. Offers plenty of privacy for the wandering vandal. But the garbage truck was blocking the alley, so I parked on the street."

"Too many witnesses."

She nodded. "All somebody would have had to do was follow me. I came straight here from work. Except there could have been witnesses here, too."

"Yeah, but it's getting dark and with the rain, visibility stinks. And—" he tried not to make it sound like a criticism "—you parked around back."

She huddled miserably.

Duncan kept the expletive he was thinking silent. Had it not yet occurred to her that the same somebody could as well have followed her home? Might already have followed her home?

"Both incidents were at the store," he said.

Her head bobbed.

"Tell me you're not in the phone book."

"No, but with the internet, it's awfully hard to keep any secrets."

He made an acknowledging sound.

"I'm glad I didn't go straight home tonight," she said in a small voice.

"No garage?"

"Yes. I would have driven right in and closed it behind me." She continued hesitantly, "So I guess this couldn't have happened at home."

"But you're afraid something else would have."

There was another of those little shudders. "Oh, I'm being silly. This still isn't anything worse than a teenager might have done."

Duncan couldn't take it. He reached across the space between the seats and pulled her against him. Her body thrummed with tension. When her cold face burrowed into his collar opening, he exclaimed, "You're freezing!"

"I'm wet."

He could feel her mouth moving against— damn it—against his collarbone. He was supposed to be comforting and warming her, not imagining other—better—reasons for her lips to be traveling down his throat to his chest.

"No kidding," he said hoarsely, his fingers tangled in her soggy hair. He moved his other hand up and down her back in what he hoped was a soothing rhythm.

Gradually the tension left her muscles until she

lay against him as if contented. It was a long time
before she asked, "Who was that you called?"

He was the one to tense slightly. "My brother."

"Really?" To his regret, she pulled away.
"But… Does that mean he's…?"

"Yeah, Niall is a cop, too. He's a detective in
Major Crimes."

"This isn't exactly a major crime."

There was his favorite word again.

"You act on behalf of the court. We take seri-
ously a threat against someone like you." That
sounded pompous and not very personal, which
maybe wasn't a bad thing.

Except, to his further regret, she disengaged
from his embrace and retreated to her own seat.
"Thank you," she said, sounding very formal. "I
appreciate all your concern."

"Hell. Tito," he said, remembering.

She made a face. "I imagine they're enjoying
the movie by now and probably didn't even notice
we failed to show up. And I have to tell you I
didn't actually want to see that movie, anyway."

Duncan laughed, leaning back in his own seat.
"Ditto."

"Really?" She scrutinized him. "I would have
thought…"

"You know, if I want to watch speeding cars
crashing into each other, I don't have to go to the
theater."

Jane giggled. It was only a small giggle, but it warmed him nonetheless.

Unlike her, he'd been aware of another SUV pulling into the parking lot. It came up behind his, and as the driver got out he set a flashing police light on the roof.

Niall.

Duncan was damn glad his brother hadn't caught him cuddling the victim of this crime.

CHAPTER EIGHT

OF COURSE DUNCAN DROVE her home and insisted on going in with her. Jane didn't argue very hard, because for the first time she felt nervous about walking into her small house all alone.

He approved the motion-activated floodlight that came on when they walked up to the porch, but seemed disapproving that she didn't have a security system, even though she doubted very many people in town did.

"You must not," she pointed out. Or Tito couldn't have broken into his house.

He patted his hip, where she'd become aware of the bulk of his holster when he held her. "I carry my own."

Jane rolled her eyes to gaze upward. His mouth tightened.

He toured all five rooms plus bathroom in her house, going so far as to open her closets and stoop to look under her bed. Painfully aware of the state of the bedroom closet and unable to recall the last time she'd so much as glanced under the bed—never mind cleaned under it—

Jane cringed. She kept quiet, though, because she *wanted* him looking. Heaven help her, she was desperately grateful to him for being here.

"All clear," he said finally. Pause. "Unless somebody's hiding underneath that jumble of shoes."

Stiffening, she said, "I suppose you line yours up in military order."

He met her eyes and said nothing. Which meant he did, she supposed. His house had been very neat and spotlessly clean.

"You probably hire a housekeeper."

"I do," he agreed. "Housekeepers usually clean. If necessary, *around* clutter."

Jerk. Jane was glad to remember how obnoxious he could be, because she was beginning to wish he wasn't on the verge of leaving her alone.

There was no way in hell she could ask him to stay, though. Excepting the snide remark or two, he was all cop now. The man who'd held her so warmly and securely in his arms was no more. Police Captain MacLachlan looked wet, tired and impatient to be gone.

"Keep the phone beside your bed," he advised. Then, seeing the expression on her face, added, "Not that there's any reason you should need it. Even if our perpetrator is escalating, he has a long ways to go before he'll be ready to confront you."

She wrapped her arms around herself. "Oh, that's a great comfort!"

The wintry gray of his eyes softened, unless she was imagining it. "Jane, we'll catch him."

They were standing by her front door now. His hand was on the knob.

"Thank you," she forced herself to say. "I mean, for…well, for everything." *Putting your arms around me.*

He nodded. Hesitated. "Jane…"

She suddenly had trouble breathing. Looking into those eyes, seeing the worry he'd been hiding and something darker yet, Jane desperately wanted him to hold her again. The silence was unnatural, as was the length of time they did nothing but look at each other and fight… what?

It's only adrenaline, she tried to tell herself, and didn't believe it, not after the way she'd drooled over him in MacDonald's. He was autocratic and brusque and close-minded, everything she despised in a man, but he also made her feel things she never had before. And, from the moment she'd seen the windshield tonight, he'd represented something else to her: safety.

He made a sound, something ragged in his throat. Jane actually swayed toward him, and then he swore, said, "Lock behind me," and left so quickly she was still trying to regain her balance.

What she was mostly left with was embarrassment.

THE FOLLOWING DAY SHE LED Detective Niall MacLachlan into her small office. Alison was here today to mind the store, and with continuing rain business was slow, anyway. Her curiosity was obvious, and Jane supposed she'd have to enlighten her and her two other employees, too, in case something happened when she wasn't here.

Niall looked enough like Duncan that the relationship was obvious if you knew to look for it. They were nearly the same height and build, both lean, solid and athletic. Their gray eyes were disturbingly alike. Niall's hair was a deep auburn, however, and she'd seen last night that his stubble was pure copper. He presented quite differently from his brother; his body language was relaxed, his smile pleasant.

She poured them both coffee, and they sat in the office, her chair swiveled to face his, which sat beside the desk. They were virtually knee to knee in the tiny space. He whipped out a spiral notebook and began to grill her.

Of course she had to take the message out. He snapped on a latex glove to carefully remove it from the manila envelope and sat silently studying it. Feeling cold, Jane rubbed her hands over her bare forearms and looked away from the disturbing, vicious chain of raggedly cutout letters.

Without any comment, Niall slid the sheet of paper into the envelope and said, "I'll have to take this."

Jane gave a jerky nod. Truthfully, she'd be glad not to have its malignant presence in her desk anymore.

He asked questions; she talked. Only when he said, "I'll need names," did she hesitate. Confidentiality was key to her role as Guardian ad Litem. Most of the people she was telling him about had vented to her, and that was all. How could she be effective if it got out that she'd named everyone who'd ever been mad at her to the police?

Niall had been watching her. Evidently reading her mind, he said, "I'll be discreet. I promise. I'll start by calling the judges concerned with any likely cases, to keep them on top of this. I can do background checks without anyone knowing, and I can likely get a good idea whether some potential suspects have moved on with their lives, no longer live in the area, whatever." He shrugged. "I'll let you know before I talk to anyone in person."

"I suppose I don't have any choice at this point."

"No." For a moment, he sounded as implacable as Duncan often did.

Jane nibbled on her lip. "Okay. Um, you probably know that Duncan's got a thing about Hector."

She'd swear she saw the light of amusement in those eyes that were so like his brother's.

"He did mention Ortez."

She explained again why Hector was an unlikely suspect. Niall made dutiful notes. She then told him about her other current case, close to wrapping up. The Joneses were, on the surface, so ordinary, starting with their name. The divorce was hideous, however. Glenn had apparently had multiple affairs and felt justified because, in his words, his wife had gotten fat and was about as appealing as "that bitch on TV."

"He used the word *bitch*."

"Yes. I don't know who he was talking about."

"Is the wife…" Niall glanced down at his notes. "Renee. Is she fat?"

"Maybe." Jane hated the word. "She told me she put on a little weight with each kid, and that Glenn was so awful she kept eating to spite him."

"Nice folks."

"Oh, yeah. The grandmother is almost as bad as the father," she said, "but it's a little hard to imagine a fifty-something woman spray-painting *bitch* on my back door."

The utter cynicism on Niall's face was unsettling. "You might be surprised."

"The father has cornered me a couple of times," she admitted. "He gives me the creeps."

"I can see why."

She told him about several other cases she'd handled the past couple of years. In one, Jane had ended up recommending shared custody, which had infuriated the mother, who had expected to gain full custody and limit her ex-husband's visitation. "Charlotte and Allen Hess. By the end, I wasn't her favorite person. There was another one," she said slowly, "where I suspect the father was sexually abusing the girl. But she wasn't talking, and there was no real evidence. I think the judge got the same vibes, though. Last I knew the dad was allowed only supervised visitation with her."

"Did you supervise it?" Niall asked, looking interested.

She shook her head. "It was going to be long-term. I only do it when it's short-term, like Hector and Tito. I would have said no, anyway, though. The father was...quite hostile to me."

Niall wrote down the name: Richard Hopkins.

Satisfied finally, he closed his notebook and said, "You've given me plenty to start with. I'll be in touch as I need to. Here's my card." He extended one to her. "The second number is my cell. Call the instant anything else happens."

She so loved the implication that, of course, something would happen. Rising with him, Jane said, "This must seem like a huge waste of time to you, compared to the kind of stuff you usually deal with. Surely vandalism doesn't generally get referred to a detective."

He looked at her straight on, and once again she had the disquieting impression he might be more like Duncan than first impressions suggested. He was utterly calm, controlled and, she sensed, as relentless as he had to be.

"No," he said, "Duncan was right. The fact that this is likely connected to your work with the court makes it a priority. A threat to you is no different than a threat to a judge, a prosecuting attorney or a police officer."

Showing him out, she was relieved to see that Alison was occupied with a girl trying on tap shoes, her mother hovering and talking about whether her toes pinched. Jane felt like she needed a few minutes to collect herself.

It wasn't any of the angry fathers she found herself thinking about once the detective was gone, however. Rather, it was the two MacLachlan brothers.

Beyond the physical resemblance, they'd seemed so different. Duncan crackled with an air of command. In his presence, no one would ever mistake who was in charge. Niall didn't give her that impression. He was way more relaxed and pleasant than Duncan ever was; she bet he was much better liked than his brother.

And yet…she'd had this weird sense that she would electrocute herself if she tried to enter his space. He had a force field around him, invisible but palpable. Duncan had let her see some emotions. Even when he was shoving them down deep, they were *there*. She wondered if anybody ever saw beyond Niall's facade to what lay beneath.

No, she thought, frowning, she was being silly—his remoteness was probably his on-the-job persona. Probably a lot of cops were like that. She was jumping to conclusions. Who knew, he might be famed for wild parties, exhibitionism and a sexy girlfriend of the month. Or—Duncan hadn't said—Niall could have a devoted wife and brood of kids.

But somehow she doubted it. Duncan MacLachlan made her mad more often than not. Niall had, instead, left her feeling chilled even though she'd liked him. And she couldn't even quite put her finger on why. She wondered how close the two men were. Having Duncan step in as a parental figure had to have put some strain on the sibling relationship.

She gave her head a shake and went to refill her cup of coffee. She needed to quit thinking about Duncan as if he mattered to her beyond being a current obstacle. Last night, for a minute, she'd thought... But he'd managed to shutter whatever she'd imagined she saw in his eyes. His curt "Lock behind me" pretty much said it all.

He might be attracted to her, but he wasn't interested in taking it anywhere. Which was smart; he liked to give orders and she'd vowed never again to take them. He'd be happiest with a sweet, adoring woman, and she...she'd be happiest with no man at all.

What she absolutely refused to think about was how long she'd lain awake last night, listening tensely to the muted sounds of a settling house, of occasional traffic and neighborhood dogs, raccoons raiding garbage cans and feral cats squabbling, the rain overrunning the gutters. Sounds that would normally be mere background. And most of all she wasn't going to think about how vividly she pictured Duncan's face, taut with some inner stress, or remembered the comfort and excitement she'd felt in his arms.

DUNCAN DROPPED BY THE detective's division midafternoon, stopping for a word here and there until he reached Niall's desk. His brother was on the phone, hunched irritably forward while he simultaneously scrolled through a website on his computer. He glanced up at Duncan, looked amused but not surprised to see him and mouthed, "Give me a minute." Then he said into the phone, "Uh-huh. Ms. Hess moved… A year ago." He took his hand from the mouse and jotted something on his spiral notebook, open to one side. "You think she remarried. Do you recall the name…? No. I see. Thank you for your time, Mr. Davis."

It took him another minute to extract himself from the conversation. Finally he ended the call and leaned back in his chair. "Captain. What can I do for you?"

It was usual for them to play down their relationship on the job, although it wasn't a secret. Duncan went out of his way to avoid any appearance of partiality, despite which he suspected that Niall had to live with the constant irritation of knowing that coworkers assumed, nonetheless, that he benefited from brotherly partiality.

"Detective," he said wryly.

Niall waited, eyebrows raised. The amusement still lurked; he wanted to make Duncan ask. Which, of course, he had to do, now that he'd come all the way down here.

"Did you get the message that was mailed to her?"

Niall opened a manila envelope and slid the

piece of colored paper onto his desk blotter. Duncan already knew what it said. What he hadn't counted on was the impact of seeing the ugly message itself. Rage rose in his throat.

"And she didn't think this was threatening?"

Niall made a noncommittal noise.

"You'll check for fingerprints?"

"No, I brought it with me so I could post it on the bulletin board. What do you think?" He carefully shook it into the envelope.

Duncan struggled to tamp down the red tide of fury. "What did you learn?"

"Quite a lot." Niall riffled several pages of his notebook. "I'm currently trying to determine which of the people Ms. Brooks named are even remotely likely to be possibles."

"You haven't eliminated any?" Duncan demanded.

Niall glanced at his watch. "I've had barely an hour since I got back to my desk," he said mildly.

"Was she frank with you?"

"I think so. Do you have reason to believe she wouldn't be?"

His mouth compressed. "No. Yes. She has qualms about divulging names."

"So I gathered. She did, however."

He nodded, relieved. "And then there's her pig-headed determination to believe Ortez is a good, kind man who's fated to be named father-of-the-year."

He probably shouldn't have said "pigheaded." That made him sound too emotionally invested.

Niall rocked in his chair, a smile playing around his mouth. "Rubs you wrong, does she?"

"Like sandpaper," he heard himself admit, then had the uncomfortable realization of how accurate that was. Sandpaper was certainly not pleasant to the bare skin, and it could rub you raw. But what it left behind could be something smooth and glossy and rich. Sensuous to the touch, when it wasn't before.

His body was beginning to crave the scrape of her personality.

Before his brother's all-too-knowing eyes could see entirely too much, Duncan said shortly, "*Have* you eliminated anyone?"

"Actually, yes. Two possibilities, a Roger Griswold, a former foster father who apparently issued some threats when Ms. Brooks encouraged the return of a child to the mother, and Jeff Cotter, a father who sued for custody of his kids and lost."

"Have they moved away?"

"Griswold did. Cotter has apparently reconciled with his ex-wife and lives with his kids. They're talking remarriage. It was the judge—Brikoff," he added as an aside, "who tells me that

Cotter claims that losing in court was the wake-up call he needed to make changes in his life. He's gone through an anger management program and is in counseling with his ex. Brikoff feels the change is genuine and doubts the guy holds a grudge against your Ms. Brooks."

"Could be deceptive."

Niall shrugged. "Maybe, but he's looking pretty unlikely."

"You'll keep me informed?"

"Have I ever mentioned that you're a control freak?"

Duncan glowered and left.

HE MADE A POINT OF CALLING Tito in the after-school hours. He suggested they shoot some baskets at the open-gym tonight at the high school, and he could tell Tito hated to say no. He wanted to stay home, however, because Raul, the former brother-in-law, was supposed to be coming by. The boy must have realized he couldn't realistically do anything to help his sister, and there had been no hint the useless ex-husband—or were they actually divorced?—was violent. He was determined to be there, though, perhaps only to glare.

"Did Jane let you know what happened last night?" Duncan asked.

"*Sí.* Yes." Tito sounded animated. "She said

someone broke her windshield while we were in McDonald's eating. That she had to have the police come. We couldn't find you after the movie, so Papa drove me home."

"You like the movie?"

Sí, sí. It was *muy bueno*. Much excitement. There had been a good deal of blood and death, according to Tito, and a train had hit a car, although the hero had flung himself out in the nick of time.

Although Duncan regretted Jane's troubles, he couldn't be sorry he'd missed the blood and death and mayhem.

Damn it, he thought; he'd forgotten to ask Niall whether the "blood" on Jane's windshield had been paint. He'd feel better to know it was. If it had been real blood, even animal blood, that suggested a greater level of intent.

He kept himself from calling Niall, though.

Instead, he phoned Jane at home.

"Hello?" she said cautiously.

"Don't you have caller ID?" he snapped.

"Duncan," she said sweetly. "How nice to hear from you." Abandoning the tone, probably as a lost cause, she said, "I don't use my home phone much. So no. I've actually been thinking of dropping the landline."

Maybe he had been rude. Rubbing his neck as he prowled through his house, his cell phone to his ear, Duncan said, "I called to be sure you're okay. That nothing happened today to shake you up."

She was quiet for a moment. "That's...nice of you. But no, except for talking to your brother, it was a standard day."

"Did Niall suggest you start parking on the street? Enter and exit your store through the front door?"

"You know there's never enough street parking downtown. The alley isn't that lonely a place. All the other proprietors park out there, too, and we all have to take our garbage to one of the Dumpsters we share."

"You don't sound willing to take any safety precautions." His irritation, he vaguely knew, covered something he was more reluctant to acknowledge. Like fear.

She didn't take it well either way. "I lock my doors. I look both ways before I step into the street. I've taken to carrying pepper spray in my hand when I scuttle across the alley. Does that satisfy you?"

No. But Duncan didn't know why. Believing Hector was responsible for the threats should reassure him. Because she'd challenged Hector's machismo, his belief that, however inadequate his status in the greater world, at home he was in charge, Hector might want to scare her. Belittle her. But hurting her, that was something else. Even stewing in his resentment, would Hector set out with malice aforethought to hurt her?

"I wish you had a home security system," he muttered.

"And I wish you'd quit saying that! All you're doing is making me more nervous."

"Nervous translates to careful."

"Is this why you called?" She sounded really mad now. "If so, can we say good-night?"

Aware he'd bungled the whole thing, Duncan again dug his fingers into the knotted muscles of his neck. "I suppose so. Just, um, don't hesitate to call if you need me. Okay? I can be there in five minutes."

There was a little silence. Then he heard a sigh.

"Sometimes you annoy me more when you're nice than when you're not."

He blinked.

"Good night, Duncan," she said firmly, and hung up. On him. Without waiting for him to say good-night, or anything else.

Weirdly, that made him grin. Sandpaper, he thought, was a hell of an analogy for Jane Brooks.

RAUL BROUGHT A CHECK THAT made Lupe's face pinch. The amount must be very small, Tito thought. She backed up and stood stiffly in the kitchen doorway, arms crossed as if she was guarding it. Keeping Raul from coming farther into the apartment. But she didn't stop him from cuffing Tito in a friendly way and then flopping onto the couch to wrestle with the little ones, making them giggle in delight. He didn't, Tito noticed, ask to see the baby. Babies were women's work; a man didn't change diapers or give bottles.

One thing Tito did know: a man should put food on the table for his family.

It was a relief when he left after only a short visit. He promised that he would come back soon, perhaps even that weekend. He had a better job now, he told Lupe, he thought he would be promoted any week, any day, and then he could give her the money she deserved.

Tito edged closer to his sister and stood at her side as she listened without expression to promises she knew better than to believe in. When the door closed behind Raul, she sagged.

"Gracias a Dios," she exclaimed. "Now, to bed! To bed," she told the little ones.

When the phone rang, she left Tito to answer it. It was Papa, who said it was Tito he had wanted to talk to, anyway. He didn't seem to remember that Raul was to have come by. Tito was disappointed that his father wasn't yet offering any help to Lupe. Of course, he was saving what money he was earning so that he could rent a place of his own, and that was important, too, but

Tito thought about how much an extra hundred dollars would make to Lupe, whose worry lines seemed to deepen every day.

Then Papa asked, as if he was only a little curious, whether Tito had found out why Jane and Duncan never came to the movie last night. When Tito told him, Papa said, "Somebody took a baseball bat to her windshield, did they?"

Tito felt a cold trickle inside, as if last night's icy rain had sneaked inside his shirt collar. His father sounded...happy.

"How do you know it was a baseball bat?" Tito asked.

"I don't, of course," his father said, too quickly. "Anything could have been used. But a baseball bat would work to do what you describe. Did she think it was only a kid? A vandal?"

Papa didn't like Jane. Tito knew how much he disliked being watched as if he needed a babysitter. But Papa wouldn't do something like that.

He had arrived late to the restaurant, though. Tito remembered being surprised. It was because of the rain, he had believed. Now he remembered how very wet Papa was when he came in. Perhaps too wet for someone who had hurried from his truck to the door. Had he seemed...pleased?

Tito felt guilty for even wondering.

He chattered about his day, what his friend Miguel had said about this girl he liked, about how the PE teacher, Mr. Speaks, had commented on what a good shot Tito had become on the basketball court. He tried to pretend he had never thought such a thing about his father, but failed.

Would Jane wonder, too? Or Duncan? Tito shivered, thinking about what might happen if Duncan suspected that Papa had taken a baseball bat to the windshield of Jane's car. Neither of the two men even tried to hide the anger they felt for each other. It scared Tito.

He thought—no, prayed—that perhaps the police who came would know what broke the glass. And if it was *not* a baseball bat, he could forget having such a dumb idea. And it was—it must be—a dumb idea.

He felt sick to his stomach when he ended the call. Tito made an excuse to his sister and turned out the lights early, pretending he was sleepy.

CHAPTER NINE

DUNCAN COULDN'T MAKE IT to the next outing. Jane told herself she was glad, but knew perfectly well she was lying.

It was soccer again. The rain had let up, although the grassy field squelched underfoot and the area in front of the goal, worn bare, was a mudhole.

When they arrived, Tito ran, yelling in delight, and slid into the mud. Hector followed, laughing, and although he didn't throw himself down, was soon mud coated, anyway. The two became distinguishable only by height.

While they played, Jane marched around and around the long field, working up a sweat, *not* thinking about Duncan or what his terse "I have to work" had meant.

If he'd been here, would he have been tempted to dive into the mud, too?

When she was a kid, she'd have *longed* to dive in. To wallow.

Another circuit. As she walked behind the goal they were using, Hector flung himself to stop

Tito's kick and slid headlong through the mud-hole. A few wet globs flew through the air and one splattered her cheek. Jane gritted her teeth, swiped it away with her hand and kept walking, although by this time her feet were soaking wet and cold and she wanted to go *home*.

Fortunately even Hector conceded he and his son were too filthy to go to a restaurant. Jane looked from Tito to the relatively clean uphol-stery in her car and decided to let him ride with his father.

"You can get *both* seats in your truck dirty," she told Hector heartlessly.

He clearly hadn't thought about the problem of getting them home, but did rummage in the bed of the pickup and found some rags and an old coat to put on the seats.

Tito had already hopped in and slammed the door when Hector said to Jane, "Tito told me about what happened at McDonald's. It was only the windshield, then? You've had it fixed?"

"Yes," she said. "Fortunately, my insurance covers it. It made me mad, though." Not for any-thing would she have told him how scared she'd been.

Frowning in apparent concern, he said, "I'm sorry we'd already driven away, but glad the cap-tain was still there." He hesitated. "Do the police think they can find who did it?"

She made her shrug casual. "How can they, unless somebody saw something? And why wouldn't they already have said?"

"Did the police look for fingerprints or anything like that?"

"Remember how hard it was pouring. I don't think they even tried." She actually didn't know what was done to her car once it had been towed, only that it had been returned to her the following afternoon with the windshield already replaced.

Hector nodded. "I must not have been parked near you, or they might have broken my windshield, too. I have only the liability insurance they make me buy. The truck is so old."

She nodded her understanding. In this state, at least, liability insurance was legally required to drive, while collision coverage was a luxury.

"It would not pay for a new windshield."

Jane summoned a smile. "Then it's lucky it was my car and not yours. It was no big deal, Hector. Although I did miss the movie."

He actually laughed, his teeth very white against his muddy face. "You would not have liked it," he said, lowering his voice as if to be conspiratorial, giving one merry glance over his shoulder at his son, who was watching them anxiously. "But Tito did."

Jane laughed, too. "Yes, so he said. And you're right. I wouldn't have liked it."

She felt better now, parting. Well, semi-parting; she followed Hector's pickup truck to Lupe's apartment building and watched Tito climb gingerly out, the mud probably beginning to harden into a body cast on his jeans and long-sleeved T-shirt. Lupe would be thrilled to see him. As he drove on, Hector waved a hand in goodbye to Jane, not seeming as if he minded the fact that she hadn't entirely trusted him to bring Tito straight home.

Had he really become reconciled to her supervision? she wondered.

Twenty minutes later, standing under a hot shower, she let herself examine her uneasiness. No, she didn't believe Hector had been the one to smash her windshield or glue all those letters to a piece of paper to spell out the ugly message. But...he could have.

And I, she realized, *will be very glad when I'm done playing the awkward third wheel. Even if I have grown fond of Tito.*

Even, she thought with a sinking feeling, though it would mean no longer seeing Duncan.

DUNCAN SAT IMPATIENTLY through the meeting that had kept him from joining Jane at the soccer field. He'd had no choice, although he hadn't contributed much to a strategy meeting called by the city attorney, who was preparing a defense against a lawsuit.

As they argued a million small points on the way to consensus, Duncan discovered that, if he turned his head only slightly, he could see the clock above the door without being obvious. Time crawled.

Probably there would be other people out on the soccer fields. Maybe. After all the rain— maybe not. Duncan discovered he didn't like the idea of Jane out there alone with only Hector and Tito, who might keep his mouth shut no matter what his father did.

He was so preoccupied, he missed whatever conclusion wrapped up the meeting, snapping back to himself only when the city attorney thanked everyone for coming and began stowing files in his briefcase as everyone else stood.

He'd call Jane. If they were going on to lunch from soccer, he might still catch them. He'd feel better, anyway, Duncan admitted, once he heard her voice.

She didn't answer. The cell phone rang and then went to voice mail. His gut tightened with anxiety. Damn it, she wouldn't have been care- less enough to have left her phone at home or in the car, would she? Duncan strode for the exit.

He was overreacting and he knew it. She'd suf- fered some petty, nasty-minded vandalism and that was all. But he couldn't get out of his mind that moment when he'd spun to see her running across the parking lot to him, fear on her face. Or her shivers when she burrowed into him.

The threat might only be implicit, but it was there.

Despite the fact that he wasn't dressed for it, he steered his SUV for the soccer fields on the outskirts of town.

Halfway there, he tried her number again, and this time she answered.

"Where are you?" he asked, pulling over to the shoulder.

"Home. Why?"

"I thought I'd join you for lunch."

"No lunch. Hector and Tito were too disgusting. They were both positively caked with mud by the time they finished."

A reluctant smile tugged at his mouth. He'd played sports in his day and never minded a little mud.

"But not you, I take it."

She snorted, although he wasn't convinced. "Soaking wet feet were bad enough."

"Ah." He realized with dismay that he'd *wanted* to meet her for lunch. To hell with Tito and his father, it was Jane he had wanted to see. Somewhat cautiously, he said, "Have you eaten?"

"No, I was about to make a sandwich." She

chuckled. "Tito was crushed because he'd counted on pizza."

"Want to go out for lunch?" he heard himself say. "Snow Goose Deli? If it's a sandwich you really want?"

The silence was long enough, Duncan tensed. Damn. Had he just asked her for a date? And was she about to say, *You've got to be kidding?*

He could let them both off the hook by adding something like, *I wanted to talk to you about Tito. Or Hector.* Make it business.

But she was already talking. "Um... Actually, that sounds nice. I was going to settle for peanut butter and jelly."

Relief, out of proportion, flooded him. "I saw the board as I passed a minute ago. The soup is curry lentil and the special is a Southwest wrap."

"Yum. Shall I meet you there?"

"No, I'll pick you up." After all, he thought, somewhat dazed, that's what a man did when he took a woman out.

She came out her front door the minute he pulled up in front. Duncan leaned across and opened the door for her. When Jane hopped in, she swept him with a glance.

"I feel underdressed."

He'd like to see her even more underdressed. Preferably naked.

He cleared his throat. "I'm the one who's over-dressed for a deli."

Slim-cut blue jeans hugged her long legs and a snugly fitting blue sweater—cashmere, he thought—barely reached the waistband of the jeans. When she twisted to reach for the seat belt—ah, there it was, a flash of creamy skin. His eyes rose to her small, high breasts, outlined by the soft cashmere. Flushed a little, she looked at him once she had fastened the seat belt.

Her eyes were a particularly deep blue, heightened by the color of the sweater. Her hair, loosely bundled on her head, was less glossy than when it lay smooth and sleek. Caramel, he decided. The perfect word to describe it.

Damn, she was so sexy he was paralyzed.

"You're staring."

He ran a hand over his face. "Sorry." *I want you.* "Long, boring meeting."

"Oh." Jane smiled. "I was afraid you'd had to go in because something awful happened."

"Something awful did," he said dryly. "Awfully boring, full of legalese." Pulling himself together, he put the 4Runner in gear. As he drove, he told her the bones of the incident that had resulted in the lawsuit. "The city will win," he concluded, "but not without killing an unconscionable number of man-hours to do it."

He was able to park only half a block from

the deli, and they walked to it side by side, Jane
at least pretending interest in storefronts on the
way. Dance Dreams wasn't on this main shopping street, where rents would run way higher.
She hadn't needed to be situated here, since hers
was a destination business not dependent on impulse customers.

"You've taken a lot of Saturdays off," he realized.

She grimaced. "No kidding. I thought about
going in this afternoon, but I'd already scheduled
staffing, so..." She shrugged. "What about you?
Do you usually work Saturdays?"

And so it went. It was strange, he thought as
they continued to talk, because they'd already
spent a whole hell of a lot of time together, but
now they were asking those first-date questions.
What do you like? Not like? How do you arrange
your life? What really matters to you?

He knew some of what mattered to her. Maybe
most of it. What he didn't entirely get was *why*,
and Duncan found he was intensely curious. The
store...well, that wasn't subtle. Nobody had fed
her dreams when she was a child, so she was
committed to making the dreams of thousands
of other little girls as beautiful as she could. The
fixing families—again, fairly obvious on the
surface. What he didn't understand was why she
hadn't tried to accomplish something miraculous

for herself. Was being a businesswoman really what she'd wanted most? And why not create her own family?

No, that he understood. When you grew up with a dysfunctional family, you were likely to eye outwardly perfect, loving families and wonder what was wrong with them behind closed doors—not so likely to imagine creating one of your own. By the time Conall graduated from high school, Duncan had been ready to swear in blood that he would never have children. Been there, done that, and his brothers had hated him for what he did. Lately he'd begun to wonder if having his own kids would be the same. It was Tito, strangely enough, who gave him an occasional pang.

His realistic side said, *More like a muscle twinge, the kind you ignored to push on for ten more bench presses, another mile, a hundred more shots from the free throw line.*

Jane had a bowl of the soup and a giant lemon-poppyseed cookie. Duncan went with the Southwestern wrap and an equally gigantic blueberry muffin. They'd managed to grab a small table to one side, out of the line of traffic. While they ate, Duncan had had to exchange greetings with a few people he knew, Jane with a couple of others, but mostly they were left to themselves.

Jane was a season ticketholder to the Pacific

Northwest Ballet in Seattle. She used her second ticket sometimes to take a friend with her, sometimes one of the older dance students. She didn't mention taking a man, Duncan noticed. Of course, most men he knew would rather go to a Seahawks game than the ballet. He admitted that he'd never seen a ballet. It occurred to him that he'd like to see one with her—to watch her face while she watched the dancers. Or maybe not; how much grief would she feel?

Was he musical? she asked. He confessed to having started the trombone in fifth grade and giving it up as hopeless by eighth. He told her about the bagpipes, too. Jane was fascinated, even more so than Tito had been, perhaps because she'd actually attended the Highland Games.

"Niall plays?" She looked delighted. "I'll have to ask him about it the next time..." The glow on her face dimmed. "That is, if I see him again."

She called him Niall, not Detective? Duncan was slammed with something he could only label as jealousy. It was unfamiliar and unwelcome.

"You got along with Niall?" he asked.

"Oh, sure." She crumbled the remains of her cookie. "I mean, it's not like we were chatting."

Still in the grip of that unpleasant feeling, Duncan asked, "What would you call it?"

"An inquisition?"

At her tartness, he relaxed. Of course Niall

hadn't tried to come on to her. Even if he'd been inclined, he was too professional for that.

"Has he told you what he's learned so far?"

She shook her head, her eyes anxiously searching his. "Do you know?"

"I talked to him this morning." Fleetingly; Niall, before his morning cup of coffee, had been short to the point of rudeness. "He's still trying to track people down. He's eliminated a few." Duncan dredged through his memory and mentioned a couple of names. She nodded. "He didn't learn anything from your car."

"Oh." Her long, slender fingers were obliterating the cookie. "Um…did he say whether the blood was, well, real?"

He hated to see the anxiety on her face. "Paint," he told her. "As you suspected. Maybe even from the same can as our guy used on your back door."

"That makes sense." She visibly processed it then relaxed. "Waste not, want not."

Duncan's mouth quirked. Nodding at her plate, he said, "I think the cookie is dead."

She looked ruefully down. "Oh, dear. I could have taken it home for later."

He was sorry then he'd said anything, because it seemed to have recalled her to the realization that they'd long since finished their lunches and perhaps it was time to go.

"This was nice," she said after they bussed

their table and he held open the door for her. "Thank you for suggesting it. I wasn't really in a very good mood this morning."

"Why not?"

"Oh…" Her gaze slid from his. "I don't know. I probably got out of bed on the wrong side."

Side by side, two kinds of awareness kicked in. One told him that she had…not lied, but evaded telling him something she didn't want him to know. That she'd had a run-in with Hector, maybe? Duncan's other reaction was entirely physical, triggered by the word *bed*. Picturing her in one came all too easily. He imagined her waking slowly, reluctantly, making grumbly little sounds as she fought off morning. He didn't know why he was so sure his Jane wasn't a sunny, bound-out-of-bed, loving-morning kind of woman. He was equally certain that she'd be sexy as hell while she peevishly roused to face her responsibilities. Her glorious hair would be tumbled all over her pillow—or did she braid it at night? Her eyes would be heavy-lidded, her mouth soft and sulky. He wondered if she liked to cuddle while she slept or would insist on complete independence. An odd thing for him to speculate about, since he didn't know which way he'd tend himself. He went home after he had sex; he didn't spend the night.

And the fact that he was painfully aroused only

because he was picturing Jane waking up in the morning reminded him how long it had been since he'd *had* sex.

Too long, apparently.

Unfortunately, his body was convinced it wanted Jane, and only Jane. He already knew how complicated that would be. *She* was complicated, about as far as you could get from his ideal in a woman.

She stopped to look at something in the window of an antique store, and he frowned, watching her.

Did he actually have an ideal, beyond knowing he was interested only in temporary relationships? Maybe not, he conceded. Physically, she did it for him. Everything about her turned him on, starting with the fluid way she moved, the graceful line of her neck as she bent to look more closely at…

He followed her gaze and saw that she was staring at an ancient pair of ice skates. They looked homemade. Clumsy, and yet—Duncan looked again at her face, to see something wistful there.

"They're too small for you," he said gently.

"Yes, they were probably a little girl's. Don't you think?"

They weren't white, so they could as well have been a boy's, and he didn't know enough about ice-skating to tell if the crude blade had been designed for hockey or figure skating. "Probably," he agreed.

She sighed. "The figure skating is my favorite part of the Olympics. Actually, I watch the U.S. and World Championships, too." More briskly, straightening away from the glass, she said, "After all, it's another form of dancing."

"Yeah, I guess so."

She didn't look back. Duncan wondered what she'd seen as she studied those ice skates. Herself, twirling on a frozen pond at home in Iowa? He realized that, for all they'd talked over lunch, neither of them had mentioned their families, at least not until Niall's name came up.

Their families were, apparently, a sore point for both of them.

"Have you ever ice-skated?" he asked.

She laughed. "A few times, with friends in college. I can go forward without falling down. I didn't get far enough to master going backward, never mind twirling or jumping." She waited while he unlocked the SUV. "What about you?"

"No, although I always thought hockey looked like fun. No local rink, though." He shrugged.

Her sigh was exaggerated. "Think of the missed opportunities. Maybe we both would have been stars."

Amused, he shook his head. "You never know."

But seeing the curve of her mouth as she climbed in, he thought, *Dreams*.

Pretty damn fragile.

WAS IT A DATE? Or a collegial lunch? Jane wasn't sure. He hadn't kissed her, although there was a second, right before she got out in front of her house, when she wondered if he was thinking about it.

She might have been the one to kill the mood, because, panicking as he turned to look at her, she'd said, "Oh, by the way, Hector suggested Tuesday night. Pizza—to make up for today—and an arcade."

Duncan had grunted. "Has it occurred to you that he's spending one hell of a lot of money on these little outings?"

Yes, it had, but even so she bristled at his tone. He refused to see the positive in anything Hector did.

"He's in the position of a divorced father who has to do something extra to make up for what he *can't* offer. Besides, there are only so many ways to entertain a twelve-year-old in Stimson." She'd looked a challenge at Duncan. "What do *you* do when you spend time with him?"

"Basketball. Soccer. Walks. I helped him with his math homework." Pause. "I admit I feed him. I told you that."

"Hector didn't finish high school," Jane said. "So maybe he can't help with the homework. And he's probably not a very good basketball player."

Her last glimpse of Duncan's face as she closed the door, he'd looked irritated, probably because she was defending Hector, whom he wanted to regard as indefensible.

Jane was disconcerted to discover she was absentmindedly sucking on a hank of her hair as she brooded. She yanked it out of her mouth and muttered, "I didn't want him to kiss me, anyway." Defiantly.

Lie. And a lousy one besides. She might be *afraid* of what would happen if he kissed her, but that was different.

With a huge effort, she managed to focus again on the order she was trying to put together for hair accessories, a really successful sideline for her store. Some of the items were practical: hairnets and pins, for example. She should be using one herself right now to keep her hair out of her face, and mouth.

Others were designed for performances: glittering snoods, fancy tiaras, crystal-studded hair fans. She was getting low on some of the items, what with the shopping rush for the upcoming recitals.

Making a decision about a particular snood, filmy black decorated with tiny, diamond-bright crystals, she clicked 10 on the order amount and moved on to a new line of hair combs she hadn't quite made up her mind about.

What would she recommend to the judge regarding Hector and Tito at the upcoming hearing? Hector *was* trying. Yes, he'd had his rebellious moments, but she couldn't really blame him. Tito sometimes seemed to be quite happy in his father's company.

She guessed what she was hanging up on was the fact that there were other times when Tito *didn't* seem as happy. *It's only been three weeks,* she reminded herself. His father had been nearly a stranger to him after three years in the correctional institute. And Tito was nearing puberty. Was it surprising that he wasn't glowing with delight because his father had reappeared in his life?

No, but… It was the *but* she kept tripping over. Worrying about. Tito seemed to be more conflicted than she would like him to be.

Was that conflict heightened by Duncan's presence on many of the outings? Easy answer: probably. But… In her worries, she'd cycled around again.

Sometimes, she thought Tito was disappointed in his father, perhaps thinking he didn't measure up to Duncan.

Who did? a small voice whispered. She shook it off.

She would love to see poor Tito filled with respect and admiration for his dad. That would be the ideal. *Lack* of respect and admiration were not legitimate reasons for her to hesitate, however. Parents sometimes—maybe inevitably—disappointed their kids. Didn't measure up in their eyes. That was life. And, reality was, Tito's situation with Lupe was maybe safe but otherwise pretty much lousy.

Frowning, Jane leaned back in her chair, not even seeing the array of glittery hair combs on the monitor.

What niggled at her was a suspicion that Tito might be at least a little bit afraid of his father. And *that* was a problem. Despite all her bravado, she'd been afraid of hers, and she never wanted to see a child who had to be.

Tito had seen Hector angry three or four times, but he'd also seen Duncan lose his temper. Tito had definitely been scared that day on the beach. So the question was, why did he seem warier of his father than he did of Duncan? Who had also, she remembered, drawn a gun on him.

Good question. One, she felt quite sure, Tito wouldn't be prepared to answer if she asked. Tito might not even know the answer.

Did he secretly dream that Duncan might yet

change his mind and take him home as a foster
son? She'd have to ask Duncan if Tito had hinted
at any such thing. Unfortunately, she couldn't ask
Duncan if he'd noticed that the boy was more nervous than he ought to be around his dad.

All roads lead to Rome...

Here she was, picturing Duncan's face, not exactly mobile or easy to read but still somehow...
expressive. To her, anyway. He could convey an
alarming amount with a twitch of those dark eyebrows or a deepening of the furrows on his forehead.

Maybe, she thought, the trouble was that it was
awfully hard to look away from him when he was
there. She thought she'd seen him close to relaxed
a few times—sitting at the picnic table that day
at the state park, for example—but the intensity
never let up.

Niall's force field said *Keep away*. Duncan's
said *Reach out a hand and touch—if you dare*.
Or maybe *she* was the only one foolish enough
to be tempted, Jane thought with a sigh.

Hair combs, she urged herself. Quit thinking
about Duncan MacLachlan. She wasn't interested
in any serious involvement with a man of any
kind, and certainly not with one used to giving
the orders and being obeyed. A man who did not
like, ever, having to bow to her will. He brought
back too many memories.

His reasons were entirely different from her father's, but were as set in stone. The *reasons* didn't matter; the result did.

Never again.

CHAPTER TEN

THE COURT HEARING TO SETTLE custody of the Jones children was hideous. None of the attorneys could control their clients. The judge had only recently risen to the bench and spent a lot of time banging his gavel uselessly while voices rose.

Jane had come to sit in near the door, not expecting to be asked to weigh in. She'd hoped to go unnoticed, but, of course, it didn't work that way.

If looks could kill, she thought, when heads turned her way after Judge Ritchie laid out the Guardian ad Litem's recommendation that the mother be awarded custody, the father visitation and the grandparents extremely limited visitation. She had a queasy memory of the word *Bitch* crudely painted on the door of Dance Dreams, the scarlet paint dripping like blood. Was one of these people responsible for it? She found herself, thanks to Detective Niall MacLachlan's cynicism, looking at Grandma's hate-filled eyes and thinking, *Yes, I can see her doing it.*

Despite shouting and the threat to file an

appeal, the judge so ruled, and Jane fled, glad to have been closest to the door. Cowardly, maybe, but she couldn't think of a reason in the world to stay to chat.

She'd have liked to use the restroom but didn't dare. All she had to do was remember the Ortez hearing, when Duncan had lain in wait outside the door.

She hurried down the carpeted hall, out the double doors and into the parking lot, doing her best to look like someone late for an appointment and not someone running for her life. Which, of course, she wasn't, even though her heart was thudding and she felt a dreadful urgency to get away before either the father or the grandmother could come after her.

She all but ran into, of all people, Niall Mac-Lachlan, dressed in sport coat and tie. For a court appearance?

"Ms. Brooks," he said in surprise. "Is something wrong?"

"No, I..." She heard the approach of footsteps and went rigid.

His eyes narrowed on a point over her shoulder.

Reluctantly, she turned. Glenn Jones, a well-dressed businessman who had been too arrogant to bother trying to charm Jane on first meeting, looked only slightly taken aback to find she wasn't alone. Face flushed with anger, eyes boring into hers, he said, "If you thought you'd sneak away without getting a piece of my mind, you're wrong…" His gaze did shift then to Niall. They all heard the unfinished quality to his sentence. *Bitch* was what he'd wanted to say. It quivered before her eyes, dripping in blood red, formed from crudely cut letters glued to paper.

Niall gently set her to one side and stared at the other man. Quite deliberately, he drew his sport coat aside enough to reveal the badge and weapon worn at his waist. Glenn's gaze dropped to them. At last displaying the first hint of caution, he retreated a step.

"Ms. Brooks," Niall asked, "is this gentleman on my list to investigate?"

She opened and closed her mouth, finally settling on an evasive, "Detective MacLachlan, this is Glenn Jones. We, er, had a family court hearing this morning."

"I see." He studied Glenn coldly. "And what is it you wanted to say to Ms. Brooks, Mr. Jones? I think I'll stay to hear it."

Glenn was too enraged to retreat. "She knows nothing about my family! Nothing." His voice was a low snarl. "But she stuck her nose in, anyway, and did her best to steal my kids from me. All that fat slob of an ex-wife of mine wants is to pay me back for losing interest in her. She doesn't give a damn about the kids. And you!" His glower found Jane. "You somehow convinced the goddamn judge to let her have *my* children."

Jane knew better than to try to argue. Truly, she did. But cowering behind someone else wasn't her style, either. "That might be because Renee gives some thought to what they need, not what *she* needs," she returned, as coolly as she could.

He took one aggressive step forward. "I'll get them back. Don't kid yourself I won't!"

Niall took a step, too, all but freezing the shorter man with a wall of ice. "Watch your tone!"

"And who the hell are you to tell me what to do?"

"Detective, is there a problem?" another voice asked.

Jane turned her head to see two uniformed officers had stopped beside the small tableau. It was one thing she liked about the courthouse; she was never truly alone.

"No," Niall said, his expression hard. "I believe Mr. Jones felt the need to vent. *And* he's now done that. Isn't that right, Mr. Jones?"

Face now beet red, Glenn muttered, "I've said what I meant to," and started to turn away, then apparently couldn't resist being stupid. "But don't think we're done," he said, with one last snarl over his shoulder.

Niall moved with shocking speed, grabbing the man's shoulder and spinning him around. In a very, very soft voice, he said, "I believe that could be construed as a threat."

For the first time, Glenn had the sense to look alarmed. "What are you talking about? I'm filing an appeal! How's that a threat?"

Niall released him with a contemptuous flick of his hand. "I do suggest, Mr. Jones, that in the future you keep your distance from Ms. Brooks. Since you're now on record issuing what, as I said, can easily be construed as a threat."

"You're crazy!" he exclaimed, and hurried toward the courthouse.

With a nod, the two officers continued on. Jane and Niall were left standing there, Niall watching with a chillingly speculative expression until Glenn disappeared into the courthouse.

"Did you know a former employee of his alleged that he raped her?" he said.

Jane nodded. "Yes. There have been other allegations of sexual harassment. Unfortunately, nobody ever quite pins anything on him. He really is a creep."

Niall turned his head to look at her. "Is the fifty-year-old grandma we discussed his mother?"

"I'm afraid so," she said with a grimace. "I expected her to chase me out, too."

The detective frowned. "Was she contesting her own son as well as her former daughter-in-law for custody?"

"Yep. Once you meet her, you almost find yourself feeling sorry for Glenn."

His rumble of a laugh reminded her of one of Duncan's; reluctant, as if he didn't do it often.

"I really don't think Glenn is the one threatening me," Jane said thoughtfully.

"I don't know. He's pretty pissed."

"So is his mother." She couldn't help a shiver, remembering that vicious stare.

"There have been no other incidents?"

She shook her head.

He contemplated her for a minute. "If I hadn't been here, I suspect he would have threatened you. Or worse."

"He's all talk." She was sure enough of that to be embarrassed at the way she'd been running away. If not for the anonymous threats, she'd have walked calmly out and had whatever conversations she'd needed to have right there in the courthouse. She explained, "This—today—it's how he operates. He intimidates people. And no, he doesn't like it if you don't let yourself be intimidated, but he always seems surprised and...I don't know. Confused. I doubt he has any follow-through in his repertoire."

Niall shrugged. "You may be right." His gaze was sharp. "If you had to take a wild guess as to who sent you that note and whacked your windshield, who would it be?"

Her fingers tightened on her purse strap. "I... really don't know. I've had quite a few people say a lot nastier things to me than Glenn Jones did."

"Oh, I can believe that. Let me walk you to your car, Ms. Brooks."

"Thank you," she said, and he fell into step with her. "You can call me Jane, you know."

"All right. Since I gather you're a friend of Duncan's."

"A friend?" Her mind boggled. "I'm...not quite sure about that."

He laughed again, and she thought maybe he did it more often than she'd suspected. "With Duncan, who is?" Something dry and almost, but not quite, hostile leaked into his voice.

Jane tried to tell herself she was imagining that weird tone. Duncan had called Niall the other night; he must trust him. And why would Niall work in his brother's department if he disliked him?

She thanked him for his intervention and drove to Dance Dreams, where she set about unpacking a shipment of spring- and summer-weight women's leg warmers in an array of delicious colors. She decided to put a couple pairs in the front window and a display of the others on a table that currently held a rather artistic arrangement—in her not unbiased opinion—of a dance bag, a couple of leotards, pointe shoes and half a dozen shoe ribbons laid out like rivers of color. She liked to change the display every few weeks.

Somehow it didn't surprise her when Duncan called a few hours later.

"Niall told me about the SOB who got in your face outside the courthouse."

"Hello, Duncan."

There was a momentary silence. "Jane."

"Yes, Mr. Jones decided to express his displeasure with the judge's decision, specifically my role in it. There wasn't anything new in that. It was nice of Niall to intervene, though."

"It sounds like it was lucky he was there. Damn it, couldn't you get an escort out to your car?"

She sighed. "Yes, I probably could, but as I told Niall, I really doubt I was in any danger. The man only wanted to yell at me."

He mumbled something she couldn't make out. Which was probably just as well. He probably sympathized with people who yelled at her. "For your safety, have you considered getting a concealed weapons permit?"

"I have never been attacked."

"You could be," he grumbled.

"Do you recommend every prosecuting attorney carry a gun? Every social worker? We all face disgruntled people on a regular basis. I'm sure I could think of a dozen other professions with the same problem. As a police captain, is that really what you want to see?"

"Damn it, you're a woman!"

He was stepping onto dangerous territory. If he suggested she was less capable because she was a woman...

"Yes, I am," she said levelly.

She heard his breath gust out. "You have no sense of self-preservation."

"I don't live in inner-city New York! This is a peaceful town."

"Not as peaceful as you'd think."

Well, he'd know. And Niall, too. What was it Niall had said?

You might be surprised.

She'd really rather not be. Or not any more than she already had been, with the string of unpleasant messages.

"I'm careful." Jane tried to sound firm.

He grunted, told her he'd see her tomorrow night at the arcade, and rang off.

Jane was left wondering exactly why he'd called.

DUNCAN HADN'T PLAYED a video game in years, not since... He had to think about it. Since Conall was fourteen, fifteen maybe. It occurred to him suddenly that his youngest brother's birthday was approaching in May. He'd be... Thirty. Duncan gave a rough laugh. His baby brother would be passing the big Three-O. Who'd have thought they would both live to see it?

There was a time he'd sent birthday cards and the like to whatever address he had for Conall. He hadn't done that in several years. This birthday, though, he thought he would, if Niall had an address for him. Not that Conall ever responded in any way, but...it seemed the thing to do. Or maybe it had to do with these unexpected pangs of emotion he'd been feeling lately. Reawakened sentimentality?

On impulse he bought a roll of quarters and challenged Jane to a few of the simpler games, including an old-fashioned pinball machine. She got into it, hunching fiercely over the machines as she operated the controls, letting out growls of frustration when she was defeated.

La guerrera indeed, he thought in amusement. Even Tito got a few laughs at her expense, which she acknowledged with good humor.

Sitting across from her at the pizza parlor felt different this time. They'd crossed some invisible divide when he had taken her to lunch. Now, everything they did together felt as if it might be a date. Except when he annoyed her, she'd become a little shyer with him, and for every time he studied her mouth, say, wondering how it would taste, he'd catch her eyeing him in return, then blushing when she was caught.

He wanted to kiss her. He wanted more than that, but a kiss would be a start. Duncan was past caring whether it was a good idea or not. Once again, he was blitzed at the end of the evening with the realization that he'd barely glanced Hector and Tito's way.

Hell of a guardian he was.

Of course, there was no chance for him to be alone with Jane in the parking lot where they all parted ways. Tito went with her, and Duncan had to stifle his frustration and go home alone.

He got a lousy night's sleep. There were noticeable bags under the eyes peering at him from the mirror when he shaved. He nicked himself painfully and had a blob of tissue blotting the blood when he went to the kitchen for a quick bowl of cereal. The coffee he could take with him.

He was thinking about his morning when his cell phone rang. He had a meeting scheduled with his counterpart in the county sheriff's department to schedule some joint training. He wanted to talk to him about their mutual participation in a regional task force, too…. Swearing, he had to hunt for his cell phone, which he hadn't yet hooked to his belt.

"MacLachlan," he barked when he'd finally found it.

The voice was very small. "Duncan?"

Fear hit him hard, a linebacker slamming a shoulder into his solar plexus. "Jane? What's wrong?"

"I, um, I'm fine. It's… There's something really awful on my doorstep. I was going to grab my newspaper and…" She made a gulping sound. Controlling tears, or nausea? "I should have called Niall and not you, huh? I'm sorry. I don't know what I was thinking. I've got his number."

She'd thought of him first. Wanted *him*. The realization was almost as powerful as that first rush of fear.

"I'm on my way." He stuffed his tie into his pocket and grabbed his gun and badge. "Do you want me to call Niall for you?"

"You don't have to come. Really, I'm not hurt or anything."

"Don't be ridiculous. Of course I am."

He expected her to keep arguing. When instead she said, almost meekly, "Thank you," Duncan felt a weird cramping sensation in his chest. "If you wouldn't mind calling him…"

"No," he said gruffly. "Are you in your house? Door locked?"

"Yes. After screaming. I don't think I ever have before."

"What's on your porch? No," he decided. "Don't tell me. I'd rather see it fresh."

"Fresh…" Her voice wavered. "I've got to go." And the silence told him she'd abruptly ended the call.

He drove too fast, using the time to call Niall. Should he reschedule his morning appointment? No, wait; this might not take long.

He barreled up in front of her house, set the brake and leaped out. He should have asked her more, he realized. Was this a crime scene of some kind? Would they need to preserve forensic evidence?

Out of habit he crossed the grass rather than approaching Jane's porch via the paved walkway. Standing to one side, he looked through the railing.

A blistering obscenity escaped him. There was a dead animal on her welcome mat. He wasn't positive what it was from here. A cat? No, maybe a rabbit? Whatever, it had been beheaded, and a huge butcher knife, glistening with blood, was stabbed into her coir mat.

Furious, he circled her house to the back door. When he pounded on it, her cautious face appeared at the window, and then she rushed to open the door and let him in.

"Did you see…?"

"I saw," he said roughly. "Damn it, Jane." Operating on instinct and *need,* he pulled her into his arms. She didn't resist. In fact, she wrapped hers around his waist and held on tight. He laid his cheek on top of her head, kneaded the nape of her neck and murmured God knows what into her hair until, finally, her muscles began to loosen.

Against his chest, she mumbled miserably, "That poor thing."

Beheading was probably a quick way to go. Wasn't that how farmers killed chickens? But he didn't point that out to her.

"Did you call Niall?"

"Yeah, he's on his way."

They kept standing there, neither apparently ready to let go. Her hair was damp, Duncan realized. It smelled deliciously of something citrus. Grapefruit or lemon, he thought. Her hair was tucked behind her ear, and he found himself fixated on the sight of her earlobe, naked where she usually wore a pretty post earring of some kind. Pearls, last night. He'd been amused by the idea of a lady in pearls doing battle with aliens in an arcade game.

So she was barely out of the shower, not yet fully put together for the day. Had she had breakfast yet?

He asked, and she shuddered.

"Coffee, at least?"

"Um…not yet." Still she didn't move, and he was glad. Her body felt perfectly proportioned against his.

The knock on the door took them both by surprise. She jumped, and Duncan turned swiftly.

It was Niall, who greeted Duncan expressionlessly but Jane with sympathy. Her face was strained, but she hadn't cried. *Not my Jane.*

Hell. He had to quit thinking that.

She chose not to follow the two men to the front door.

Niall opened it, and they both studied the exhibit so carefully arranged to terrorize her. Once past the first sickening sight, Duncan frowned, wondering how he—whoever *he* was—knew that she wouldn't have left through the garage without ever seeing this. Or at least not seeing it fresh.

Fresh. The poorly chosen word knocked at his consciousness. Oh, damn. Her stomach had probably heaved when he said that earlier, on the phone.

Niall speculated aloud. "Did he ring the doorbell or knock? Is that how she found this?"

"She came out to get the newspaper." Which still lay on the porch, a few feet from the bloody tableau.

Niall made an acknowledging noise. After a minute, he said, "Do you suppose he's been watching her and knows she comes out every morning to get her paper?"

It was an ugly thought.

"Interesting timing," Duncan said.

Niall glanced at him. "Following the scene at the courthouse, you mean? Yeah, but that doesn't necessarily mean anything. If she had her dates right, she's getting approximately a message a week. This one is right on time."

Duncan swore.

Niall had lowered himself to his haunches, where he could inspect the knife more closely. "They're getting more explicit."

The head had been set to face the door. The animal was definitely a rabbit, with long, velvety ears and now-glazed eyes. Duncan doubted this had been a wild rabbit. It had the fat, plush look of a domestic one, which would further sicken Jane if she thought about it. Not a pet stolen from some kid, he hoped.

God. Please don't let it have been stolen from a neighbor kid.

Niall made the decision not to call for a crime scene tech. He'd come prepared to remove the mat, animal and knife himself, the poor damn rabbit and the mat to be disposed of, the knife to be examined for fingerprints. As carefully staged as this had been, the knife would be clean.

Duncan grimaced, eyeing the thick, vividly red blood. *Well, not clean.*

He found Jane sitting unmoving at her kitchen table, a cup of coffee in front of her and gaze fixed on some indeterminate point. It swung to Duncan as soon as he appeared, but she didn't say anything. She didn't have to; he saw the horror in her eyes.

"Niall is…removing everything. I'm afraid you'll have to buy a new doormat."

She sagged slightly. "Okay, this time, I'd have to say it's a threat."

"You think?" he said, deeply sardonic.

Color was seeping into her cheeks. Her eyes flashed at him, and he saw that her hand was almost steady when she lifted the mug for a swallow.

He got the cup she'd poured for him, and they sipped in silence for some time.

When Niall eventually appeared, it was to tell her he'd cleared the porch.

"Knocked on a few doors, too. Lady across the street is pretty sure she heard a car stop out front and then leave again about forty minutes ago, but she didn't think enough about it to look out the window. No one saw anything. I've still got to find the paperboy…"

"Papergirl," Jane corrected him.

He nodded, dumping sugar into his own coffee

and leaning against the counter. "I can't imagine she wouldn't have stopped if she'd seen."

"No," Jane said dully. "Are there, um, bloodstains on the porch boards?"

Niall shook his head. "If it helps, I don't think the, er, deed was done there. It would have been way messier if it had been." Bloodier was what he meant. "Too risky," he continued. "It would have taken too long, for one thing. And the rabbit might have been..." *Noisy.* He didn't finish; didn't have to. He cleared his throat then, after a prolonged silence, said, "I'm sorry."

She gave a stiff dip of her head and sat staring into her coffee.

"You didn't hear anything earlier?" Niall asked.

"No. I haven't been up that long. And I took a shower first. I really hadn't been downstairs more than a minute. I like to read the paper while I eat breakfast."

"Is that your habit?"

Her face blanched at the realization that she'd likely been watched. "Yes."

Duncan reached across the table and took her hand. She gripped tight.

"Do you get up about the same time every morning?"

Her desperate gaze was fastened on Duncan's face even as she answered his brother. "Yes."

"First thing I'll do is see if I can locate Glenn Jones and his mother," Niall said.

Duncan looked at him.

Niall got the message. "And Ortez." He shrugged. "Unfortunately, this is a lousy time of day to pin down alibis."

Hope in her voice, Jane said, "Hector has several roommates."

Niall glanced significantly at the clock on the stove. "What do you want to bet he was on his way to work right about when this was deposited on your doorstep? Grandpa probably wouldn't rat out Grandma, and Jones lives alone." He set his empty mug in the sink. "It'll be a miracle if any of them can prove he or she wasn't here this morning."

The hope died on her face. Niall made his excuses and left with a promise to keep her in the loop. Duncan lingered.

"Are you going to work?"

She nodded.

Okay. Hell. She wasn't going to like this.

"I want you to get a home security system."

To his relief, she gave a slow nod. "I'd rather spend the money on a few weeks on a Hawaiian beach, but..." Her shrug was helpless-looking enough, it kicked up his rage again. He didn't like seeing her afraid. "Do you recommend any particular company?"

"Yeah." He found her phone book and circled a couple of ads. "Use my name to get quick service."

"Thank you."

"Why don't you get ready for work?" he said gently. "I'll follow you there. And home tonight."

She bit her lip and nodded again instead of arguing.

He wanted to beg her to get mad.

What he really wanted was to take her home with him. He knew without asking that she'd say no, though. Duncan didn't know how he was going to drive away tonight, leaving her alone.

"Did you get breakfast?" she asked. "There's... oh, cereal and oatmeal, if you can help yourself while I put on makeup and stuff?"

He looked at her more closely. She must not wear much makeup, he thought, because the lack wasn't noticeable. She didn't need it, with that beautiful, fine-textured skin and thick eyelashes a shade darker than her hair. He supposed she'd want to dry her hair, though, and put on earrings....

He saw for the first time that she was wearing slippers, fuzzy and pink. Really girlie.

Pink tutus, he reminded himself, were her business. He found her to be unexpected on a lot of levels, and this was one. A gutsy, stubborn, outspoken woman who was also unashamedly feminine.

Suppressing the new attack of awareness/lust, he nodded toward the stairs. "I'll have another cup of coffee, if that's okay with you. Take your time."

She gabbled a few things about getting the cereal out for him, or maybe cooking, and finally allowed herself to be persuaded that he could take care of it himself. He managed not to say, *I pretty much lost my appetite, thank you.* As she so clearly had.

He called and postponed his meeting, then went out to collect her newspaper from the newly bare front porch. He had time, barely, for that second cup of coffee before Jane reappeared, all put together. Hair a shiny curtain, simple gold studs in her ears, possibly a hint of blush on her cheeks and real shoes on her feet.

He'd liked her damp and unfinished.

Duncan pushed his chair back and stood. He should head for the door, remind her to lock up behind him on her way to the garage—but he couldn't seem to move that way. Or move at all. He couldn't look away from her. This time, it wasn't the curve of her mouth, the grace of her carriage, her glossy hair or vivid blue eyes that kept him staring and immobile. It was his painful awareness of her tension, her brittleness. A vulnerability she so rarely revealed.

"Oh, hell, Janc." The words exploded from him. He took a step finally, but toward her instead of away. Their bodies smacked into each other, but comfort wasn't the goal. Getting closer was. Melding their mouths was. The voice of reason lost to primal need.

CHAPTER ELEVEN

HIS FINGERS SANK INTO her hair, the thickest, most gloriously textured silk Duncan had ever touched. His hands were shaking. Jane wound her arms around his neck and rose on tiptoe, her head tipped so that her mouth could meet his.

He'd never kissed a woman like this. Everything he felt was in his touch: stunning physical hunger, tenderness that wrenched him inside out and fear. He was afraid for her, and—God—afraid *of* her. His mind never turned off. Never. But now it did. He was all feelings, sensation. The shape of her head, that hair slipping over his fingers, the shyness of her tongue and the cinnamon taste of her mouth. They were in contact, from thigh to breast. She was leaning as hard into him as he was into her. One of her hands gripped around his neck, while the other had grabbed onto his hair. She made little sounds he couldn't even name, but they increased his desperate need of her.

The tumult wasn't all physical, though. The best of it—the worst—was inside, where he wasn't himself anymore, standing alone. He was melting down, heart and lungs and soul, like hot candle wax, and who knew what shape he would end up.

The kiss went on and on, broken by ragged gulps for air. Once he closed his teeth on her deliciously soft earlobe and the dainty earring that decorated it. One hand left her hair to lift her hips higher against his, tighter.

He needed to be inside her. He wanted to bear her to the floor, but a voice of reason suggested a sofa, a bed. Someplace soft. She deserved soft.

Duncan lifted his head, looked down at her face flushed with passion, mouth swollen, eyes the deepest blue he'd ever seen, and he thought, *Dear God, what am I doing?*

She stared up at him. Her pupils flickered; dilated then contracted. She began to pant, then shuddered and pushed away from him.

"Oh, no," she whispered.

No? Oh, no? Was the idea of making love with him that horrifying? Stiff with affront, he let her go.

"I'm sorry," he said. "I didn't intend…"

"No, I was practically climbing inside your skin." Her teeth sank momentarily into her lower lip. "It's…it's got to be the adrenaline."

She was probably right, the reasonable side of

him concurred. No kiss could be the emotional conflagration that one had seemed to be.

Back off. Think about this. Don't do anything stupid.

He grimaced. *More stupid than you already have.*

"Are you all right?" he asked gruffly, seeing her grab one of the kitchen chairs as if for balance.

"Yes, of course." She swallowed. "Um…I need to find my purse. And…" Her head turned; he had the sense that she was looking blindly. "Only my purse, I guess."

She did find it. And then, as if nothing at all out of the ordinary had happened, Jane let him out the front door and locked it behind him. He waited in his SUV until she reversed her car out of the garage. They both watched until the garage door slid down. Then he followed her to the store, hovered in the alley while she parked beside the Dumpster and let herself in the back door.

She gave him a small, uncertain wave and disappeared inside.

Only then did Duncan let himself sag forward until his forehead bumped the steering wheel and his eyes squeezed closed.

He couldn't afford to feel like this. Because she had looked so vulnerable, her innermost self unguarded, he had sprung himself wide, too, but he couldn't do it again. He couldn't. It was too dangerous. He couldn't trust anyone, not that much. The panic somersaulted sickeningly in his belly. He hadn't felt so exposed since his mother said the terrible words: *I'm leaving. You don't need me anymore.*

Had she really believed that?

Did it matter? What mattered was that she'd left him not only with the burden of his brothers, but with an achingly deep certainty that he never wanted to be stripped so bare again.

He would never fail a trust. Not the way *she* had. Not the way his father had. But the flip side was, he would never again depend on anyone else.

He was coming frighteningly close to letting himself do that.

Stupid, stupid, stupid.

Eventually he was able to loose his hands from their death grip on the steering wheel. Fortunately, the store had no windows to the alley. No one at all had seen him wrestle with his demons.

The ten-minute drive to the Sheriff's Department where the meeting was to be held gave him time to lock himself down.

THAT HAD TO BE THE WORST start to a day ever. A personal best.

Find a beheaded rabbit on your doorstep. Dis-

solve into a puddle of terror. Oh, and then channel all your angst by throwing yourself at a man who is absolutely, one-hundred-percent wrong *for you.*

Not that the throwing part had been all one-sided. In her immediate, postkiss shock, she hadn't let herself remember quite how not-one-sided it had been, but as the day went on and she opened herself to remembering, Jane could say with absolute assurance that Duncan had kissed her with equal enthusiasm.

So—why had she felt such a huge rush of shame when he'd ended the kiss? Why had she been so sure she'd made a fool out of herself? Or...was that it at all?

She didn't know. Probably because she wasn't thinking rationally. About anything.

Thoughts pinged around in her head like the ball in that pinball machine. She'd believe she was settling to some kind of conclusion and... whack! She was off again. Replaying every minute, in brief, jerky segments. Showering—she tried to rewind time and strain her ears for any unusual noise at all. Right before she turned on the water, had she heard...? And then, oh, God, there was the moment of opening the front door, lifting her foot to step out and seeing...*that*. Her pulse had zoomed, zero to sixty, in the one shocking second. Foot yanked back, door slammed, locked, her trembling on the inside for that paralyzed moment. Calling Duncan, that awful moment when she'd had the dry heaves after he said, "Fresh." Falling against him the second he arrived, needing his strength, his heartbeat. *Him*.

She settled the best when she thought about Duncan. As if, even at this distance, he made her feel safe.

Why him? She didn't know, only that from the first time she saw his picture in the newspaper, she'd felt unexpected things.

That's only lust.

But it wasn't. It never had been, not entirely. He wasn't even handsome, not really. She thought it was the guarded way he'd looked at the camera, as if he'd rather its eye had never found him. She'd felt a kind of recognition. Except it wasn't only that, either, because his brother had something of that same look, and she didn't want to throw herself at him.

But then, he didn't look at her the way Duncan did. Maybe, feelings like this had to be mutual.

He was as reluctant as she was, though. Maybe more so. He'd kissed her as if he was starving, not for any woman but for *her*. Only then his expression had gone almost entirely blank. She'd all but heard the steel reverberating when the barrier came down.

That might have been her fault, because she'd

been so shocked at herself. Except it was just as well, wasn't it?

Whack. Her brain bounced another way entirely.

How I dread having to go home.

And yes, Duncan would probably walk through her house again. She felt quite sure he wouldn't kiss her again, though. And then he'd leave, and she'd be alone.

Growing up, what she'd wanted most was to live alone, to be subject to no one's authority. Sometimes, still, she put on her leotard and danced in the middle of the night because she could. She had pizza for breakfast or ice cream for dinner or turned the music really, offensively loud. When she wore a dress that clung to her curves or bared a whole lot of skin, she smiled at herself in the mirror and thought, *Up yours, Dad.* Not healthy to still be rebelling at her age, but she had a lot of years to make up for. She was her own woman now; that's what counted. She answered only to herself.

And now she had to fear going home to her own house, to her own solitary self.

She called the home security company Duncan had mentioned first, and the man agreed to meet her at home at five-thirty. If she was lucky, Duncan would stay to consult with him.

But, of course, there was no way any alarm

system would be installed tonight, or probably even tomorrow or the next day.

She had friends with whom she could stay temporarily. But knowing *he* likely had followed her from work, first to McDonald's and then home, reminded her that he could follow her again. It would be horrible if she brought her troubles with her and visited them on someone she cared about.

She could brace a chair under her bedroom doorknob. Sleep with a fireplace poker clutched in her hand.

Beg Duncan to stay?

That's what she was afraid she would do. So afraid, Jane knew she wouldn't.

Couldn't.

NIALL SLAPPED HIS HAND on the table and roared, "For God's sake, sit down!"

Duncan jerked, pulled out a chair then changed his mind. He didn't even know what he was doing here, at his brother's place. Place, not house, unless you were talking about a fairy-tale gingerbread house, or a child's playhouse. Tucked neatly in behind a modest, 1940s-era bungalow, the cottage was small enough to give Duncan claustrophobia. He told himself that's why he was pacing.

"I don't plan to stay," he said.

In complete exasperation, Niall said, "Tell me again why you're here?"

Yeah, why are you?

"To light a fire under your ass, why else?" Except that wasn't really why he was here and he knew it.

Because I need you to tell me what to do?

Niall growled. "Go home. Go for a run. Call that kid you like so much. He'd probably let you beat the crap out of him on the basketball court."

The muscles in Duncan's jaw flexed. "I have to stay available."

"You could do that at home."

He'd stayed home yesterday evening, after he followed Jane from work and walked through her house to reassure her. After he consulted with the security guy and overrode all Jane's objections to his suggestions. Once home, he'd made himself some dinner, sat down with it, eventually scraped most of it in the trash.

Leaving her had been one of the hardest things he'd ever done.

"Will you be all right?" he'd asked, and, holding open the front door, she'd smiled and given a sturdy nod.

"Of course I will." With an almost-mischievous grin, she had added, "I have you on speed dial now, you know."

"Good," he'd said hoarsely, and her smile had ended up dying in the face of his grimness.

If he'd seen the slightest sign she would welcome him he'd have offered to stay despite his own deep qualms. But he hadn't mistaken the horror with which she'd jumped away from him after he kissed her, and she was working damn hard now to convince him she was relaxed and absolutely fine. *Nope, don't need you,* her body language insisted.

So be it, he'd told himself, and gone home where he'd tried to eat, tried to watch TV, tried to read. Tried to sleep.

This afternoon he'd gotten hung up in some meetings and the best he could do was excuse himself for a minute in the early evening to call Jane to make sure she'd made it safely home.

She was apparently peachy fine. "Niall already checked in," she told him.

When he got free, Duncan drove first by Jane's house. There were lights on—in fact, so many her house shone like a beacon. *Here I am.* No, she was defying the darkness with light. He wondered if she would sleep with them on, too, or if she would convince herself that was silly.

He had actually gotten as far as his own house and slowed to pull into the driveway before his foot resettled on the gas and he kept going.

Tomorrow was Friday. He wished it was Saturday, when Hector was thinking maybe a movie again if it was raining, as the forecast promised. Tito liked going to the movies. This was ridiculous—Duncan couldn't keep taking Saturdays off, but this one he would. To be with Jane.

"I don't know what I'm doing," he said.

"What?" His brother looked at him, startled.

This was why he'd come.

His skin felt too tight, hot. *Hell.* This was worse than standing up in front of the class to give a presentation when you weren't prepared. Worse than walking toward a crazy, armed man, your hands raised as you offered yourself in exchange for a sobbing hostage.

"Has Conall ever, uh, had a long-term girlfriend?"

"What?" Niall said again, but his expression had become wary.

"Have either of you?"

His brother's fingers drummed on the table. "No." There was a small silence. "Women, yes. Long-term, no." He frowned. "I don't think. Conall hasn't said, anyway."

"Do you think you ever will?"

"God, no!"

So I'm not alone. Weirdly, Duncan was appalled. He'd rescued his brothers, and yet they were as screwed up as he was.

Really? You're surprised?

This was the most personal they'd gotten in probably fifteen years. Which was pathetic. Here was Duncan, filled with anxiety, and Niall twitching like a kid undergoing the inquisition.

Duncan swore and sank down on the chair he'd pulled out.

Niall cocked his head, an expression of sheer amazement on his face. "You've fallen for her. Jane."

"I swore I never would."

"But you did," said Niall, irritatingly persistant.

"I can't go anywhere with it. I can't..."

"Let her in?"

His jaw hurt. There went the enamel on his teeth. "Trust her. I can't...trust anyone."

They stared at each other, two men who knew each other too well, and yet not at all.

"You were an adult when Mom left."

Duncan let out a huff of almost humor. "Eighteen? An adult?"

Niall gave his head a shake, rubbed a hand over his face. "I didn't think..."

"What?"

"About you." He came close to a laugh, too. "Man, does that sound self-centered. It is, isn't it? Oh, shit, who am I kidding? I was. I just, uh, thought..."

"That I was the tyrant and you were the victim?"

"Something like that," his brother mumbled.

"You *still* think that?" Duncan asked in disbelief.

"No. I don't think about the time after Mom left any more than I can help. Do you?"

"No," Duncan admitted.

They sat in silence for a long time.

Why have we never talked about this?

Because they were men? Because Duncan didn't talk about feelings? Didn't admit to having any? Crap. He had no idea.

He groaned. "I didn't mean to start this. But I…"

"Don't know what you're doing. Yeah, you said that." One corner of Niall's mouth twitched. "Maybe a night or two with her would cure you."

"Maybe." He'd been trying to tell himself that. But… "I don't think so. I'm afraid I'd only get in deeper."

"And you can't walk away. Not now."

"No. What if this psycho actually comes after her?"

Niall did not rush to reassure him. "We have a seemingly limited pool of suspects."

"Probably. Maybe. Did she talk about *every* case she's worked? What if this is about something else entirely?"

"Unlikely." But Niall's fingers were beating a rhythm on the table again. His one nervous habit.

"'Bitch, you think you can do anything you want' sounds a lot like somebody didn't like her butting in. Unless she makes a habit of interfering…?"

"Didn't you ask?" Duncan said with quick anger.

"More or less. She said no."

Neither spoke for a minute, maybe two. Finally Niall said, in a strange voice, "You're trusting me with Jane, right? I mean, with her…well-being."

Was he? The concept was unexpected. Duncan's eyebrows knit.

When he didn't say anything, Niall gave his patented, humorless laugh. "Or not."

Still disconcerted by the whole idea, Duncan found himself slowly admitting, "Yeah, I guess I am. You're…a hell of a cop."

"And your brother."

They looked at each other cautiously.

"Yeah. And my brother."

What was Niall suggesting? That Duncan *could* trust him? Or that he already did, and hadn't noticed?

"What's your worst memory of me?" He hadn't known he was going to ask until the question was out, lying there like a defective cherry bomb.

Niall's body coiled as if he wanted to leap away from it. Duncan could almost see it vibrating on the table. From Niall's expression, he did, too.

Finally he let out an expletive. "That's a hell of a thing to ask."

"Forget it. Forget I asked." Once more filled with foreboding and restless energy, Duncan pushed back the chair and stood.

"No." His brother moved his shoulders as if to force them to relax. His expression had morphed into something strange. "Funny, I thought choosing one worst memory would be harder than it is."

Duncan clenched his jaw, one way of bracing himself.

"But what jumps to mind first is you coming to pick me up at juvie. Telling me Dad had been put away for ten years, that Mom was gone, *kaput*. It was only us, and I was answerable to you now. Things were going to be different. I'd toe the line or else. I was going to class, getting my grades up, mowing the lawn…" He laughed at that point. "What did I know, being fried because you were ordering me to take responsibility for the lawn." He shook his head. "You threatened me, and I could tell you meant it. Mom never did."

"I know."

"I told myself it was BS, of course. You wouldn't wreck my car so I couldn't drive it if I got out of line. So what, you were bigger than me? You couldn't really *force* me to do everything you told me to do."

But he could. He had. He'd been his brothers' worst nightmare.

They were both quiet for a while. Duncan itched to pace again, but didn't, only stood there gripping the back of that chair.

"I imagine you can figure out what some of my other worst memories are," Niall said dryly.

Yeah, that wasn't hard. He'd actually been surprised that one of their explosive encounters hadn't made the grade as Number One Worst.

"You going to ask me what my best memory is?" Niall asked unexpectedly.

"I…didn't plan to. I wasn't sure there would be one. But okay. What's your best memory of me, the tyrant?"

"This is leaving aside some of the early good stuff. When you taught me to pitch, and spent hours every night catching for me. Helped me get that heap of crap I called a car running."

Duncan nodded. He had a lump in his throat. It felt like mumps. He'd never had mumps.

"My best memory… No, I have two. But the first one is you coming to pick me up at juvie."

"What?"

"Yeah." Niall's fingers played a quick tune. "Strange, huh? But see, here's the thing. You came. I knew, I always knew, you didn't have to. You'd been dying to leave for college. I was… jealous, because you were so close."

Now totally unable to speak, Duncan could only nod.

"I told myself I didn't believe all that crap you were threatening, but I'm pretty sure that deep inside I did. And what it meant was, you weren't leaving. I didn't want to believe every word you said, but I did, too. Because it meant…I could trust you. You were digging in, for me and Conall."

A sound ripped its way out of Duncan's throat. Raw, inarticulate, pure emotion.

Niall's eyes shied from his face. It was a minute before he said, "The other time I remember was college graduation. Not high school. That time you looked happy, but I figured it for relief. One of us was out of your hair. No longer your responsibility." His mouth twisted into something resembling a smile. "And then you wrote me the first check for tuition. Anyway—fast-forward four years. Graduation day, me getting my diploma with honors. I looked over, and saw you crying." This grin wasn't twisted—it was broad, and affectionate. "Yeah, I saw you. It blew me away. My big brother crying because he was proud of me. That was, um…" He cleared his throat. "I think maybe that was the moment I knew I wanted to, uh, follow in your footsteps." He gestured hastily. "Becoming a cop, I mean."

Assuming responsibility for other people. Trying your damnedest to rescue them.

Shit. Duncan was suddenly afraid he was about to cry again. This—what Niall had said—was a gift. *It was all worth it,* he thought giddily.

Feeling out of control, clumsy, he shoved away from the chair and stumbled back into his antsy circuit of the too-small room. While his back was to his brother, he gave his cheeks a quick swipe and was dismayed to feel moisture. God. He *had* cried.

Niall wasn't looking at him when he turned that way again. He sat with his head bent, one hand beneath the table, the other open on it. His whole pose was relaxed, pensive, but from this angle Duncan could see the hand on his thigh, not quite out of sight. It was fisted tight.

"Thank you," Duncan said hoarsely.

Niall's head came up. There was alarm in his eyes, but also... A glitter of emotion to match what Duncan felt. They stared at each other, leery, embarrassed, but also without the barriers Duncan had barely known were there. It was as if a door had been unbolted, flung wide-open. He felt a weight in his chest.

My brother. For the first time in forever, those two words didn't mean "my responsibility." Or "my burden." They meant... Dazed, he shook his head. He wasn't entirely sure. Except that his brother was someone he could trust, who maybe—certainly—had mixed feelings about him, but who was also conscious of that bond. Who would cover his back without hesitation, as he would Niall's.

"I think I'm in love with her," he said, and Niall only nodded.

"I noticed."

Duncan hesitated, gave a nod of his own and left.

He still didn't know what he was doing with Jane. But he thought he was closer. Which scared the crap out of him, but not having the right to stay close to Jane and keep her safe…

He groaned and got behind the wheel of his 4Runner. He felt so strange. As if he'd been frozen, and now with one gentle but strategic tap he had shattered into hundreds, thousands of pieces. Some were melting. He didn't understand any of it.

How was it that what he once would have seen as duty, as burden, wasn't? That now it was something he craved?

The kiss?

Partly. It had contributed, yes. But whatever this was had started the first time he saw her, when she knocked at his door and he opened it. The cracks in the ice had spread when she stood up to him. When she shamed him that day at the beach. When she let him see some of her own hidden hurt.

Yesterday, driving away from her house and leaving her alone, that was the tap that had broken his ice. He wondered if she could melt it entirely.

If the creep stalking her actually got to her... His hands convulsed on the steering wheel. It would not be a failed responsibility. Or not *only* a failed responsibility.

It would be a new Ice Age.

CHAPTER TWELVE

TITO SAT IN THE HALF-EMPTY movie theater watching the action on the screen without pleasure. *Pretending* to watch. Last time they saw a movie, he had glanced over his shoulder once or twice, trying to pick out Duncan and Jane from the other dark figures nearby and failing. But he hadn't seen them, not knowing they weren't there, and had forgotten them altogether.

This afternoon, he could see them without even turning his head. They sat right across the aisle. Papa had snarled something under his breath when they chose their seats, so close. It had made Tito's skin prickle. He wished his father wouldn't be…so angry. He didn't like him when he was that way.

For a while, Duncan and Jane had shared a small popcorn that rested on his knee. After a shake of her head, he'd set it down on the floor to one side. Not long ago, he had laid his arm over her seat, behind her shoulders. Tito couldn't tell where his hand was—dangling in air? Curled around her upper arm?—and he didn't know why he cared. So what if Duncan liked Jane? If he was here not for Tito's sake, but for hers? *I have Papa.*

But Tito was having one of his mixed-up days when he wished he didn't. Papa's mood had been dark, which made him snarl at Jane and glare at Duncan. Everything about him made Tito feel itchy, like he wanted to squirm in his seat until he was as far from the man beside him— his father—as he could get. Papa stank, as if he should have showered this morning. Tito didn't like the way he looked, from the stubby square- ness of his hands to the grease on his chin he hadn't wiped off after today's burger and fries. He was so short, so *squat.* Tito stared unhappily at the movie screen, wondering if *he* would look like that. He wanted to be like Duncan instead, tall and lean, with that long-legged stride and watchful way of turning his head. Duncan had... had dignity. *La dignidad. Sí.* Staring blindly, Tito examined the concept. Maybe Papa had lost his in prison, or had never had much to start with... Tito didn't know.

This tug-of-war inside him was making him feel sick to his stomach. *La familia* was most important. He knew that. He was lucky that his father was willing to do anything to *be* his father. Think of Raul, how worthless he was.

But Tito's whole body wanted to strain toward Duncan, right there across the aisle. And yet he was ashamed of himself, because he was supposed to love his own father. *Why don't I?*

He stole a glance at his father, whose hand was buried deep in the extra-large popcorn tub, and whose face glistened even more now.

Tito shivered, and looked away.

"I'M GOING TO CHECK IN AT the store," Jane said, almost patiently, "and then I'm having dinner with friends."

Tito waited at her side, his dark eyes moving from her face to Duncan's. Hector had already driven away, his truck giving a throaty belch of black smoke and shuddering as it joined the line of cars leaving the theater parking lot. Duncan had walked Jane and Tito to her car and now gripped the top of her door, keeping her from shutting it. He stared forbiddingly down at her.

"You'll be going home in the dark."

Unease snaked up her spine. "I left inside and outside lights on. I won't be late. I should be home by seven-thirty or eight. The last thing that happened…" Oh, Lord, Tito was listening. She didn't want Tito to know about the rabbit. "That was in the morning." She didn't want to admit she'd rather not spend the whole evening at home alone.

Duncan had a few more things to say about her carelessness where her personal safety was concerned, then at last, scowling, closed her door while she was still midword arguing.

Jerk.

"What did you mean, 'the last thing'?" Tito asked anxiously.

"Oh. Um. It was like the broken windshield, only less destructive." *Except to the rabbit, who was dead.* "Somebody seems to be playing mean tricks on me."

"They didn't break a window at your house?"

"No. Whoever it was left me a, well, a message on my doormat." She summoned a smile for his benefit. "Nothing you need to worry about, Tito. Don't kids play practical jokes on each other that aren't always funny?"

His face twitched as if a few electrical impulses had gone astray, and he ducked his head but finally bobbed it. "Yes." He was quiet until she had made the turn out onto the main road.

Tito might not have noticed that Duncan's black SUV loomed directly behind them. By chance? Jane almost snorted at that.

"You don't know who's doing it?" The words burst from the boy, betraying an intensity and anxiety that made her turn her head and study his face briefly before she once again had to pay attention to the road.

Tito couldn't be responsible for the things that had happened…? Relief flooded her on the heels of that foolishness. Of course not. She'd picked him up and driven him to McDonald's the night her windshield was smashed. He'd been with her every minute. And the rabbit… How would he have gotten away from his sister's scrutiny on a school morning, across town and then home or to school with no bloodstains to betray him? Besides, she liked Tito. She couldn't imagine him doing *that* to some poor animal.

But was he smart enough to wonder about his father? Had he, too, thought about the fact that Hector had arrived late to McDonald's and come in soaking wet? It hadn't occurred to Tito then, Jane thought; he'd gone off to the movie happily with Hector. But later, especially if Hector expressed some anger at Jane for the way she insulted his honor, his ability to care for his family…. It was possible.

She changed the subject and chattered away about school and Lupe and his two nieces and nephew until she dropped him off.

Jane hadn't told Duncan she was driving all the way to Bellingham for dinner with her friends. Austin taught psychology at Western Washington University and his wife, Susan, worked with United Way. Austin had been Jane's friend from college; they'd dated a couple of times, given that up as a lost cause and settled for being good friends. Susan and she had become even better friends.

Over dinner, she told them about the dead rabbit on her doorstep and all the rest, although she kept her tone light. *Icky,* it implied, *but I'm not scared.*

Before her eyes, Austin clicked into professional mode. "Jane, you took Psychology in college. This kind of stalker can be exceedingly dangerous."

"Surely not a stalker," she objected. "It's not like I have a *relationship* with this…person. Whoever he is obviously doesn't imagine that I'm his in any romantic sense."

Austin was shaking his head. "This guy—and shakes are good it *is* a man—is obsessed with you. Doesn't have to be romantic. The obsession is the meaningful part."

The scary part, too, it seemed. Austin had quite a lot to say about stalkers. She began, with exasperation, to think he was as bad as Duncan. Susan wasn't much help, since she worked with a woman who'd been stalked and terrorized by an ex-boyfriend.

Wasn't dinner with friends supposed to be relaxing?

By the time she said good-night, Jane didn't feel very relaxed at all. At this time of evening, I-5 was surprisingly lonely heading south. In this

twisty, mountainous, wooded stretch, the freeway shrank to two lanes each, north and south-
bound. Dusk turned into dark as she drove. Her
tension, subdued for most of the day, crept out of
hiding and tightened her, muscle by muscle. By
the time she left the freeway for the even-darker,
even-lonelier drive east toward Stimson, she felt
as if she hadn't worked out in months and had
foolishly tried to make up for the lack. She was
knotted, taut, heading toward will-I-be-able-to-
get-out-of-bed-tomorrow stiffness.

Pulling into her own driveway, watching her
garage door lift silently, she realized she was
scared.

Would she be less scared if she'd come straight
home at five-thirty and spent the evening, as
she had the last two, trying to avoid casting any
shadow as she passed windows, afraid to turn on
the TV for fear she wouldn't hear breaking glass
or the clunk of a door lock being breached?

Monday the security system was to be installed. *Only tonight and one more night. Thank
God.*

The garage was bare of anything that didn't
belong. After pressing the button on the remote,
she watched in the rearview mirror as the door
closed in its torturously slow way. Nobody had
slipped inside. She relaxed marginally. Safe,
so far.

She sat there for an embarrassing length of time, reluctant to get out of her locked car. If only Duncan was here to walk through the house with her. She thought she could survive being alone again, if only he were here now.

Well, he wasn't. And she wasn't about to call and beg him to come.

Finally she got out, purse clutched in one hand, her pepper spray in the other. She closed the car door behind her as quietly as she could—*as if someone in the house wouldn't have heard the garage door opening and closing,* a voice in her head mocked. The house was truly silent when she let herself in. The hum of the refrigerator turning itself on made her jump. She walked through the downstairs, leaving her purse on a table and picking up the fireplace poker. Two weapons now: poker and pepper spray. She'd read somewhere that pepper spray could madden an attacker instead of stopping him. *No, no. Please don't let that be true.*

Not until she'd flung open closet doors and verified that they were empty did she begin to relax. She didn't quite have the nerve to throw open the front door to see if anything was on the porch.

It was still early to go to bed. *But...I have to look up there. Can't sit down and read, or make myself a cup of tea, until I've checked under beds. Under my piles of shoes.* That was supposed to make her smile, and didn't. *Until I know for sure that I'm alone.*

She was less frightened, though, as she started upstairs. Honestly, why would somebody lie in wait for her there instead of downstairs? Right behind the door she had to open to come in from the garage, for example?

Her house was really a story and a half. Upstairs consisted only of a guest bedroom, her bedroom and a bathroom. Guest bedroom first—like the downstairs, it was clearly untouched. She made sure her back wasn't to the door to the hall when she stooped to look under the bed and quietly slid open the closet door. Bathroom, then; she could see through clear glass into the shower, thank goodness. No Alfred Hitchcock scene here.

Jane did wish she'd left her bedroom door completely ajar and not open only a few inches, the way it was. Why she'd half closed it that morning, she couldn't imagine.

For some reason her heart had once again begun to beat harder, faster. She'd shut the bedroom door last night when she went to bed and braced a chair however uselessly under the knob. But when she went downstairs, come morning? She'd set aside the chair, pulled the door open and… She couldn't remember.

The hand holding the iron fireplace poker high

was shaking. So was the one clutching the spray, the hand she used to nudge the door open.

The first thing she saw was the shards of her chair. Then her bed, the bright matelassé coverlet slashed into ribbons. The vicious, ugly words written in blood on the wall above the bed.

Her scream gurgled in her throat as she backed away so fast she bounced off the wall on the other side of the hall.

Duncan kept her on the line as he drove with screaming siren and flashing lights through dark residential streets. Right before he tore out of his house he'd used his landline to call Niall, who would approach Jane's from the other direction. Maybe a patrol unit would already be there; Duncan didn't know.

"Keep talking," he said urgently into the phone. "Let me know you're all right."

"I am." Shuddering breath. "I don't think anyone's here, Duncan. He would have come out of the bedroom, wouldn't he?"

Yeah. Of course he would have. Duncan didn't say, *I wonder how long he waited for you.* Because this creep hadn't had any way of knowing Jane had plans this evening, had he?

Red dripping, still wet... Probably paint, she had concluded earlier. Like before. But he'd been able to hear the doubt in her voice. This paint was…thicker, she said, and he'd have sworn he heard her teeth chatter, too.

The house was a beacon again tonight, lit top to bottom. Duncan slammed to a stop in her driveway, cut the siren but left the lights flashing and ran for her front door. She opened it before he got there. He took the steps in two strides and Jane leaped into his arms. She was shaking, or he was. Probably both.

He heard a siren and chose to wait there, on the front porch, for his brother.

Niall drove up right beside Duncan's SUV. He took the time to turn off lights and siren before crossing the short distance to her front door almost as precipitously.

"You're armed?" he asked Duncan. "Have you gone through the house?"

They did it together, after gently placing Jane with her back to a wall right inside the front door, which Niall locked. They covered each other, one at a time, and silently and smoothly cleared the house, room by room, whether Jane had already done it or not. Somebody could have been upstairs, waiting for a chance to slip out as she succumbed to hysteria. Maybe he had only wanted to see her terror.

Duncan didn't let himself be sickened by the sight of Jane's bedroom until he was sure the nutcase who'd gone berserk in here was gone. Then he let his gun hand sag to his side and *looked*.

The words on the wall, Duncan thought, weren't the worst of it, even though the sharp, metallic tang in his nostrils told him that the dripping red *was* blood.

Niall, grimly silent until now, said, "Somebody hates her big-time."

Her clothes had been torn from closet and dresser and slashed like the bedding. For some reason Duncan's gaze fixated on a dainty blue satin bra with both cups hacked in a telling display of frenzy. A few perfume bottles and the like on the dresser were smashed. So were the mirror above the dresser and the oval, freestanding, floor-length one. Jagged shards clung to the oak frame.

Almost nothing in the room was undamaged, except the windows and blinds.

He was sane enough to know he didn't want to risk being seen by a neighbor.

"Glass breaking would have made some noise."

Niall grunted. "We might get lucky." He tilted his head. "The troops are here."

After a last look at the devastation, Duncan followed his brother downstairs, where Jane was letting two uniformed officers inside.

Niall dispatched them immediately to knock on neighbors' doors. Duncan had gone straight to

Jane, who stared up at him with eyes near black with shock, and wrapped an arm around her, pulling her to his side.

"You're coming home with me," he said gruffly.

She didn't argue, only gave a little shiver and said, "I suppose I should pack some things."

Duncan's eyes met his brother's over her head. After a moment, he asked, "How far did you go into the room?"

"I didn't go in at all. I saw enough..." She broke off. Her fingers clenched Duncan's shirt under his jacket. "There's more."

"Yeah, I'm afraid so." When he hesitated, she tipped her head to stare at him.

"What?"

"You're going to need a new wardrobe."

She stared. Swallowed. "Paint? Or...?"

"He cut your clothes up. I doubt he had time to get everything, but... He did a lot of damage. Smashed mirrors and the bottles on your dresser, too." He paused. "You can sleep in one of my T-shirts."

Her self-possession remained formidable although he could feel the quivers running through her body. She gave a stilted nod. "Maybe I could...get some things out of the bathroom?"

Duncan raised his eyebrows at Niall, who nodded. "Sure," he said easily. "You got a bag you can use, so you don't have to go in the bedroom?"

"Oh. Yes. I keep my suitcases in a hall closet."

He accompanied her while she retrieved an overnight-size bag from the closet and packed a few things in the bathroom. He noticed she was careful not to so much as glance toward her bedroom as they came and went.

"Do you need us?" Duncan asked Niall, who shook his head.

"Jane," Niall said gently, "I think you'd better plan to stay with Duncan for at least a couple of days. I'm going to treat your bedroom like a full-blown crime scene, plus we'll need to figure out the entry point and hope for fingerprints. I don't suppose you accidentally left the front door unlocked?"

Her scathing look brought a fleeting grin to his face. "Didn't think so."

She left her keys for Niall, and then Duncan hustled her out the door and bundled her into his SUV, not letting her do more than exchange a couple of words with the next-door neighbors standing in a fearful cluster out on their lawn, staring.

"You doing okay?" Duncan asked her a couple of times during the ten-minute drive, and she nodded or mumbled assent.

They were almost to his house when she said, "It wasn't paint, was it?"

He didn't want to lie to her, ever. "No. I don't think so."

"Where would you *get* so much...?"

"Kill something." He glanced sidelong at her. "An animal." They weren't dealing with a serial killer here, he reassured himself. The blood had to be from an animal, although something bigger than a rabbit, he thought. At least raccoon-size, given the volume of blood used.

She hunched farther in on herself, for which he couldn't blame her. When he parked in his own garage, she sat like someone in a waking sleep, waiting until he came around and opened her door. As he herded her into the house, she seemed more docile than grateful to be here.

"You had dinner," he remembered, awkwardly.

Jane swallowed, as if she'd rather not have thought about food. "Yes. Thank you."

"I think a hot shower or bath would be good for you. You've got to be suffering from some shock."

"That...would be good."

He delivered her and her overnight bag to the guest bathroom, checked to be sure there were towels and shampoo and anything else she'd want, then went to get something for her to wear. He didn't have anything like a robe. Sweatpants, maybe? Flannel pajama bottoms? He had a couple of pairs he rarely wore. Eventually he offered a pair of each along with a T-shirt and some warm socks, all of which she accepted without comment. Then he went to the kitchen to heat water for tea or coffee and waited.

She was so long he went down the hall, but he heard water running in the bathtub so he didn't knock to say, *You okay?* Of course she wasn't. *He* wasn't okay. Duncan had seen a lot of ugly things in his career in law enforcement, but this one had been a strike against Jane, and that made it different. This was probably like a doctor whose wife had been diagnosed with some insidious disease. Cancer. That doctor wouldn't be cool and thoughtful. He'd feel like any other scared husband.

She's not your wife.

No. But right now, she might as well be, for the impact her shock and fear were having on him.

The sound of the bathroom door opening brought his head around. Jane appeared hesitantly in the kitchen, her cheeks flushed pink from the bath and her hair hanging loose and damp. She'd decided on the green plaid pajama bottoms, which didn't fit her too badly, what he could see of them. She was long-legged enough, they didn't even bag at the ankles. His T-shirt hung to nearly midthigh on her, though.

Giving an uncertain smile, Jane said, "I don't suppose you have a ponytail holder? I didn't think to grab anything."

"Uh…" He touched his own head, his hair tousled but short. "No. Would a rubber band do?"

"They break your hair. I'll leave it loose."

"Tea?" he offered. "English Breakfast or herbal."

She decided on herbal. "I don't need any more adrenaline," she said ruefully.

He didn't, either. Duncan poured himself the English Breakfast, anyway. He couldn't remember why he'd bought the herbal. It tasted like tainted water to him. It was probably worse now, as it had been sitting in the cupboard so long.

His socks looked cute on her, he decided, when she hoisted herself onto a tall stool at the breakfast bar. Saggy on her much-smaller feet. Even so, he could see her toes curl over the rung.

Setting out a saucer for their tea bags, he carried both mugs to the breakfast bar and hitched himself onto the one right next to her. Jane stared into her steeping tea with unwarranted concentration. Duncan had gotten to the point where he was trying to think of something to fill the silence when she spoke, so quietly he barely heard her.

"I feel so violated."

He swiveled so he was completely facing her. After a minute she raised her head to meet his eyes.

"That's normal," he said. "People sympathize when your house is broken into, but they're talking about your new flat-screen TV and the hassle of dealing with an insurance claim. Unless it's happened to them, they don't think about what it feels like. And this…is worse. Way worse."

She bit so hard on her lip, he almost protested, expecting to see blood. "If only it wasn't my bedroom," she burst out.

God. He wanted to take her in his arms and not let go. But she was holding herself together, and he sensed that she needed to keep on doing that.

"I know."

She shuddered and reverted to staring at her tea. He watched for a couple of minutes then lifted her tea bag out of her mug and dropped it on the saucer. "Drink," he murmured. "The warmth will do you good."

They didn't talk much. He had the furnace cranking so that he was sweating, but she seemed comfortable. The tea helped, he thought, maybe only the comfort of cradling a hot mug, breathing in the steam, sipping. It occurred to him how rarely he'd had a woman in his kitchen. Beth Pannek, a lieutenant on the traffic side who, along with her husband, a county deputy, had become friends. A couple of others who'd come to dinner, none to spend the night. He didn't bring women here for sex.

He'd never had one sitting here in his kitchen wearing his pajamas.

Duncan couldn't tell if she had any consciousness of him as a man right now. He shouldn't be thinking about how much he wished he was taking her to his bed, but he couldn't help himself. Where was his vaunted self-control?

Slosh, slosh. Iceberg becomes ice cubes become meltwater.

And he wasn't as disturbed about it as maybe he should be. He wanted her, yes, but…mostly he wanted to hold her. Waking and sleeping. Something he'd never done.

"I wish I had a sleeping pill to offer you," he said finally.

Jane gave him a funny smile that was all askew. "I wish you did, too. But I think I'm ready to go to bed, anyway."

"Okay." Careful not to touch her, he showed her to the guest bedroom, something he'd never quite figured out why he needed. He wasn't a sociable man. Nobody had ever slept in that bed. He'd never envisioned having guests. He'd also never asked himself why he'd set it up for guests. With faint shock he realized it had something to do with his brothers. He'd kept Niall's room in the old house while he was in college, so he had someplace to come home to. Conall's in turn, even though Conall never did come home. He'd wanted them to know they *could,* even though after he had the new house built he never actually said, *I always have a place for you.* He tried to imagine showing Conall to this room, and gave a grunt that earned him a startled look from Jane. "Sorry," he said. "Just…had a thought."

Her eyes widened. "About what happened?"

"No. About my brothers. Nothing important."

"Okay." She peeked into the bedroom, and he wondered if he ought to offer to look under the bed for her, but she only said, "Do you mind if I leave the door open?" and went in.

"Of course not. I'm, uh, right across the hall." He gestured. "If you need me, call. I'm a pretty light sleeper."

Jane nodded, her smile genuine if strained. "Duncan…"

He cut her off quick. "If you're going to thank me, don't. No thanks. Good night, Jane."

She surprised him by stepping closer, rising on tiptoe and kissing his cheek, the touch of her lips so soft it was barely a whisper. Then she whisked into the room and went to the bed. Duncan retreated before he had to watch her actually snuggling under the covers.

WAS IT ANY SURPRISE THAT sleep eluded her? Jane tried to think about anything or everything *but* that awful scene in her bedroom, but the result felt like a too-fragile leaf circling in an eddy, being pulled inevitably toward the center where its fate awaited, like it or not.

As always, she did best when she turned her thoughts to Duncan. Not so much wondering about him—she was getting a pretty good idea why he wasn't married, for example. The tension between him and Niall wasn't that hard to read, either. Sibling tension wasn't meant to get stirred into the push-pull between father and son.

Jane frowned in the darkness. Did that have anything to do with why her sisters had rejected her long-distance overtures with such vehemence? Did they think she was trying to be something to them that she wasn't? After a minute she thought in resignation, *Who knows?* More likely they were comfortable in the pattern of their lives. Neither had been born rebellious, the way she had.

Back to Duncan. The Duncan here and now, right across the hall from her. He'd stayed up a while longer, after showing her to the bedroom. But not long ago she'd heard his footsteps. He'd paused outside her bedroom door, as if listening for her breathing. The hall light went out. After a pause, the bathroom one went on.

A night-light for her. Huddled under the covers, she was grateful.

More light, from his bedroom, she supposed. The sound of a distant toilet flushing, and then his light went out. She thought it was that, rather than his door closing.

She'd rolled so that she faced her own open doorway. Through it she knew she was looking through his, at an angle. Maybe straight at his bed, where he might be stretched out staring her way thinking about her....

Jane muffled a moan.

What would he do if she crept in there on silent feet and stood like a child beside her parents' bed and said, "Can I sleep with you tonight?" Except she didn't feel childlike. She wanted to feel safe with him, but she also wanted...more.

Stupidly more. The kind of *more* that would return to haunt her. He threatened her determination to hold on to her independence as no man ever had. And all she had to do was think about the way he snapped out orders and took for granted that they'd be followed to know how wrong he was for her.

Maybe she was getting drowsy. She could *think* without hurting anything, couldn't she? Or *picture?* How Duncan's harsh face would look relaxed in sleep, for example. She lingered over that one. Or his body, sprawled across the bed. But he'd said he was a light sleeper, which didn't suggest much relaxation....

Jane drifted.

She woke screaming, horrors flash frozen on her retinas, blood splattering her.

CHAPTER THIRTEEN

"JANE! SWEETHEART, you're all right. You're only dreaming." Hard arms closed around her; Duncan's heart slammed beneath her cheek when he pulled her face against his chest. "Shh, shh, shh. It's okay, honey. You're at my house, remember? I'm here."

He was. She latched onto him with a ferocity that might have shocked her any other time. Seen dimly in the fall of light from the hall, he was half sitting on the edge of the bed. She scrambled onto him and her arms wrapped him so tight it was a wonder if he could breathe.

Continuing to murmur comforting words to her, he turned them both so he could lie down on the bed beside her. She was still mostly on top of him, but he couldn't mind much or he would have set her to the side. Instead, his hands were moving up and down her body now, crooning in a different way from his deep, velvety voice.

She was whimpering, Jane was dismayed to realize. She made herself stop, but the result was some hitching breaths that could have been mistaken for sobs. Maybe *were* sobs.

"Cry if you want," he said against her ear. "It's okay."

"No." She sounded funny; raspy. "I…I think I'm all right now. I…I don't know…"

"Bad one, huh?"

"Yes." She squeezed her eyes shut trying to see it, and realized the nightmare had faded, the way they did. "All I can remember is blood."

"I'm not surprised."

After a minute she mumbled, "Thank you."

"For?"

"Um…"

"Offering myself up?" Was that a hint of amusement?

She bobbed her head. She was starting to be a little embarrassed, but not enough to make herself let go and roll away. Instead, under the pleasure of his hands kneading a tight muscle here, squeezing another there, her body began to loosen. She wasn't grabbing on to him so tight anymore. She concentrated on the feel of his hands on her, strong and gentle at the same time. And his body beneath hers. What was he wearing…?

Nothing on top. All that separated her from the solid beat of his heart was skin, muscle and bone. If she moved her cheek, the least little bit, she felt the silkiness of chest hair. And she could see his small, flat nipple.

With alarm, Jane realized that she was suddenly, acutely aroused. No in-between state; one minute, sagging in relief, the next quivering with the need to touch and kiss and merge. What if he guessed...?

Her eyes widened at the feel of the hard ridge beneath her belly. Whether he knew what she was feeling or not, *he* was aroused, too.

Bad idea.

Don't care.

He'd quit crooning at some point and been doing nothing but breathing. Now, though, he made a sound. It rumbled from deep within him. A groan.

And his hands. They hadn't stopped. They still kneaded and caressed, but one of them wrapped her hip and one buttock. The other, *oh,* it was skating up her side to the plump swelling of her breast, what he could reach of it with her flattened atop him.

The need to touch in turn had become irresistible. Her hand slid over the powerful muscles in his chest so that her fingertips could lightly explore his nipple. And...she wriggled, trying to crawl higher on his body so she could put that ridge somewhere it could do more good.

Duncan muttered some kind of blasphemy, his

voice deeper and darker, and then he was forcibly lifting her so that she straddled him the way she longed to, and so that their mouths could meet.

The kiss, only their second, wasn't tentative. It seemed to take up where the other had left off. Or as if it never *had* left off. Hungry and practiced and insatiable. His tongue explored her mouth and then gave her a chance to do the same, though it never ceased its stroking. His hands had slid now beneath her borrowed T-shirt and stroked her bare, exquisitely sensitized skin. Then one delved beneath the waistband of the pajama pants and gripped her butt, moving her against him. No, helping her own movements find a rhythm, one that had already flooded her with heat and raw need.

Duncan yanked the T-shirt over her head, lifted her and reared up enough to close his mouth over her breast. No preliminaries here, either; he suckled hard, and a thin, high cry escaped her.

They rolled so he could wrestle her pajama bottoms off and take her other breast in his mouth. The deep, rhythmic pull matched the coordinated way their hips pushed at each other.

Almost sobbing in her desperation, Jane struggled with his pajama bottoms. He kicked them off in the end and was between her legs in the blink of an eye. She had to be sopping wet. The blunt tip of his penis felt so good, so… Jane strained upward, trying to draw him in.

He pushed, then swore. "I have to go find a condom." There was nothing velvety about his voice now. It could have stripped varnish.

"No!" She grabbed frantically at him when he would have withdrawn and tried to pull him deeper.

"Jane!" Duncan sounded desperate.

It was an effort to shape words, but necessary. "I'm on the pill."

He said something, she didn't know what, but it didn't matter because instead of pulling back he was thrusting hard.

This was nothing like her few and unsatisfactory attempts to explore her sexuality. It was all sensation, so powerful she didn't seem to exist as a conscious entity. There was no perfect rise and fall, taunt and satisfy; it was more like a struggle, something so primitive there were no words for it. The hunger, the frustration and satisfaction, and drive toward a cataclysm she wanted, oh, she wanted…

When it came, she was shocked. Her mouth opened on a silent cry. This was no enjoyable little *pop!* like champagne bubbles when the cork came out. Her body arched and spasmed as a flash flood of white-hot pleasure tore through her, from her core outward. He made a guttural sound, thrust even harder a few times and then went rigid.

She'd somehow lost all strength. Her arms fell from him to flop onto the bed. His full weight sprawled atop her. Neither moved, but to gasp for breath.

Brain function was slow returning. Tiny niggles first—the sandpaper texture of his jaw against her throat and chin. The tickle and heat of air his lungs pumped out. Twinges in muscles she hadn't known she had. Then awareness of her full body, starting with a delicious lassitude. And something that was almost joy, but was physical, tips of her toes to the tips of her fingers and to the hair on her scalp.

No wonder people would do anything *for this.*

He stirred, as if his brain was coming online at the same time, and then with a groan levered himself off her. Jane was startled by the sense of loss, cured when he scooped her up tight to his side, her head planted on his shoulder. Cuddling her.

Had this been out of the ordinary for *him?* She couldn't ask without sounding pathetic.

She felt the moment Duncan began to actually think. Without moving, he tensed. Panic jumped in her chest. Would he want to get up and return to his own bed, leaving her alone?

"Are you..." she stuttered, and couldn't finish.

His head tilted. "Am I what?"

"Leaving?"

"No." His arm tightened and his other hand came up to stroke her hair from her face. "I won't leave you."

She almost shuddered in relief. The plunge from the heights and climb up again had left her dizzy.

"Then...what were you thinking?" She had to ask.

His head cocked a little more, as if he was trying to see her face. He cleared his throat. "I don't know if I was thinking." Pause. "Feeling instead."

She nodded, wanting to say, *Feeling what?* but knowing better.

They cuddled, and breathed, seemingly locked in silence. Only then, out of nowhere, he said, "Like nothing I've ever felt before."

Jane's throat seemed to close. Did he sound as unnerved as she was?

Maybe, but...he'd been honest. It would be cowardly to be any less.

"Me, too," she whispered.

His lips brushed her hair. "I'm glad," he murmured. Then, "Shall I get up and turn off the light?"

"Not unless it bothers you."

He shook his head. She lay there listening to

his heartbeat, reveling in the startling heat of his strong, solid body and the security of his embrace, and sleep crept up so stealthily, she hardly knew when it pulled her under.

"YOU'RE DRESSED." DUNCAN heard the flatness of his own tone and hid his wince. Way to go.

He'd heard the shower earlier, but hadn't expected her to be in her own clothes, makeup applied, even a pair of dainty gold hoops in her ears.

Having barely walked into the kitchen, Jane stared at him with astonishment. "Um...yes."

"You're not thinking of going to work."

She stiffened. "It's Sunday, so no. If this was Monday, my answer would be yes."

"Do you think that's smart?" It had to be said, even if he got her back up. The only common sense she'd displayed so far was in calling him when she got in trouble.

"I own a business, Duncan. Do you want me to hang a 'Sorry—open again whenever' sign on the door?"

"Until this is settled..."

"Dance Dreams is my livelihood." *And more.* She didn't have to say that.

Save the argument, he told himself. "If not work today, why get dressed up?"

"These are the only clothes I have, remember?" she said, expression even more brittle. She quit hovering and circled the breakfast bar. "Do you mind if I get myself a cup of coffee?"

He spread his hands. *"Mi casa su casa."*

The flash of her eyes might have been sardonic, but she said politely enough, "Thank you."

As Jane poured herself a cup of coffee, Duncan popped a raisin cinnamon bagel into the toaster when she said that's all she wanted.

"Actually," Jane said, "I was hoping you'd give me a lift to my house. I thought I'd take my car and go shopping. I need to start replacing the basics."

"You might find a fair amount of your clothes can be salvaged."

"Do you really think so?"

He couldn't look right into her eyes, deep blue and clear, and lie. "I...didn't look into every drawer or lift the piles."

She made a sick sound and closed her eyes as if gathering strength. "What about my shoes? Did you notice them?"

"They were soaked with blood," he replied, hurting for her.

Her whole body jerked, as if he'd hit her. Duncan made a helpless sound and pulled her into his arms. She clung, but only briefly. When she stepped away, her face was pale but set.

"Will you give me a lift?"

His jaws ached. He gave a short nod.

"Okay." The bagel popped up, and she turned away to butter it as if nothing out-of-the-way for a typical Sunday morning had happened.

Was making love Saturday night typical for her? She was on the pill. He didn't know why the idea bothered him; he really didn't think he held a double standard concerning sexual mores. It was only that he—*oh, hell, face it*—didn't like to think of her in another man's arms.

"I hope you don't regret last night," he heard himself say stiffly.

"I suspect you're more likely to regret it than I am," said Jane, giving away absolutely nothing.

"What's that supposed to mean?"

"You wouldn't have been in bed with me at all if I hadn't woken up screaming bloody murder."

Maybe he was mistaking wariness, or even shyness, for a rebuff. He wasn't the only one feeling uncertain this morning, Duncan belatedly realized. Instead of greeting her with a smile and a kiss, he'd gone on the attack.

"I wanted to get in that bed with you when I tucked you in."

She went very still. Then her eyes, wide and dilated, searched his. "Tucked me in?"

"Well, not quite." His mouth was lifting into some kind of smile. "I didn't dare. If I had, I wouldn't have been able to leave. I had myself convinced you didn't need that."

With a soft explosion of air, Jane flung herself at him. They hugged, hard. Tipping her head, she smiled at him, though it wobbled on her lips. "Turns out," she whispered, "that it was exactly what I needed."

"Jane." Only, *Jane.* He kissed her. Not so much with passion, although it was in the mix. Rising to the top was tenderness, his need to protect her and, maybe most of all, this confounding need she'd provoked in him since their first meeting.

She kissed him with, he sensed, as much feeling. The touch of their mouths was strangely soft, a lingering and soothing and sampling that, as far as he was concerned, could have gone on all day. Into the night.

His cell phone rang. Since it lay on the counter about two feet away, they both jumped. Reluctantly, he let go of her and reached for it.

Niall.

"What did you learn?" Duncan demanded.

Beside him, Jane smothered a giggle. When he rolled his eyes toward her, she murmured, "Hi. Thanks for calling."

Duncan grimaced. "Thanks for calling."

His brother laughed. "Did somebody prompt you?"

Duncan made a purely masculine sound Niall could take as he pleased.

"Entry was through the back door—jimmied

lock. Lots of fingerprints, but I'm betting they're all hers. I'll need to get a comparison print from her. Ah…ditto for her bedroom. Obviously, she doesn't even have a housekeeper."

Or a lover. Duncan briefly exulted in the thought, until it occurred to him that, like him, she might prefer to have her sexual encounters away from her own home. Her haven.

"No info yet on the blood. I'll let you know."

"Okay. We can pick up Jane's car, can't we?"

"Yeah, sure. I took a look in the garage, but I don't see any sign our guy was out there at all. Not for more than a look, anyway."

After ending the call, Duncan repeated the gist to Jane.

"I don't have any plans today. I could come shopping with you."

She blinked. "You're a man."

"And?"

"Men don't like to shop."

"I don't usually," he admitted. "Today, I want to."

"You mean, you want to play bodyguard."

Offended, he thought, *Play?* Fun and games, this wasn't. "If that's how you prefer to look at it."

She looked at him. Really looked at him. "I didn't mean to insult you."

"You shouldn't have to do this by yourself."

Jane leaned into him, hugged him and said simply, "Thank you."

"We can pick your car up on the way home."

"Okay." Her voice was thick. She made a funny little snuffling noise, then straightened with a shaky smile. "What say we hit the road, then?"

At her request, he drove her to Skagit County, where an outlet mall drew shoppers from Canada and farther for designer goods. Jane decided to hit the lingerie store first. In some alarm, Duncan decided to wait outside on one of the benches put there for that purpose. Laughing, Jane disappeared inside for quite a while, reappearing eventually with a good-sized bag that Duncan stowed in the rear of his 4Runner.

That was his role, he realized quickly: Sherpa. Occasionally she asked his opinion, which was a greater pleasure. She'd emerge from a dressing room, twirl in front of him, and he had an excuse to let his eyes linger on how a pair of low-cut jeans perfectly outlined her perfect ass, or how a soft sweater draped over her breasts and bared her delicate collarbone and long white throat. He agreed with all her choices.

"Um…shoes next," she finally decided, and Duncan shook his head.

"Lunch next."

They had to leave the outlet mall for that. He took her to a nearby soup-and-sandwich place.

Somehow, over lunch she got him talking about his brothers. Sneaky, the way she went about it, asking first about the little stuff, whether he was jealous when they were born, the closeness he'd had with Niall and the distance from Conall, six years younger.

"Too far apart in age, I guess," he admitted. "I think... Oh, hell I don't know for sure, but Mom said things that made me suspect Conall was an accident. She...always seemed ambivalent about him."

"That's sad," Jane said finally. Her attention was utterly on him, to the point where, in that way she had, she'd begun to crumble her food rather than eat.

He reached across and rescued her sandwich. She laughed ruefully and took a bite.

A few minutes later, she said, "I was the oldest in my family, too, you know." A shadow passed over her face. "I wished I could have taken my sisters with me when I left."

"It wouldn't have gone well if you had," he said harshly then moved his shoulders in discomfort. "No. Maybe you'd have done better than I did."

"What do you mean?"

So he told her. How they'd clung to him briefly, scared he'd leave; how it had felt, as if he was being smothered in responsibility, as if their neediness adhered to his flesh like Velcro he'd yearned to rip away and instead had endured.

"Then they started to relax. To test me, I suppose. To get angry when I reacted differently than they had expected or wanted."

"You weren't Mom or Dad."

"No." Talking about it made him feel a little as if he were ripping some of that Velcro from his bare skin right now, tearing up strips that bared the muscle and blood beneath. Not making him naked; no—worse. "If I was going to do it at all, it was going to be right," he said. "No more trouble with the law, no more booze, drugs, parties. Conall was twelve," he added as an aside. "Twelve years old, and he liked beer. Too much."

"So you did do it right," Jane said softly, eyes drenched with compassion.

"Oh, I did it. But right?" He shook his head. "There had to be a better way. Niall speaks to me, Conall doesn't."

"What...what happened?"

This was one of his worst memories. The realization that he couldn't watch them every minute, that persuasion wasn't working, that, in the grip of grief and resentment and hormones, they were incapable of listening to the voice of experience—from an eighteen-year-old!—or of achieving perspective themselves. That, if he was going to keep them out of trouble and following his orders, he could only do it with fear.

Of him.

He'd picked his moment. He had grounded Niall, whose brand-new driver's license was, so to speak, burning a hole in his pocket. Niall told him he could shove his rules you-know-where and walked out the door. He drove away and didn't come home until three in the morning. He wasn't staggering, but he'd clearly been drinking.

"He was nearly my size. I couldn't turn him over my knee."

Jane nodded. Neither of them were eating anymore. He was grateful they'd arrived at the sandwich place late enough the lunch crowd was mostly gone. Now they were the only customers left.

"I dragged Conall out of bed. I wanted the demonstration to work on both of them. I grabbed a baseball bat, went outside and took it to Niall's car. I'd…helped him restore it. We'd worked on it for months. Rebuilt the engine, painted it…" He had to stop for a minute. "I took the baseball bat to it. Windshield, hood, trunk. I beat the shit out of that car. Nobody would ever be driving it again."

He could still remember the looks on their faces as they stood like terrified children on the lawn, Conall a scrawny thirteen-year-old, Niall still skinny but coming into his adult height and bulk. Conall had started to cry, but Niall's expression, by the time Duncan was done, had been closer to hate.

And fear. Oh, yeah, he'd made them afraid of him. They'd stayed that way long enough. There had been battles, but nothing so hideous again. Niall had closed himself to the big brother he'd once worshipped; Conall had gotten into sports, found new friends, graduated in the top ten in his class, his defiance of Duncan constant but petty.

"Didn't the neighbors…?"

"Call the police?" Duncan gave a short laugh. "Oh, yeah. I had a lot of explaining to do. But I owned the car. Thanks to my mother, I owned the property it was on."

"Your father didn't…?"

"No, the house was always in her name. She didn't trust him. Couldn't trust him."

And then had been untrustworthy in her turn. *The MacLachlan legacy,* he thought.

"I see." Jane was gazing at him with an expression he couldn't read. Not contempt, which he'd half expected. Not fear, because he was the kind of man who had used violence as the prod to push his brothers into the future. Not…anything he could figure. "You did that in cold blood," she said, her tone odd. "Not because you were mad that night and had to take it out on someone or something."

"No." True confessions sucked. "You're smarter than they were." Or knew him better? That was an unsettling thought. "I planned it. I almost pushed Niall into defying me that day, that way. It was a setup."

Her smile was as strange as her tone. "You're an interesting man, Captain MacLachlan. Not quite what meets the eye."

"Is anyone?"

"No." Her expression became, if possible, even more veiled. "I don't suppose any of us are." After a moment, her mouth quirked. "I think I'm rejuvenated enough to tackle shoe shopping. What about you?"

A fate worse than death. No, he realized; a worse fate would be letting her go off shopping alone. Alone, needing to replace the shoes drenched in blood by someone who hated her guts.

"Why not?" he said.

Her knowing chuckle lightened his mood, impossible though that should have been.

Déjà vu.

It was Tuesday morning, and the review of the custody on Tito Ortez was in front of His Honorable Judge Edward Lehman. He was once again

peering over reading glasses at the six people
seated around the table in his courtroom—the
one difference being that this time he'd requested
Tito's presence. The judge had been reading
Jane's report, which made her nervous. It was not
one-hundred-percent complete. At the same time,
she'd expressed enough reservations... Well, she
had no idea which direction he would leap. Or
even which way she thought he ought to leap,
which was unusual for her.

She wasn't the only nervous one. Not the caseworker; she was surreptitiously scanning a file
on another case. *She* hadn't had much to do with
the matter of Tito Ortez this past month. A visit
or two to Lupe's home, to ensure his well-being.

But Tito himself was hunched as small as he
could make himself, and that was small. With
his shoulders rounded and his head bent, the
effect was turtlelike, except that Jane suspected
he knew quite well he had no shell to hide within.
No, as a minor he was completely vulnerable to
the decisions of these adults.

Lupe was fidgeting. Hector sat impassive, reminding Jane again of a Mayan figurine, sul-
lenness set in stone. She could all but feel his
anger, barely contained. It was enough to make
the small hairs on her arms rise.

And Duncan... Jane didn't know. They'd arrived separately, even though they'd slept to-

gether. And made love. Mostly, made love. In theory, she could go home today. The home security system had been installed on her house yesterday. Duncan and Niall had both tested it and deemed it adequate. Jane hadn't said anything last night about going home, though, and neither had he. She'd told herself she couldn't face her bedroom until it had been scrubbed and everything that was damaged hauled away, but a cleaning firm that apparently specialized in crime scenes was coming that day. By tonight it should be bare. Mostly empty. Ready for her to fill the drawers with her new clothes.

Which brought her, reluctantly, back to Duncan and the present.

Didn't know? Of course she knew what he was thinking. He hadn't relented in any way toward Hector. If anything, the threats to Jane had hardened his stance. Hector was still his primary suspect, if not Niall's.

Maybe her skin wasn't prickling because of Hector's suppressed emotions. Maybe it was Duncan's she felt instead.

Or also.

The judge had already asked questions of Lupe and of Jennifer Hesby, the caseworker. Now he said, "Mr. Ortez, thank you for the copies of the pay stubs. I see nothing to indicate you've yet rented a home for yourself and Tito?"

Hector's face flushed. "I had to buy the truck, and then there were repairs on it and tires. It had to be safe, for my son."

Judge Lehman waited patiently.

"No," Hector finally said, in a strangled voice. "Because I couldn't have Tito at home, I have to take him out to eat a lot, and to movies. With the rain, I had to think of things we could do inside."

"Children are expensive to raise. Particularly teenagers," the judge observed.

"A few more weeks…"

"You may recall, one of my stipulations was that you have a home to offer Tito before I granted you custody."

Hector simmered in silence.

"I see that Ms. Brooks had to curtail your home visits at your daughter's apartment."

"The apartment is so small! All we did was…"

The judge's sharp gaze sliced off the beginning of an impassioned defense.

"I think we must once again continue any final decision. Mr. Ortez, when do you anticipate being able to make first and last months' rent on a place of your own?"

Hector flattened both hands on the table. He was sweating, his dark eyes fixed in a kind of desperation on the judge's face. "Only a few more weeks. Perhaps a month. Not that long… Tito could come stay with me now. Two of the men have left. I now have a bedroom he could share."

Tito shriveled even smaller. The judge's gaze flicked to him and then to Duncan, seated beyond Jane.

"Captain MacLachlan, you don't properly have a place in these proceedings. However, through the perspective of your relationship with Tito, how do you believe the visits have gone?"

Jane tensed. With all her being, she prayed for him to be honest, fair. To be the man of honor she wanted him to be. Like Tito, she bent her head.

"Mr. Ortez didn't cancel a single visit," Duncan said slowly. "I...have come to believe that he loves his son."

Her muscles began to unwind.

"However, I'm still not convinced he's Tito's best alternative."

Jane went rigid again.

"I've seen several displays of Mr. Ortez's anger. To my knowledge, Tito has to this point been compliant. I have grave reservations as to what will happen when he defies his father, as will inevitably happen."

The thought spurted into Jane's head. *Maybe you should teach him violence as a parental tool.* She was immediately horrified at herself. It was unfair even to think that; Duncan had been in a quite different situation. The violence had been...

staged. His brothers had never been at risk. Not the way he feared Tito would be.

Assuming he actually believed any such thing, and wasn't saying what he was out of dislike, or jealousy, or because he didn't like the way Hector talked to her. Or because he believed, with utter narrow-mindedness, that Hector had scrawled obscenities on her bedroom wall in blood. Used serrated scissors or shears to shred her clothes.

No. Not Hector. She didn't believe it.

Still, she shivered.

"Ms. Brooks?"

She looked up reluctantly. "Mr. Ortez is unquestionably under a great deal of stress right now. I can hardly blame him for feeling some resentment of me, given my role. His behavior toward his son has been entirely positive, however, aside from encouraging him to break   "
the rules? "—the parameters of the court-ordered visitations."

The air stirred beside her. She'd pissed Duncan off, no question.

"Hmm." Lehman appeared to think for a minute, during which they all stared at him, except Tito, still curled in on himself. Finally he said, "We'll continue the supervised visitation for one more month. At which point—" he leveled a look at Hector "—I anticipate you will have a home to offer your son? Ms. Brooks, can you do this?"

Oh, God. She didn't want to. But she'd never bailed midstream. "Yes. Of course."

An explosive exhalation beside her brought her head around so that she could see the fury gathering on Duncan's face. She quickly looked away and saw instead Hector's walnut skin flushed nearly purple. Veins bulged out on his temple.

"Very well." The judge's gaze swept over them. Narrowed slightly. He only banged his gavel, nodded, rose and walked out.

"Gotta run," Jennifer muttered, apparently impervious to the atmosphere. "Lupe, I'll call you. Jane, you, too." Briefcase snapped shut, she hurried out.

Jane touched Tito's shoulder. Somehow he hunched farther, so that her hand barely grazed him before falling away. Jane met Lupe's eyes, black with worry, and said, "Lupe, did you understand all that?"

"*Sí.* Yes." In Spanish she said, "I hoped..." but stopped, leaving unsaid what she had hoped for. "Tito, come, let's go."

The boy pushed back his chair and stood.

Jane did the same without looking at Duncan. She walked into the hall and ached to keep going, out to the parking lot. But no. She might be able to prevent a confrontation between the two men.

This wasn't like after the Jones hearing, when she hadn't seen that she could accomplish anything good.

Hector's callused hand grabbed her shoulder and swung her around. "You lied to me!"

As if in slow motion, she saw the alarm on Lupe's face, saw her put an arm around Tito and pull him away. Jane was dimly aware that other people were in the wide corridor. Heads were turning. A uniformed bailiff started down the hall toward them.

Duncan was there first. With a snarled, "I warned you to keep your hands off her," he wrenched the smaller man away from Jane. Hector stumbled against the wall, hitting hard. With scarcely a pause, he flung himself forward with his fists raised.

CHAPTER FOURTEEN

"PAPA!" TITO AND LUPE cried simultaneously.

The bailiff was still coming. Had he broken into a run? He wouldn't get there in time, Jane realized. Other people were backing away. Violence flavored the air, like ozone after lightning. What was Duncan doing?

Standing solidly between her and Hector, of course. He hadn't lifted his fists or reached for a weapon, but he was balanced lightly on his feet. Hector would be hopelessly outmatched. And then arrested, for assaulting a law enforcement officer. What had Duncan once said? *I played right into your hands*. That's what Hector was doing; playing into Duncan's hands.

Jane stepped between the two men.

Somehow, she never knew how, Hector stopped. No blow connected.

"Goddamn it, Jane!" Duncan grabbed her and tried to lift her away.

She fought him. "Did you set this up, too?" she snapped, and hated herself when she saw his face. When he backed away.

She made herself turn from him and look instead at Hector. "I didn't lie. You knew you had to be able to provide a home for yourself and Tito. You knew that violating part of the judge's orders would have consequences."

His smoldering gaze was aimed beyond her, where Duncan stood. "If *he* has his way, I'll never have my son. He's exactly like those police officers that arrested me. Like all the guards in that place." He symbolically spat to one side. "He makes himself feel big by trying to make everyone else small."

"I think—" she had to swallow "—Captain MacLachlan loves your son. He is looking out for him. You should be glad there are more people than only yourself who care about Tito."

"Tito has family. He has a father. Why would he need someone who tries to keep him from his family?"

Unexpectedly, Duncan spoke. "I want you to live up to your responsibilities, Mr. Ortez. I want you to be the kind of father who worries less about how big or small he feels, and more about what is best for his boy."

A fine speech, if it hadn't been spoken with such deep contempt.

"Like you, who are so big you have to hide behind a woman?" Hector snarled. "A man needs to be a man in his son's eyes."

Apparently neither man saw the boy huddled in his sister's arms, or the expressions on both their faces.

"Please don't have this argument in front of Tito," Jane said desperately.

She couldn't see Duncan, didn't know how he reacted to her plea. Hector glared at her.

"*I* am his father." He turned to Tito and Lupe. "It is time that you choose. Is it that you wish your father had stayed out of your life? This man gives you an hour here and there. How long will he bother? But if you have more faith in him than you do in me, your father, now is the time to say so. I will not keep fighting for you."

Jane cringed. Oh, poor Tito! How could Hector do this to him?

"Come," Hector said to his daughter and son.

Lupe started forward, trying to urge Tito with her. His feet seemed rooted to the floor. He stared in panic from his father to Duncan and back again.

"You don't have to make a choice," Jane said, trying to inject urgency into a voice she also kept gentle. "This isn't an either/or, Tito. It's not. You can love your father, and still want to be friends with Duncan. Your father is speaking out of anger."

Tito looked at her for a minute, his eyes filled with despair and confusion. She couldn't tell if he'd really heard her, taken in what she was trying to say.

"Family doesn't matter so much to you, then?" Hector made a sound of disgust. "I should never have left Mexico for a place where people think a man of dignity can be treated like a child."

"Children," Duncan said with scorn, "don't knife a man to death."

Jane wheeled around. "What's wrong with you? Do you only want to win? Is that all that matters?"

For one tense, angry moment his eyes glittered at her. The next, a shutter seemed to close over his expression. He looked at her, hard and cold and utterly aloof.

Hector turned away and started down the hall. Small, stocky and roughly dressed, he did have a kind of dignity, but Jane felt mostly frustration.

Tito gasped, broke free of his sister and, with only one wild glance at Duncan, ran to catch up to his father. Hector laid an arm over his shoulder and whispered something in his ear. Lupe hurried after them. Neither Jane nor Duncan moved until the small family had disappeared through the glass doors.

"I have to take him to school," Jane said, recalled to her responsibilities.

"You do that."

She felt as if her chest were being crushed. "Duncan…"

His seemingly uninterested gaze met hers. "I'm not much in the mood to talk to you right now. I'll catch you later." He nodded and strode in the other direction, reminding her the courthouse was linked to the public safety building where his department was housed.

He never looked back.

DUNCAN WALKED STRAIGHT through the building, aware he passed people he probably should have greeted, but he was so frozen inside that, by the time he shut himself alone in his office, he couldn't have named a one.

He stood for a minute, not having the slightest idea what he'd intended to do when he got here.

Sit down.

All right, I can do that.

He looked at his computer and couldn't remember if he'd left it on. What difference did it make? Right now, he was incapable of doing any meaningful work.

Because it was easier and less painful, he thought about Tito first. He wasn't surprised that, when push came to shove, the boy had chosen his father. Really, what else could he do? Hector was right. Who was to say that Duncan would stay interested in a kid who wasn't his own, wasn't even his brother?

Wasn't family.

So why the hell did it hurt so much?

He realized he was bent forward as if protecting his soft inner core.

Too late. Maybe he'd been wrong; maybe thinking about Tito wasn't less painful than thinking about Jane.

But even thinking her name told him he hadn't been wrong. This pain was sharp and deadly. The way she'd looked at him.

Did you set this up, too?

Well, he'd wondered what she thought when he told her the harrowing story of scaring his brothers into obedience. It was plain enough now; he'd disgusted her. As he'd disgusted himself. What he'd done that night was despicable.

But what else could I have done?

He had no more idea than ever.

It worked, didn't it?

Oh, yeah. But at what cost?

He heard her voice again. *Do you only want to win? Is that all that matters?*

The pain in his belly could have been a bleeding ulcer. Or a knife that had slid between his ribs. Duncan ignored it. He sought for his familiar dispassionate outlook. Was she right about him? God knew, he was an intensely competitive man. Above all, he hated to lose. Was that how he'd seen Hector? As his competition for the affections of a scrawny, needy kid?

Duncan stared into space, stunned by the fact that instead of an answer, he had a vacuum. *I don't know.*

But then he reexamined everything he'd said and done today, and couldn't see what he could have done differently. He *did* believe Hector loved his son. As Jane had reminded him, Hector was in there trying, unlike Duncan's father.

No, he thought, frowning, that wasn't quite fair. In his own way, Rory MacLachlan had loved his sons. When he wasn't in prison, he spent time with them. Duncan was the one to reject Rory, once he figured out that his father's love had one gigantic limitation: he wasn't willing to work a hard, honest job for his sons' sake. He needed too much to feel like a big shot, someone to whom money came easily, a man who was above the law and petty questions of morality.

It wasn't Dad's brand of love I rejected, Duncan realized. *It was Dad himself. The kind of man he was.* Now, why should that be a surprise? In the end, hadn't all three MacLachlan boys become their father's antithesis?

Okay, but Duncan's father wasn't the point; Tito's was. And Duncan did have grave reservations about Hector's temper and the potential danger to Tito. Duncan wasn't so sure that Jane could see the difference between Hector and him, and that was part of what hurt. The difference was the ability to control himself, to channel his anger into constructive action. Duncan didn't lash out. Hector had shown once, in a big way, that he did.

Duncan hadn't moved in a long time. He sat in his chair, looked at the far wall of his office without really seeing it and thought bleakly, *Was I supposed to let Hector manhandle her? Hurt her? Is that really what she wanted?*

If so, she didn't know him. Or, face it, didn't like who he was.

He tried to remember a particular moment last night: her face after he'd kissed her, when they had drawn apart slightly and looked at each other. His fingers had been tangled in her hair, cradling her head. She was so beautiful.

But the picture wouldn't form, blocked by a more recent one. The way she'd looked at him today, in the hall outside the courthouse. She'd been angry and upset. Duncan frowned. More upset than his behavior warranted? He was a cop. Of course he wasn't going to let Hector grab her or give her hell.

Niall had stepped into a similar situation, he remembered. She hadn't been exactly grateful, from what Niall said; she'd apparently been

pretty confident she could handle the situation
on her own. But she hadn't been furious at Niall,
either, even though he'd actually threatened the
guy who'd stormed after her. So why was she so
pissed at Duncan?

He didn't get it. Suspected he never would.

All I can do is what I think is right.

No matter what, he would protect her. From
Hector, or anyone else.

If she'd let him.

JANE HAD A SINKING FEELING when she saw that
lights were on in Duncan's house when she arrived at the end of the day. She let herself in with
the key he'd given her. Of course they had to talk.
She owed him an apology for what she'd said
about his setting up that scene. She'd betrayed
his confidence. She hadn't meant it, either. Jane
didn't even know why she'd said it.

She called, "Hello."

"I'm in the kitchen."

Can't chicken out. Dropping her purse and coat
on the sofa, Jane made herself follow the sound
of his voice.

He was putting something in the oven. It was
in a ceramic casserole dish with a lid on. She
couldn't tell what it was. Maybe one of the dinners his housekeeper made and froze for him.

Duncan closed the oven door, straightened and turned to face her. His expression was guarded.

She had to start somewhere. "Thank you for recommending that cleaning firm. They called to say they're done. They didn't even have to re-paint."

His dark eyebrows drew together. "You're not thinking you'll go home."

"There's no reason I can't." She didn't actually want to go home, but that wasn't the point.

"No reason?" He stared at her like she was an idiot. "There's every reason! Of course you'll stay here until Niall arrests that nutcase."

If there was one thing calculated to get her back up, it was being told what to do. Who did he think he was, God? *I have spoken.*

No. Don't overreact.

"I spent a whole lot of money on a home security system so no one can surprise me again. Why did I waste the money if it's still not safe for me to go home?"

Duncan leaned against the counter. "It's a sensible precaution if you're going to keep taking these kind of cases." His tone was exaggerated, as if he were lecturing a sixteen-year-old who'd done something foolish and potentially dangerous. "It is *not* adequate protection when someone's after you who has already painted your bedroom with blood."

She swallowed the taste of bile. Her mind wanted to shy away from the memory of those hideous scarlet words on the wall. The thick texture of the—not paint—blood. Dripping. Like the words spray-painted on the door of her store, and yet...not like.

"Thank you for the reminder," she said sharply. "Apparently you need it."

He wasn't like her father; *he* hadn't bothered to lecture. His word was law, often laid down in Biblical language. His voice had thundered out, "In this house, so shall my word be." But Jane was having a bad case of double vision. One man seen through the filter of another.

"What were you so mad about today at the end of the hearing?" she heard herself ask. "Why aren't you happy that Lehman ordered another month of supervised visitation?"

"Happy?" Duncan pushed away from the counter. "When you'd opened your mouth and said, 'Oh, yes, Your Honor, I'd like nothing better than to continue to enrage some homicidal maniac!'" His voice had risen to a roar now.

She refused to retreat one iota. She'd never been able to. You gave up one little piece of yourself, one bit of independence, and the next thing you knew, it was all gone and you were nothing. A doormat. Her mother, her sisters. Most of the women in the congregation. All purpose and will given into the keeping of others: men.

"Why won't you listen?" Jane cried. "I've told you. Hector's not..."

She might as well not have spoken.

"I'll tell you one damn thing. You're done with the Ortez case. You won't be supervising any more visitations."

Jane was too shocked to do more than whisper, "What?"

"I called Lehman. Told him what's been happening." He paused. "Why haven't you?"

"Because I don't believe Hector has anything to do..."

Duncan talked right over her. "He agreed that you shouldn't be put at risk. He's going to assign someone else."

She'd never known it was possible to see red. Literally.

"Let me guess," she said flatly. "A man."

"That's right. A man."

Jane hadn't known disillusionment hurt so much. Except she knew quite well it wasn't anything that simple. Dear God. How had she let herself love a man who, like her father, needed to dominate and control any woman in his life? Or did he need to dominate and control *everyone?* Either way, she couldn't bear it.

"None of those decisions are yours to make,"

she told him, her eyes dry and burning, her heart as arid. Death Valley. "How dare you go behind my back to the judge?"

"Decisions? One. One decision. Not decisions, plural. And my job is to keep you safe. Continued involvement with Hector Ortez endangers you. Lehman agreed, I might add."

She shook her head. "I will discuss it with him in the morning. This was none of your business, Duncan. It never was."

"Wasn't it?" He looked so damned confident. Angry, too, but mostly sure of himself and his right to do as he saw fit with her life, all in the name of taking care of her.

He was no better than her father.

"No." Hungry and bitter both, she took in his face: heavy brow, creases worn by the burden of responsibility, blunt, battered bone structure. And she grieved. "I'll say this clearly, once only. It is *not* your business. *I'm* not your business. Thank you for what you've done for me. Obviously, I gave you the wrong impression. I'm correcting that now."

Those winter gray eyes narrowed. "What the hell are you talking about?"

Jane walked out of the kitchen. She went straight to her bedroom—no, not *her* bedroom at all, his guest room. Grabbed the overnight case and took it to the bathroom. The *guest* bathroom.

With a couple sweeps of her hand, she dumped her toiletries in and turned. Duncan blocked the door.

"Excuse me," she said politely.

"You're not leaving."

"Oh, yes, I am. Get out of my way."

In a remote part of her mind, she saw how stunned he looked. She couldn't let herself think about it, not really. She hurt enough already. Jane marched into the bedroom and began scooping clothes into the shopping bags they'd come in.

"You intend to go home," he said in disbelief.

"Yes."

"Goddamn it, Jane! What are you going to do, sit on the front porch and wait for the bastard to come?"

"I'm going to retreat behind my very expensive new security system." Her arms were full now. She started toward him, willing him to step aside. "If I hear anything I don't like, I'll call 9-1-1. Like I should have done in the first place."

He stepped out of her way.

At the front door, she struggled to free a hand to turn the knob but managed. After dumping everything in the trunk of her car, she turned around and went in to get the next load.

It took three trips. Duncan stood right inside and watched her come and go. With the last arm-load, she swept past him, but stopped momentarily on the threshold, locked in place by a spasm of anguish.

Thank you. No, she'd already said that. *Goodbye.* Why bother?

After a moment, she unfroze her muscles and kept going.

The first time she'd loved anyone since she hugged her little sisters goodbye, and it *hurt.* It hurt so terribly much.

WHAT IN HELL HAD HAPPENED?

His front door still stood open. Jane was gone. He'd caught a glimpse of her car as she reversed into the street, then accelerated forward.

It felt like a hit-and-run. She'd driven over him, been aware of the bump of the tires and kept going, anyway.

He hadn't known devastation like this since his mother said, "I'm leaving." Since he had stood there in the silence after she went and seen his fate.

After a while, he closed the front door and went to the kitchen. If he'd ever needed a drink… Or five or six or ten. But he didn't go to the cupboard where he kept a bottle of whiskey, or to the refrigerator for a beer. Getting drunk solved nothing.

He should call Niall and tell him what she'd done. But he didn't reach for his phone, either.

The only thing he did do was pull out a chair from the kitchen table and sink into it.

She was gone.

Was it his fault? He'd spent eighteen years telling himself it wasn't his fault his mother had abandoned her family. She'd told him he was a good boy. No, it was Dad's fault. Niall's. Conall's. If Conall had only cleaned up the kitchen that day, the way she'd asked him. If Niall hadn't chosen right then to get tossed into juvie. If they'd been home, if she'd had to look them in the eye, would she have gone?

Did I blame them? he wondered dully.

Yeah. Maybe.

This was different. He couldn't summon any anger at all. He knew Jane well enough to have guessed how she'd react to him telling her what to do instead of suggesting. To him calling Lehman behind her back. Why had he done it?

Because she was too reckless to take sensible precautions. Because keeping her safe *had* to come first.

Because... His heart constricted. *Because I don't know any other way.*

No other way to protect someone he loved. No other way to...hold them. He was good at building Cold War style concrete walls topped with multiple strands of barbed wire. Maybe necessary for Niall and Conall. Maybe not.

It worked.

As a management style in a police department, it worked, too. It was all he knew.

The last time he'd trusted someone, she left.

He hadn't trusted Jane, and she'd left, too. Probably ripped to shreds by the barbed wire. Devastated, he still knew that she hadn't stormed out in a fit of pique. She had been genuinely hurt. Maybe even as hurt as he was.

Would saying "I'm sorry" be good enough? Duncan couldn't imagine. Not when he didn't altogether understand why she'd gone off the deep end like that. Yeah, he'd been dictatorial. The admission didn't come easy to him, but he knew he had overstepped.

Not because she was a woman, whatever she thought. Because he loved her. For the first time in his entire, lonely life, he loved a woman. And he'd lost her because he was who he was, and didn't know how to be anyone else.

But that wasn't the worst part. No, the really bad part was that by now she'd have reached home. She was all by herself in that goddamn house, having to walk into a bedroom stripped nearly bare, put her clothes away in empty drawers and a closet that should have held her long-accumulated possessions. Having to make up that bed, imagine sleeping in it tonight.

She was completely vulnerable, and it was his fault.

Eventually Duncan did pick up the phone. He told Niall, "Jane's gone home. She's there by herself."

Strange how silence seemed more alive when it was conveyed by a telephone connection. At last Niall said thoughtfully, "The security system is good."

Duncan grunted his opinion. It wasn't good enough. It didn't stop someone smashing a window and climbing in. It made noise; it's main use was for repelling burglars. No one would slip in and out by stealth. No, Jane wouldn't come home to any more surprises, at least not ones left indoors. But her stalker was flat-out crazy. If he'd worked his way up to the final act, he wouldn't care about walking away afterward.

"Couldn't you talk her into staying on with you for now?" Niall asked.

Up and pacing his kitchen, Duncan admitted, "I pissed her off. We had a court hearing today. Lehman wanted her to supervise another month of visits between the Ortezes. I called the judge later, told him what's been going on and got her taken off."

His brother let out a low whistle. "Without talking to her first?"

"I talked. She wouldn't listen."

"And there's the brother I know and love," said Niall, sharp-edged.

"What the hell's that supposed to mean?"

"You know what it means."

He felt hollow. Carved out like a jack-o'-lantern. He didn't answer.

"Ortez isn't our guy," Niall said.

"What?"

"I got confirmation this afternoon. There's no way he could have done Jane's bedroom. He was at work all day, even had lunch there. Someone went off and grabbed burritos for everyone. The boss had given permission after closing for Hector to use the lifts and tools to work on his truck. A couple of guys hung around and helped him."

Duncan closed his eyes. "You're sure?"

"I'm sure."

He swore. "Then who?"

"I'm down to a couple of good possibilities. The one that makes me uneasiest is a guy named Richard Hopkins. There was an ugly court battle over whether he'd be allowed to see his daughter. Apparently everyone concerned thought he was sexually abusing her in some way or another, but a physical exam didn't confirm and the girl wasn't talking although she started puking every time about an hour before Daddy was due to pick her up for visits. Jane put a lot of pressure on the judge in the case, and in the end he ruled all visits had to be supervised. The father was steamed."

"How long ago was this?"

"Two years. Jane didn't supervise the visits— she says she doesn't do long-term ones like that, and especially when one party is so hostile to her. Here's the thing, though. The visits got less and less successful. Hopkins got madder and madder. Started not showing sometimes, much to everyone's relief. Then, when the daughter refused to see him one time because she had something going on—this was a year ago, and she'd turned thirteen—he dragged her out kicking and screaming. Threw her against the wall when she fought him. She had several broken bones. He lost all visitation, needless to say. Mom and daughter quietly moved, afraid enough of him to try to disappear. After that, child support was supposed to go through the state, but Hopkins quit paying it, left his job and dropped off the map. He may be trying to find his ex and their kid." Niall paused. "Or he may have channelled his rage at Jane, if he blames her for everything that went wrong."

"Find him."

"You think I'm not trying?"

Duncan rubbed his neck. "No," he made himself say quietly. "I know you are. I'm…" He couldn't finish.

"Scared out of your skull? I know. Duncan,

you've got the power to arrange some patrol unit drive-bys. If the guy is lurking, we might get lucky."

"I can do that." *I can also go sit outside her house and watch it. All night.*

How long could he do that and still do his job during the day? And what would Jane say if she spotted him?

He knew. I'm *not your business.* She couldn't have been any clearer.

But what if this guy got to her? Duncan felt as if he was being ripped in half.

"Thanks," he said gruffly to his brother, and ended the call.

CHAPTER FIFTEEN

SLEEP ELUDED HER.

Gee, what a surprise. It didn't help a bit to pop out of bed, pad downstairs and check the security system control panel to be sure it was engaged. Several times.

She wasn't trying to sleep in her own bed; the guest room looked way more appealing. It's true her own bedroom was spotlessly clean. But she thought she might paint it after all. Maybe even have the carpet torn up and replaced with hardwood. She'd thought about doing that, anyway, someday.

Although she lay tense, listening for every sound, it wasn't fear keeping her awake, she finally admitted. Or...not *only* fear.

No, it was Duncan. Seeing his face as he realized she was really walking out on him. She'd been shocked by how much he looked like that expressionless stranger who had met her at the door the first time she went there to talk to him. The man who didn't look as if he knew how to smile—although he'd surprised her. Icy cold, controlled and guarded. His face had since become so much more readable to her, or perhaps he had let himself open to her.

No longer.

She kept replaying the whole scene. What he said. What she said. The awful part was, the more times she ran through it all, the more clearly she could see that she'd screened everything Duncan said and did through the filter of her childhood, of her greatest fears.

He was controlling, manipulative, impatient. But he wasn't like her father, either. Seeing that was hard for her. Friends told her how, when they went home for the holidays, they found themselves reverting to old, often immature patterns. Long-forgotten resentments rising. Conditioned responses taking over. Well, Jane didn't go home for the holidays. But she did have conditioned responses, and Duncan had a way of tapping them.

Aching inside, she tried to figure out why she hadn't told him off. Fought to defend her competency. Convinced him to butt out. He was used to being in charge, used to being obeyed, but she'd discovered before that he was educable. Her father could never have said, "I was wrong." Or, "I don't like it that you won't do this my way, but I'll let you try your way even if you fail." Duncan, she thought, had acted out of fear for her, not of

her and what her defiance represented. That was
the difference between him and her father.

One of the differences.

She struggled to articulate the bigger difference. Something someone had said recently had
almost triggered a revelation. She hadn't had time
to let it catch hold...

Her eyes opened in the dark when the memory
flooded back. It came in Hector Ortez's voice.

*He makes himself feel big by trying to make
everyone else small.*

That was what her father had done. He wasn't
confident enough in himself to make any judg-
ments of his own. He believed in their small
sect's version of God, the leader's interpretation
of the Bible, his dictates on morality and propri-
ety and politics and everything else, because Dad
desperately needed someone to tell him what to
do. His security lay in living within certain rigid
rules laid out by someone else. And yet, deep
within, he must know the truth: if thrust out into
a world where he had to make his own decisions,
he would be lost.

Like everyone else, he needed to feel strong.
Big. He could only do so at his family's expense.

Jane lay stiff, staring at nothing—no, at the
past—and marveled. She'd never understood
before quite what a threat she was to her father.

He had acted the despot out of weakness.

Duncan had become dictatorial out of strength. Strength, she thought, and a powerful sense of honor.

He had become the man he was because he couldn't walk away from his brothers. Because people depended on him, because he felt responsible even when others would shrug and figure, *It's someone else's problem.* As with Tito.

And her.

Would she feel the same about him if he didn't adhere so unshakably to what he thought was right?

She'd turned to him every time she was scared. Flung herself into his arms, leaned on him, accepted his protection and his expertise. And then—*oh, what an idiot I was*—she'd expected him to stand back and let her decide what she needed and didn't need to stay safe. Boy, had she sent mixed messages! *Duncan, please come, I'm scared.* And then, *This was none of your business. It never was.*

Of course it was. She'd made it his business. She'd given herself fully to him, and known when she was doing it that he would do whatever he had to do to keep her safe.

Tears blurred her eyes. With shock, she swiped at them.

Duncan felt responsible for her, yes. He wanted her, too. She knew that.

But he hadn't gone shopping with her because he thought she needed a bodyguard, or because they'd made love. He'd done it because he believed she had needed him, and he was right.

She didn't know a single other man who would have willingly spent *six hours* shopping with a woman, waiting patiently while she tried on clothes and shoes, ferrying packages to the car, giving his opinion on which shirt looked better, all to be nice.

Duncan had probably never given a woman flowers. Soft words weren't his style. Had he ever in his life said "I love you" to anyone?

Why hadn't she seen that taking her shopping was better than the biggest box of chocolates or bouquet of red roses ever? That it was the kindest, most loving thing anyone had ever done for her?

She turned her wet face into the pillow, knowing that she loved him and that maybe he had loved her, before she had misunderstood him so dreadfully, lashing out over and over. Because she was scared to have become so vulnerable to Duncan.

Was she capable of that much trust? Even if he would forgive her?

STAN'S AUTO REPAIR WAS a big place with four bays, a sparkling-clean front office complete with tidy waiting room, free coffee and pop machines, and what looked like a dozen employees all wearing dark blue coveralls. Duncan walked in feeling unaccustomedly self-conscious.

A big man who looked Samoan, maybe, or Hawaiian, smiled at him from behind the desk. The name "Tupa" was embroidered on the breast of his coverall. "How can I help you?"

"I'm looking for Hector Ortez."

Tupa's gaze dropped briefly to Duncan's waist, and he realized his suit coat hadn't covered the badge he wore on his belt. Tupa's face had hardened when he met Duncan's eyes again.

"He in trouble?"

"No. Nothing like that." Duncan managed a relaxed smile of his own. "His son Tito thinks someday he'll kick my butt on a basketball court."

"Ah." Friendlier again, Tupa said, "I'll get him."

When Hector came through the door to the garage, his expression was stoic, closed. A cop, Tupa would have said. Whether it was Duncan or another officer didn't matter; Hector had reason to distrust all of them.

"Is something wrong?" he asked. Alarm flared on his face. "With Tito?"

Duncan shook his head. He glanced to see that Tupa had discreetly withdrawn to a desk with a computer out of earshot. "I was actually, uh, wondering if you take a long enough lunch break that we could talk."

Hector stared at him.

"I'd like to tell you where I'm coming from." He cleared his throat. "Why I worry about Tito."

He wouldn't have been surprised to be re-buffed, but after a minute Hector nodded. "I have half an hour. I could take it right now."

There was a panel truck parked by a gas station a block away that served great Mexican food out the side that rolled up. Hector suggested it, and Duncan nodded. He grabbed a burrito or a que-sadilla there regularly.

Once they had their food, they sat at one of several plastic tables set up beneath an awning stretching out from the other side of the truck.

Duncan opened the bottle of lemonade he'd bought, took a long drink and began talking. He told Hector about his own father, about having to take responsibility for his brothers and why. He admitted that Tito had reminded him of his youngest brother in particular, small for his age, desperately in need of direction. And then he told him about Jane's problems.

"You seemed angry enough at her, I had to wonder," he said bluntly.

"I am angry because of everything that has happened. I was defending myself and yet I went to prison. I have been stripped of everything. I thought at least I had my family. My children. I don't understand why this judge wants to take them from me, too."

"I really don't think he does. I spoke the truth yesterday. I believe you love Tito and can be a good father to him. None of us want to take Tito from you. I only fear your anger." He hesitated. This was really what he'd come to say. "I think Tito does, too."

Hector drew away, clearly offended.

"I ask only that you think about it," Duncan said quietly. "Jane was right to yell at both of us. We were scaring Tito, and I think Lupe, too. You don't want your son or daughter to be afraid of you."

Hector became quiet. Duncan let that silence lay for a while as he unwrapped his burrito. Finally he ventured, "His grades seem to be improving."

"He tells me that, now he is paying attention, the math is easy for him." Hector shook his head. "It never was for me."

Duncan laughed. "I think Tito is a really smart kid. Persuading him to pay attention, to try, is the real trick."

The conversation went easier then. Hector confided his worries about Lupe and her children, Duncan told him how fierce Tito was talking about his former brother-in-law, Hector even asked what Duncan's brothers now did. When Duncan told him they were cops, too, he nodded. "They do the same as you do because they admired you," he said, as if it were a given.

"Or because we all wanted to make up for our father's crimes."

"But you say this Conall was only twelve the last time he saw his father." Hector shook his head. "Only a boy. No, I think *you* are his father. You should be proud."

Taken aback, Duncan didn't try to argue further. A few minutes later, they dropped their wrappings in the garbage can and walked back to Stan's Auto Repair together. Duncan didn't say again, "Please think," but they parted amiably.

He drove to the Public Safety Building aware of a peculiar sensation lodged under his breastbone. Hector, he admitted, had caught him by surprise.

Duncan was proud of Niall and Conall. He'd had a grim sense of satisfaction at a duty performed when they both turned out okay. But it had never once occurred to him to feel proud because they'd chosen to become cops, too. Not in his wildest dreams had he believed either of his brothers admired him.

Was it possible?

I think you *are his father.* It occurred to Duncan how much he wished he could talk to

Conall about it all. Maybe...have a beer with *both* his brothers. As a family.

TITO WAS SURPRISED WHEN he came home to see his father sitting on the couch holding baby Felicia while Yolanda and Mateo clutched at him and chattered. Good smells came from the kitchen.

Tito hesitated, his eyes flicking this way and that. If Jane was here, she must be in the kitchen. Or had Papa decided he no longer needed to listen to her?

But his father smiled at him and said, "Don't look so worried. I called Jane today and asked if I could come here in the evenings, if I promised to be here only when Lupe is also."

Surprised, Tito nodded. He silently stowed his basketball in the small closet and then went to the bathroom.

Papa wouldn't lie, would he? Churning inside, Tito wondered. He couldn't betray his father, no matter what; he already knew that. Family was family. He didn't think Duncan would want to see him anymore, though, and that hurt.

Through the door, he heard Lupe's raised voice calling him. Although he wished he didn't have to eat with the family, Tito went out to join Papa and the others at the table. Felicia usually cried during dinner, but cuddling with her *abuelo* must have put her in a good mood; she seemed happy lying in the playpen and gnawing on a cloth doll. Tito pulled out his chair and sat, head bowed, while Lupe asked for blessings.

Lupe had made *chili verde*. There were warm, homemade corn tortillas, too. Tito ate hungrily, watching his father out of the corner of his eye.

Papa had opened a Mexican beer, but he took only sips. When Mateo spilled his milk, Papa waved Lupe to stay and mopped up, then filled the glass halfway full again. He even put his hand on Mateo's to help him lift it to his mouth.

Not until the little ones were done eating and had left the table with Lupe's permission did Papa say, "I've been thinking."

Lupe and Tito looked at him.

"Lupe, it's okay if you say no. If you are happiest living here. But I think it must be hard for you, with so little help from Raul. What I was thinking—" he took a deep breath as if for courage "—is that perhaps we could rent a house big enough for all of us. One with a yard for the children. Some nights you wouldn't have to pay for child care because I would be home. And perhaps Tito would help, too."

Tito felt a strange, warm rush of feeling. Papa did want to help his daughter. And Tito hadn't wanted to leave Lupe alone, or not see the little ones very often. Mateo and he…they were tight. Boys needed a big brother to look up to, didn't they?

"I also want to tell you I'm sorry that I got so angry yesterday morning. That I scared you. I was wrong. It's true that I should be glad other people are trying to do the right thing for you, Tito. I think I was jealous because Duncan—" he said the name awkwardly, as if it didn't fit the shape of his mouth "—went to school so much longer than I did. He has money and is important. But…he could be a good friend for you, Tito, and I should be glad of that."

Should? The word caught Tito's attention like a burr grabbed fabric. Did that mean Papa really wasn't glad?

Maybe, but at least he had admitted why. He'd come right out and said he was jealous. It took a brave man to admit that. Tito felt his eyes sting. He ducked his head. Men didn't cry.

Lupe was talking excitedly. A real house? With a yard? Perhaps the neighbor lady could come there, to their house, to babysit when Papa couldn't and Lupe had to work. "Tito, what do you think?" she asked at last.

He had overcome the desire to cry by then. He squared his shoulders and sat with pride. "I think it would be great if we could all live together. A family. I'd like that."

His father smiled, such a big smile Tito suddenly remembered the papa he'd loved when he was still a little boy and life was less complicated.

"Duncan said he would like to keep spending time with you, if you want," Papa said. "You like him, don't you?"

Tito swallowed. "He's been nice to me. And I'm getting really good at basketball!" He eyed his father nervously. "He helped me with homework, too. Especially math."

"Ah." Something flickered on his father's face. Sadness, perhaps, but also acceptance. "I thought so." He looked again at Lupe and then at Tito. "Well, then. No more movies this month, Tito, or hamburgers and pizza. I must save my money for the house so we can all be together. Okay?"

Lupe glowed, looking more like herself. Younger.

Tito grinned at him, pleasure bursting inside him. "Okay!"

Papa might be short and not so good at basketball. He might not be able to answer every question the way Duncan could. But Tito felt so proud. His father had showed that he was a strong man. A big man, not a small one at all.

And I can still be friends with Duncan, too.

He was old enough to know that life wouldn't always be so perfect. Old enough to know that his father would disappoint him again in the future, and that he would probably disappoint Papa, too. Still feeling warm inside, he grappled with the notion as he jumped up to help Lupe clear the table.

Mistakes were okay, he finally thought in amazement. It was admitting them and doing better that made a man. The kind of man he, Tito, wanted to be.

MIDMORNING, JANE TOOK a call from Niall who told her that Hector definitely was out of the running as her stalker. She thanked him and left a message for Judge Lehman, telling him that she wanted to continue supervising Tito's visits with his father.

Hector himself called her in the middle of the afternoon to ask her permission to have dinner with his family. He sounded…humble, she finally realized.

"I'm ashamed of the way I acted yesterday," he said. "I upset everyone. Tito wouldn't even look at me afterward." He hesitated. "I didn't used to be angry all the time. I don't like it."

Wow.

"We all understand why you've been angry," she said. "I've never told you this before, but I read the transcript of your trial. I think it was wrong that you were convicted. I believe you were only defending yourself."

"I was drunk," he said simply. "Foolish drunk. To have gotten into an argument with someone like him was stupid. I never meant to kill him."

"I think Tito will figure that out."

"I don't want him to think that's how a man acts."

"Have dinner with your family tonight." She was smiling despite her bleak mood. "In fact, why don't we resume the original plan? You can have dinner there as long as Lupe is with you and Tito."

"Thank you." His voice sounded thick.

Only after hanging up did she start to wonder what had effected the sea change in him. What if he was playing her? Was he gloating, thinking, *stupid woman?* But, despite her qualms, she didn't believe it. She thought he'd been sincere.

Take off your rose-colored glasses, Duncan would say. Had said. Her answer was, *Not happening.* The greatest miracle in her life was that she *could* believe in people, and she intended to keep right on doing so.

So why hadn't she believed in Duncan?

But she knew. Of course she knew. Having faith in people one step removed was way easier than when *she* was the one who might get hurt.

Call him.

She thought about it for the rest of the day. After closing, she went so far as to drive over to his house but saw no lights on inside. On a rush of guilty relief, she realized he might not be home for hours. Of course, she couldn't sit out here waiting forever. Maybe it would be better after all if she phoned him. He might not actually want to see her. On a wash of misery, Jane admitted that she could hardly blame him if he didn't.

She went grocery shopping, loading up her cart until the total bill startled her. Too many comfort foods, but she refused to regret buying them. If she'd ever needed comfort, it was now.

It was getting dark by the time she reached home. Jane eyed her house uneasily as she pulled into the driveway and waited for the garage door to lift. She'd feel better if she'd left more lights on. Especially the outside lights. She grabbed her cell phone from her purse and clutched it in her hand.

It was still there when she drove into the garage even before the door was all the way up, then hit the button on the remote to reverse it. In the rearview mirror, she watched as it went down again, finally settling into place with a clunk and sigh.

Okay. Tension trickled out of her and for a moment she leaned back and closed her eyes. She was securely locked in again. Time to pull herself together. Jane popped her trunk, grabbed her keys and purse and got out of the car, then remembered she'd left the cell phone on the seat and leaned in to get it. She dropped it in the loose pocket of her linen jacket.

She was bent over the trunk, reaching for grocery sacks, when she heard a whisper of sound behind her. A footstep? A fireball of fear went off inside her and she tried to spin around. She bashed her head on the trunk lid, saw stars—and hard arms closed around her from behind. Something sharp pressed against her throat. A knife blade.

"Did you expect me, bitch?" the man murmured in her ear.

The grocery bags fell from her hands.

DUNCAN DIDN'T LET HIMSELF express his restlessness in any physical mannerisms, even though he was bored out of his skull. A meeting regarding the regional drug enforcement task force that should have taken an hour had stretched to two and a half. The county sheriff was an elected position, which might explain why the current sheriff had risen beyond his level of competence. His main goal here seemed to be ensuring that the sheriff's department got ample credit for any arrests even though Whatcom County, also involved, was a far larger agency. The several larger cities within the region had collectively provided as many officers to the task force as each of the counties had.

Duncan caught a grimace on the face of one of the police chiefs, who then looked embarrassed to be caught. But, damn, would somebody shut this guy up?

The Whatcom County sheriff obliged by heaving himself to his feet. "Lowell, sorry to break this up, but I have business this evening. We've covered the main points, haven't we?" His gaze traveled the room. There might have been a twinkle in his eyes at the multitude of vigorous nods. "Good," he said. "I suspect we can clear anything else up by email. Great to see you all in person."

Chairs slid. Empty foam coffee cups hit the metal bottom of the trash can by the door. There wasn't quite a jostle to escape the room, but close.

Duncan didn't hurry to his SUV. His house would be empty and dark. Jane's, he thought, would probably be bright enough to be seen from a satellite. He didn't like thinking about how scared she'd be. He kept hoping— unreasonably, he knew—that she'd call. Say, "I didn't mean it." Or was he supposed to do the apologizing?

But he was uncomfortably aware that a call from him could be construed as harassment, given how blunt she'd been.

Obviously, I gave you the wrong impression. I'm correcting that now. I'm *not your business.*

Oh, yeah, she couldn't have been much clearer. He checked his cell phone even though he would have felt it vibrate. No missed calls. With a sigh, he unlocked the vehicle door and got in. There were probably a couple of people here who wouldn't have minded joining him for a meal, but he wasn't in the mood. He'd find something in the freezer at home.

SHE KNEW THAT VOICE. Richard Hopkins. Of all the people she'd dealt with as Guardian ad Litem, he'd made her the most uncomfortable.

"Drop your purse," he whispered. When she didn't unclench her fingers fast enough, the knife bit into her skin and she felt a trickle of blood run down her neck like beads of sweat. "Now."

The purse fell with a clunk. So much for hoping to slide her hand in and find the pepper spray.

She tried frantically to think. The alarm would blare soon if she didn't turn it off. Would he know that? Did it matter? Maybe he intended to kill her here and now.

It did matter, because he nudged her toward the control panel. "Do what you have to do," he told her. "I'll slice your throat if that thing starts screaming."

Maybe it would be better if he did slice her throat now, versus taking his time about it. Jane shuddered. No. Wasn't there a chance that he didn't actually intend to kill her? Despite his every hint to the contrary?

Blood, viscous and pungent, splattered and sprayed on the walls.

A hint, Jane thought hysterically. That was like calling death "passing away."

She felt the bump of the phone in her pocket as he turned her. Her adrenaline surged. With Duncan on speed dial she could push only two buttons...but Richard would hear the ringing. She imagined him slamming the cell phone to the concrete floor of the garage. Having to watch her only link to the outside shatter.

Oh God oh God oh God please help.

Text. Could she text silently, by feel alone? Did Duncan have his phone set to ring or only to vibrate when a text came in? She'd bet on the latter. But...could she do it by feel alone? Her breath hitched in a near sob. She didn't dare swallow. Step by terrifying step, she was being pushed to the control panel by the door leading into the house.

What if she thought she'd succeeded in texting him but really had pushed the wrong button? Or whatever he got was incoherent? Though that would alarm him, wouldn't it? Or what if he tossed his phone aside the way she'd seen him do when he got home and didn't notice that it had vibrated?

She had to try.

She tapped the sequence of numbers on the control panel first and saw the light flash to indicate it was satisfied. They could go in, where normally she'd reset the alarm by the front door. But she wouldn't be doing that, would she?

Jane stumbled on the step and the blade bit deeper. In her fear, she felt it as no more than a sting. She had her right hand in her pocket, where she started pushing buttons. *Oh God oh God, she'd forgotten the tiny beeps.*

"Why do you blame me?" she asked loudly. "I don't understand. I haven't been in the picture for years."

Focus. Remember what the screens look like. She thought she had clicked on a New Message screen that would go to number one on speed dial— Duncan.

She kept talking. "You could have built a good relationship with your daughter."

Her thumb kept moving. She scraped her feet to drown out the tiny beeps.

Help home

That was surely enough. Please let that be what she'd actually typed. Send. One last small beep.

"What was that?" Richard snarled. "Was it that damn security system? Are you trying to trick me?"

"No." Terror made speaking hard. "It's off. I swear. I didn't hear anything."

"Where's your phone?" he said suddenly.

"I don't have one anymore here in the house."

"I know that!" he shouted. "Your cell phone."

"In...in my purse," she whispered. "I think. Maybe in the car. Or...or it could have fallen in the trunk."

Oh, God, she now had a new fear. What if it rang? *Pretend you didn't know it was in your pocket.* What else could she do? Hide it somewhere, if she got the chance? No, she might have a chance to use it. Another chance.

Her eyes burned with unshed tears. *Duncan, check your phone. I need you.*

CHAPTER SIXTEEN

DUNCAN THOUGHT ABOUT MAKING a sandwich, but scanned the entrées his housekeeper had frozen for him. One label caught his eye. Creole Chicken. After a moment, he took it out, read the instructions and put it in the microwave. He'd started it whirring when his cell phone gave a little bounce on the tile countertop and hummed.

Text message.

Jane had never texted him. He couldn't imagine why she would. Niall, maybe? Frowning, Duncan reached for the phone.

His heart jumped when he saw that the message actually was from Jane. He opened it.

Hflp homf

What the hell...? He stared for an instant without comprehension. Then...

Help. Oh, shit, she'd been trying to type *help*. Typing blind?

Swearing, hand shaking, he dialed his brother's phone number. Niall answered on the first ring.

"Where are you?" Duncan demanded.

He had a flash, remembering the way Jane teased him about never starting a conversation with *hello, hey, how are you.* He could hear her laughing. He bypassed fear and went straight to anguish.

"On my way home," Niall said. "Why?"

"I got a text from Jane. It says 'help home.' I'm—God—close to fifteen minutes away."

He'd gathered his keys and was blundering into the garage. The door rose.

Niall's voice was crisp and hard. All cop. "I'm two."

"No siren."

"No siren."

"If the security system is on…"

"Either way, I'll break a goddamn window."

He was backing out of the garage, careening into the street. "I love her," he said hoarsely.

"Yeah." Duncan had never heard the tone in his brother's voice before. It was…gentle. "So you said."

Choked, Duncan got out a thank-you.

"See you there." Niall ended the call.

Duncan drove like he'd never driven before, his mind consumed by fear and the realization that he couldn't save her. Only Niall could, if they weren't too late already.

THE SILENCE AS RICHARD pushed her toward the stairs was unbearable.

She asked, wishing she didn't sound so tremulous, "What are you going to do to me?" Better to know. Wasn't it?

She had yet to get a good look at his face. He'd stayed behind her the whole time, knife blade to her throat. His breath was hot on her neck. Bad breath, as if he hadn't bothered to brush his teeth in a while. Actually, *he* smelled, that awful fetid odor of someone who hadn't showered in way too long.

"What I want to do is take everything away from you, the way you did to me." The way he talked was odd. Slightly singsong. Or maybe it was Jane's hearing.

She reluctantly took the first step. The angle of the knife changed. Richard wasn't very tall, she remembered. He was having to reach up when she was a step above him. Was there any way she could take advantage of that?

"But you don't have anybody to take away," he continued, sounding mad about that. He shoved. "Move! No children. I would have liked to kill your child, so you know what it feels like."

"Your daughter…" *Don't swallow, don't swallow, not with a knife at your throat.* "Susie's not dead."

"She's dead to me. She screamed, 'I never want to see you again!' To *me*."

Wow. Imagine that.

Duncan, please.

"As long as she's alive, there's hope." Jane winced at her own platitude. It was true, oh, yes, it was, but it still sounded like a greeting card.

"She was everything to me. *Everything*."

Her throat hurt. How deep was he cutting? "Your children," she gasped, "aren't supposed to be everything."

"I loved her!"

His roar made her jump.

"You turned her against me. It was you and that bitch Joan."

His wife. A petite woman who, Jane remembered thinking, had been quiet and self-effacing until the day she realized her husband was looking at their daughter, touching her, wrong. And then she had become a lioness. So different from the women who refused to see, refused to believe, because it would disrupt their lives.

"Why are we going upstairs?" she asked.

"I want to kill you in your bedroom."

"I've cleaned it up."

"Did it scare you?" he asked with creepy interest.

Why not be honest? "Yes."

What if she fell against him? Would her weight

send them both tumbling down the stairs? But with the blade biting into her throat, all his arm would have to do was tighten momentarily.

Reach up and grab his wrist? Jane tried to remember how strong he'd looked. He was about Hector's height. But Hector was muscular, stocky. Richard Hopkins had been fairly slight, she thought, but then recalled that he was a runner. He'd talked once about competing in the Boston Marathon. Wiry and strong, then.

When he leaned in to snarl in her ear, "Quit dragging your feet," she felt the scrape of his unshaven jaw. Niall hadn't been able to locate him. What had he been doing, hiding out in the woods up the hill from her street?

She was getting light-headed. Hyperventilating. How long had passed? Five minutes? Twenty? She had no idea.

She sent a plea out into the ether. *Duncan.*

Only a few steps to go. Then the length of the hall. Even if help came now, Richard could so easily slit her throat before anyone could possibly reach them.

I'm not weak, she thought. Dance had made her strong. If no one came—or if someone did—she would fight. Grab his wrist and twist away. Kick him. She had especially strong legs. Maybe she should have fought sooner.

No—help might be on the way. It could be

here. While there's life there's hope. An hysterical bubble of laughter tried to rise from her chest.

They walked down the hall, shuffling their feet in tandem. He wasn't letting any distance open between them. She was sick to her stomach now, too. *It's his breath, his odor.* If she started to heave, would he back off in instinctive repulsion? It wouldn't be all that hard to do.

Duncan, where are you?

DUNCAN TOOK A CORNER so fast, the SUV might have been on two wheels.

Niall should be there by now. More than two minutes had passed. Three, four, at least. Had he gotten into the house? If it was empty, he'd have called. What was he *doing?*

The light turned yellow ahead. Duncan slammed his foot down on the accelerator and tore through the intersection.

JANE WAS STARTLED BY THE reflection in the dark window. Not sharp like in a mirror. The mirrors this man had shattered in a fit of rage. No, what she saw was shadowy, insubstantial, like a pair of ghosts.

Only…it seemed as if something *else* was moving out there. Not a tree limb; the old maple in her backyard wasn't close enough to the house.

Was it another reflection? Someone behind them who'd slipped into the room?

As if she heard a sharp, warning voice, she thought, *Don't let him notice.*

"Please," she whispered. "If you love Susie, you'll see I was trying to help her. Maybe I was wrong, but…but I was trying to do the right thing."

"The right thing?" Spittle dampened her neck. "Taking her away from her father, who loved her?"

Had his hand relaxed the slightest bit?

"I didn't know," she mumbled. Oh, but she had known. She had. "Love" shouldn't be sick and perverted. His own daughter.

Her eyes strained to see past the reflection in the glass. And she saw it—a face. A sudden movement. Outside? She grappled with the idea. How could anyone be looking in her second-story window? But someone was. Which meant, whatever she was going to do had to be…*now.*

She reached up and grabbed Richard's wrist and forearm. Simultaneously, the window glass exploded inward. She couldn't get a good grip. His hand seemed to be slippery. Her vision wavered. She was screaming, pushing his hand away from her neck for all she was worth, but her legs didn't want to support her anymore.

"Police! Drop it!" a voice barked. *Not Duncan.*

As if engaged in a terrible dance, Jane and Richard swayed. Was she winning? They were twirling, and then there came a crack of thunder and with his arm wrapped around her his weight bore her down. The floor ascended or she descended, Jane had no idea. It was like a kaleidoscope, spinning, and why was her face *wet?*

A DRIVE THAT SHOULD HAVE taken fifteen minutes took nine.

Duncan pulled up to the curb a block away and ran. He had almost reached Jane's house when his cell phone rang.

"I shot him," Niall said baldly. "He's dead. Jane's...bleeding. I think she's okay, but she went down hard and either hit her head or passed out." He paused. "Are you close?"

"Outside."

The tension in Niall's voice scared the crap out of Duncan. *Bleeding.* He'd given up praying a lifetime ago, but he was doing it now.

"Good," Niall said. "I don't want to take pressure off her wound. You don't have a key, do you?"

"No. I'm coming through a window."

"Open the front door for the EMTs."

The next-door neighbor's kid had left a tricycle out in the front yard. Duncan grabbed it on the run, leaped onto her front porch and slammed the trike through the front window. No scream of an alarm; it had been disabled somehow. Niall? No. He must have broken a window, too. The alarm should already have been on.

Duncan didn't give a shit, and knew on some level that he was distracting himself. He'd never been more scared in his life than he was of what he'd find upstairs.

He unlocked and flung open the front door. Already he could hear the distant wail of a siren. No light on in the kitchen. He took the stairs three at a time.

Light spilled from the bedroom at the end of the hall. Jane's bedroom. He could hear the murmur of Niall's voice. His own steps slowed as fear swelled in him like nothing he'd ever felt before.

"Hey, it's okay, it's okay," Niall was saying. "You're going to be fine. Hang in there, honey. Duncan needs you." More raggedly, "Damn, I wish you'd open your eyes. Don't even *think* about dying on us. No, I didn't say that. The cut's not that deep."

When Duncan went into her bedroom, blood dominated his vision. Too much blood. She was soaked in it. In his horror, he didn't even waste a glance at the body slumped a few feet away. He hardly saw his brother, kneeling beside her, his hand seemingly wrapping her throat. It was Jane. Only Jane. Completely still.

It looked like Niall had tried to wipe her face clean. But her hair glistened dark. Duncan heard himself groaning as he, too, fell to his knees beside her.

"The blood's not all hers," his brother said. "Most of it isn't hers. God. I had to wait until they turned. You know what head shots are like. I was so afraid of the bullet ricocheting off his skull. I got him through the temple. His head just, uh…"

"Where's she bleeding from?" Duncan asked, his own voice unrecognizable.

"Neck. He had a knife to her throat. It was… blood was running down her neck."

The siren screamed to a stop outside. Doors slammed. Noise and voices downstairs. Niall yelled, "Up here!"

They came, two paramedics with a stretcher and the tools of their trade. Duncan and Niall had to give way. The two, man and woman, checked her airway, asked questions about any possible head injury, cleaned up blood with wipes so they could see better and applied a thick white dressing to her neck. Then they were lifting her and carrying her downstairs, moving fast.

Duncan blundered to his feet and followed.

"Let me drive," Niall said. "You're in no shape."

Duncan shook his head. "You shot a man. You need to stay here, control the scene."

His brother looked distraught. "Yeah. Okay."

They were on the front porch. Other sirens were closing in now. One of the EMTs was closing the back door; the other, the woman, was inside the ambulance with Jane. The driver leaped in.

"Go," Niall said roughly, but Duncan turned.

He reached out a hand. Niall's was slick with blood when it met his but he squeezed tight. "Thank you," Duncan said roughly.

That was the moment he knew he was crying. He didn't care, only let go of his brother's hand and ran for his 4Runner to follow Jane to the hospital.

JANE OPENED HER EYES TO the unexpected sight of white curtains pulled around her bed.

Hospital. Why...? And then she remembered.

She must have made a sound, because suddenly Duncan was standing beside the bed. He looked bad. Every line on his face, and right now there were too many, was worn deep. His eyes were bloodshot. His jaw was dark with evening beard.

"You're awake."

She blinked a couple of times. "I'm alive."

A ragged laugh escaped him. "Yeah. God."

"It was Niall," she realized. Her neck didn't

feel so good; she reached up and found a thick dressing on it. Her hand trailed a line…an IV, she saw. Her forehead wrinkled in perplexity. "How… Um, how did he come through the upstairs window?"

Duncan gave a harsh exhalation. "He climbed your house. I guess he saw through the front window that you were starting up the stairs. With the downstairs window frames, the clapboard and the back porch overhang, he said there were enough footholds. He's done some rock climbing. Even so, I don't know how the hell he managed it." He reached over the railing and smoothed hair from her forehead. His hand shook. "I wish you hadn't had to see…" He stopped. Muscles knotted in his jaw.

"See…?" She thought about it. After a minute, she said, "I didn't actually see much of anything. I never even saw his face." It was her turn to brake on a surge of fear. "Where is he?"

"He's dead. Niall shot him. That's what I'd rather you hadn't seen."

Still, his hand stroked, the rough-gentle pads of his fingertips soothing, pressing. Her eyes drifted closed. That terrible explosion of sound. The rain that had fallen. The stumbling, surreal descent to the floor.

"It was blood," she whispered, her eyes opening. "Yes."

She shuddered, her whole body—toes to a quick chatter of teeth.

"You shouldn't have been alone." Torment deepened his voice, darkened his eyes to charcoal. "It was my fault. You wouldn't have left if I hadn't been such an idiot. I'm sorrier than I can ever tell you."

"No." *Tell him. Now.* "It was me. Ever since I left, I've been trying to figure out how to explain. And...and hoping you'd listen."

His jaw worked. Those eyes, so full of emotion, held hers. Then he said, "Let me get this railing down." His hand left off its caressing briefly. With a rattle, he lowered the bed rail and started to drag a chair closer.

"Will you sit here?" Jane tried to smile. She patted next to her. "On the bed?"

His smile wasn't any better than hers. "I can manage that." His hip pressed her waist. The fabric of his dark trousers pulled tight across his thigh muscles. His hand found hers and gripped tightly.

"Am I okay?" Jane couldn't figure out why she didn't feel worse.

Another shaky laugh. "Yeah. You bled quite a bit. He cut you." With his other hand, Duncan gently touched the dressing on her throat. "You hit your head when you went down, too. Minor concussion. But you'll be out of here in the morning, if you feel ready to go."

But not home. Oh, heavens. Would she ever feel safe in that house again? It had been bad enough after the break-in, after the devastation in her bedroom, but now...

She nodded slightly. "Of course I will."

"I should call the nurse. They'll want to know you've regained consciousness."

"I...okay."

He restored the rail first. She had her temperature taken, lights shone into her eyes, her knees and elbows tapped while her limbs jerked. Eventually the medical personnel went away again.

Duncan drew the curtain closed so that no one passing in the hall could see her bed. Then he lowered the rail again and sat beside her. His hand found hers as if it were the most natural thing in the world.

"Shall I get my apologies out first?" he asked.

"No. Let me." It took her a while. Her voice got hoarse as she talked, telling him about her family. Her mother, a shadow, with no needs or demands or personality of her own. Her father's thunderous insistence on instant obedience to his dictates. Her own rebellion, begun when she was so young she hardly knew what had motivated it. "I...you flipped all my switches," she said. "I thought you were like him."

"Maybe I am." His shoulders had a rigid set. His hand released hers and he'd managed to erase some of the expression on his face.

"No." This was the most important thing she had to say. "It took me most of the night to figure out that you're not anything like my father. It was what Hector said about a man who could only feel big by making other people feel small. That was Dad. You had to be strong because you were needed. Your brothers needed a rock and you provided them with one." Her lips curved. Maybe this was the wrong moment to tease, but she couldn't help herself. "It maybe got to be a little too much of a habit."

Some of the tension left his shoulders and he smiled wryly. "My brothers have suggested as much."

"You and Niall seem so close in some ways."

He grimaced. "And in other ways we're complete strangers. A few weeks ago, I'd have told you that we were barely acquaintances."

"And now?" Something told her this mattered.

"Now…" He was the one to bend his head this time. She watched him struggle to frame his thoughts. "I suppose we're brothers." Duncan sounded surprised. "I didn't realize how much I trusted him. Tonight—" his voice had become raw "—I had to trust him. I couldn't have gotten to your house in time."

She reached for him. Their fingers meshed.

"You did," she whispered. "You saved me because you saved Niall. You know he became the man he is because of you."

"Hector said something like that. I'm still not sure I buy it, but—" he cleared his throat "—I think that at least we're fixing some of the things wrong between us."

Jane gave his hand a squeeze. "I'm glad."

"I should let you sleep." But he didn't move.

"You're probably tired."

He didn't say anything for a long time. When he did, it was a complete non sequitur. "I'm not an easy man."

Jane's heart hit a bass beat. "I'm not such an easy woman, either."

He didn't give any sign of having heard her. "I don't know how to be different, Jane."

Was he saying that he wanted to be? For her sake? Voice thick with hope, she said, "All you have to do is listen to me."

His eyes met hers. "And what if I don't? What if I'm afraid for you and think I know best?"

"Then...then I should yell at you and *make* you listen. Instead of walking out."

"I love you," he said hoarsely then visibly braced himself.

Emotion flooded her, honey thick, unfamiliar. She was perilously close to crying. "I never thought…"

He looked wary. "I'd ever be idiot enough to say something like that to you?"

Jane struggled to sit up. As if instinctively, Duncan reached for her. To help her, because that's what he did.

"That I could love anyone," she said. "I think I was afraid I'd become like my mother. I'd start agreeing and conciliating and…lose myself."

Duncan gave a bark of laughter. "You?"

That was all he had to say. *You?* As if the idea were ludicrous. And it was, she realized. Tonight she'd realized she wasn't weak. She'd fought for her life and won. Not alone; maybe she'd have lost if she'd been alone. But she'd done her part. And she hadn't been alone. If Duncan meant what he was saying, she didn't have to be alone. It wasn't so much him she'd been afraid to trust, Jane realized; it was herself.

And…I can. I do.

She was sitting all the way up now, her arms wrapped around Duncan's torso, her cheek pressed to his neck and jaw. She felt his mouth against her hair. Kissing her.

"I love you," she said. "So much."

The strength and ferocity of his grip was all Duncan, the man she knew, but his voice wasn't.

It shook, like his hands had earlier. Jane heard naked vulnerability.

"Don't make me drop you off at your house. Come home with me. Please, Jane."

She smiled even as she started to cry. "Yes. I want to."

"We can rip up the carpet in the spare room. Put in mirrors and bars and whatever you need to dance."

She gulped and bobbed her head.

He was rubbing his cheek against her, rocking her slightly. "Jane?"

She sniffed and wiped her tears on his T-shirt. "Yes?"

"Do you want children?"

Jane drew away and looked at him. "Don't you?"

The furrows on his forehead had deepened. "It…never occurred to me. I never expected…" He was obviously bewildered. "I never thought I'd marry. And I…God. I figured I'd be a lousy father."

Tenderness filled her. "I don't think you'd be lousy at all. Look at Tito."

He didn't appear convinced.

"Although you might want to curb the tendency to snap out orders."

It was the right thing to say. Duncan laughed. But a moment later, he'd gone solemn again.

"I...wouldn't mind trying. But I don't know how much I can change."

"Oh, Duncan." Tipping her head back to kiss him pulled at the wound on her neck and made her realize that her head throbbed, but she did it, anyway. "You don't have to change," she murmured against his mouth.

He cupped her cheek and kissed her, slow and sweet. Loving. And he was smiling when he lifted his mouth. "Easy enough to say now."

There was that blasted sting in her eyes again. "Just...keep loving me."

She felt his sigh. The rise and fall of his chest, the stir of air against her skin. He said, "If there's one thing I am, it's stubborn. I latch onto an idea, I don't let it go."

"And you've definitely latched onto me."

Another rough laugh. He was getting good at laughing, she thought. Doing it more often. Oh, Duncan, who says you can't change?

"Yep." His mouth found hers again. It stayed tender; nuzzled, nipped, savored. And the next thing she knew, he was gently easing her against the pillow. The expression on his face was enough to stop her heart. When she first met this man, she'd never have guessed he could look like this: open, warm, affectionate. Defenseless, even as he was harnessing the passion that he felt, too. "I won't be letting go," he said. "Except temporarily. You, love, look like hell. I'm going to get off this bed and let you sleep."

Panic darted through her. Jane refused to give in to it. "You should go home and get some sleep, too," she said with a smile.

"I may get some sleep, but I'll be doing it right here." He kissed her again, softly. "I'm not leaving you. I don't want to let you out of my sight. I may have to drive you to work and pick you up afterward for a long time to come."

"What you mean is, you'll drive me crazy."

"Yeah." There was a rueful, almost-but-not-quite-amused tone to his voice. A glint of self-awareness in his not-so-cool gray eyes. "I'm good at that."

The painkiller they'd given her earlier must be taking effect. Jane felt drowsy and astonishingly at peace. Their hands were still linked, although he'd settled into the chair beside the bed now.

"I'll yell at you," she told him, although the words slurred.

"And I'll listen," Duncan said, voice a caress.

Smiling, Jane closed her eyes. They were still holding hands when she fell asleep.

* * * * *

LARGER-PRINT BOOKS!
GET 2 FREE LARGER-PRINT NOVELS PLUS
2 FREE GIFTS!

⬧Harlequin®

Super Romance®

Exciting, emotional, unexpected!

YES! Please send me 2 FREE LARGER-PRINT Harlequin® Superromance® novels and my 2 FREE gifts (gifts are worth about $10). After receiving them, if I don't wish to receive any more books, I can return the shipping statement marked "cancel." If I don't cancel, I will receive 6 brand-new novels every month and be billed just $5.44 per book in the U.S. or $5.99 per book in Canada. That's a saving of at least 16% off the cover price! It's quite a bargain! Shipping and handling is just 50¢ per book in the U.S. or 75¢ per book in Canada.* I understand that accepting the 2 free books and gifts places me under no obligation to buy anything. I can always return a shipment and cancel at any time. Even if I never buy another book, the two free books and gifts are mine to keep forever.

139/339 HDN FEFF

Name   (PLEASE PRINT)

Address   Apt. #

City   State/Prov.   Zip/Postal Code

Signature (if under 18, a parent or guardian must sign)

Mail to the **Reader Service:**
IN U.S.A.: P.O. Box 1867, Buffalo, NY 14240-1867
IN CANADA: P.O. Box 609, Fort Erie, Ontario L2A 5X3

Not valid for current subscribers to Harlequin Superromance Larger-Print books.

**Are you a current subscriber to Harlequin Superromance books
and want to receive the larger-print edition?
Call 1-800-873-8635 today or visit www.ReaderService.com.**

* Terms and prices subject to change without notice. Prices do not include applicable taxes. Sales tax applicable in N.Y. Canadian residents will be charged applicable taxes. Offer not valid in Quebec. This offer is limited to one order per household. All orders subject to credit approval. Credit or debit balances in a customer's account(s) may be offset by any other outstanding balance owed by or to the customer. Please allow 4 to 6 weeks for delivery. Offer available while quantities last.

Your Privacy—The Reader Service is committed to protecting your privacy. Our Privacy Policy is available online at www.ReaderService.com or upon request from the Reader Service.

We make a portion of our mailing list available to reputable third parties that offer products we believe may interest you. If you prefer that we not exchange your name with third parties, or if you wish to clarify or modify your communication preferences, please visit us at www.ReaderService.com/consumerschoice or write to us at Reader Service Preference Service, P.O. Box 9062, Buffalo, NY 14269. Include your complete name and address.

HSRLP11B